The Debt]

Keelan LaForge

Printed in Belfast, United Kingdom.
Cover Design by James, GoOnWrite.com

Dedication

For all the mental health patients not getting
the treatment they deserve.

PROLOGUE

J oel folded the paper back along the creases already made by a disturbed hand. He handed the note to his partner.

"Seems pretty clear-cut to me," he said.

"Why would he put the wallet under a rock?" Sam asked.

"Guess he didn't want anything to blow away. If he took it with him, it would have been unreadable by now."

Joel leant over the railing of the bridge and looked at the crew lifting the corpse from the water.

"This is the easiest part," Sam said. "When we don't know the details of who they are and why they did it."

Joel shrugged. "The guy obviously wanted out. At least he left this world by choice. That's more than most of us can hope for."

The limp form looked colourless and inhuman. It made it just slightly easier to look him in the face once he'd been flipped over. He hung as lifelessly as a fish caught from the river for dinner. The coroner zipped him into a body bag, wheeling him off the scene.

Joel placed his palm on Sam's back. "Let's go and take a closer look."

They approached the cordoned-off bank and a teenage boy was sitting on a nearby bench, a blanket wrapped around him, vaping like life depended on it.

Joel looked questioningly at the police officer on the crime scene.

"This is the boy that called it in."

"Hey, thanks. Looks like you've had a rough night."

"I've had better," said the kid, releasing the vapour.

"Let me know when you're ready to give your statement."

"I'll give it now. Get it over with. Sleep's suddenly looking unlikely."

"I'll get your name and address first and then I'll ask you some questions."

After pencilling down the boy's credentials, Joel asked the obligatory questions.

"What exactly did you see?"

He looked the boy in the eyes, seeing in them the death of innocence, and flicked his eyes back to his pad.

"I was just going for a walk along the towpath and I saw him jump."

"Did you see anything before that?"

"No. I just looked up the second he jumped."

"Did he shout anything when he fell?"

"No, he was weirdly quiet – I'll never forget how calm he looked as he did it."

"So, it was a suicide?"

"Well, what else could it be? I saw the guy jump into the river from a hundred feet up. He was alone. He looked peaceful before he even hit the water."

"What time did this happen at?"

"It must have been 12pm"

"And what had you out so late?"

"It's the shortcut I take to get back from my girlfriend's house."

"What age are you?"

"17."

"Did your parents know you were out?"

"No."

"Ok, if you tell us the name of your school, we can phone them to explain why you're not there tomorrow."

"Thanks – can I ask you something?" said the boy.

"Of course."

"Do you think he felt anything?"

"I doubt it – when you hit the water at that speed, it's like hitting concrete."

"It doesn't feel like things will ever be the same again – life feels crueller."

"They won't, but you're just finding out what other people find out further down the line. Eh - I'll take you home in my car – talk to your mum. Would that help?"

The boy nodded. He picked himself up and started to unwrap himself from his blanket, to hand it back – it was police property.

"Keep it – you look like you need it. We'll talk about the rest on the way to your house."

Joel led the boy to the car, leaving Sam to take care of the rest. The river looked beautifully still; like a coverlet for all the victim's pain that had now been absorbed into its depths.

• •

I sat on the plush carpet of grass with Molly. We were in the Botanic Gardens and it was the best day of the year. The place was bustling with tourists, students and families. Considering that fact, I was in a surprisingly good mood. I looked around at the summertime flower beds. They were brightly blooming and so Molly seemed to be too in her summer dress with her flushed complexion. It felt like such a good day that nothing could threaten it. But it's always when you think such thoughts that something shows up to prove you wrong.

On the other side of the railings, just feet away, there was a man sitting alone on a bench outside the Palm House. He had a bald head that shone like polished silver. He looked neither happy nor unhappy, like an emotionless type. But there was something about his eyes that unsettled me. They were piercing, not so much colour-wise as focus-wise, and they were looking straight at my girlfriend. I was used to her getting looks from strangers. She stood out in a way that made her impossible to ignore. But there was something more sinister about this man. I put my arm around Molly, and he shifted on the seat. I tried not to stare at him for too long. It's better with these types to ignore them and hope they'll go away. To them, I know that attention is the same thing as encouragement.

 "Why don't we take a walk around the ravine?" I asked Molly.

"But aren't you enjoying sitting here?" she asked, tilting her head to one side. She did that because she knew it made it impossible for me to tell her no. But that day, I knew we had to move.

"I need to walk around – I'm getting restless sitting here."

She glanced in the direction of the man watching us.

"Ok," she said.

She got to her feet and swept the loose grass off the backs of her legs. I could still see the man eyeing her out of the corner of my eye. I wasn't going to give him the satisfaction of a glance. I took Molly's hand and led her across the grass and away from her observer. I knew that no matter how much time passed, I'd never forget his penetrating eyes.

CHAPTER ONE

Pierce

I waited for my name to be called. It was one hell of a wait – three years to be exact. I'd been groping for some form of treatment every one of those days that nearly added up to a round thousand. Finally, the day I'd expected the first day I'd walked into the emergency room was upon me, and I didn't know if I had the strength left in me to summon up the words I needed to say. I'd been assigned a psychiatrist. I looked around the room at all the other patients. Their suffering was more obvious than mine. They rocked backwards and forwards in their seats, foreheads pressed to palms, tremors that travelled the full length of the room; everyone could see their anxiety, their anguish, the acuteness of their conditions. I was a different case. I held it all inside. That was one of the reasons I'd had a terrible time getting treatment. I looked down at my clothes; they were grubby, but, like my girlfriend said, I just looked like a typical twenty-something guy: unkempt hair, holey jeans, sullen expression. That was what she told me; I tried hard to smile, but maybe I never quite pulled it off. Maybe she just didn't get why I couldn't. Whatever was eating me up on the inside was imperceptible to her, never mind to a strange doctor that had only minutes available to assess me.

I tapped my foot on the floor. If anyone had been watching, maybe they would have noticed my agitation coming through. Or maybe they just would have thought I was enjoying my music. My headphones were on and I was listening to a punk band. I kept my eyes glued to the door, in case I missed something important. I could lipread my name well by then; I lipread it every time Molly tried to get my attention, every time I was too far gone to hear her. The visitations were becoming more regular. Since I was a kid, there was a voice in my mind that didn't sound like my own. He had always been fully grown, even when I wasn't. At the age of three, I remember hearing him. His voice was more distinct to me than those of my own parents. He was more persistent than the most pronounced of their parental pestering ever was. Day and night, he made his appearance. He didn't care about the hour at which he came. Every night when my mother left the room, he was waiting for me at the window, lingering at the velvet curtains, like he was checking they were securely shut, so no one could see us. He remained at the curtains - that physical form that I assigned to the voice, like he was tucking me in, but without the comfort. Then, his eyes were upon me; like his forehead was pressed to mine, talking so loudly I could hear his voice resounding in my brain. I shared a room with my sister. I wondered how she was never woken by him. I never woke her either; I wanted to spare her the terror.

I'm twenty-seven years old now and my companion hasn't aged a minute. He stays constant and adds a new frown line to my face each year. I'm not sure what peace sounds like, but I keep hoping one day I will. I've been told once I get the right treatment, the voice will finally be silenced for good. A fix-all – that's what I need. I just haven't been able to get access to someone able to prescribe it. Mental health issues are rife in this small country. With a population not far over a million, half of its inhabitants seem to be under the weather; figuratively and literally. Maybe that's what causes a lot of the problems: the souls start to match the pallor of the grey skies.

I know my problems aren't more important that anyone else's, but I'm still desperate for someone to help me. Still, I've tried to be patient. But three years is a long time to wait patiently when you're losing the will to live.

A guy about my age enters the room. I can hear him even through the heavy drone of bass in my ears.

"It's pissing it down," he shouts, taking his hood down and leaving a trail of droplets on what-was a recently mopped floor.

He sits right beside me, uncomfortably close. He doesn't look the type to notice boundaries: in space, in sound, in etiquette. The diversity of the issues being treated there surprises me. I look around the room at the uniform seating, the tables cluttered with issues of "Psychology Plus." Maybe the staff are hoping we'll find our cure between their pages and leave them in peace to do their paperwork. That's one constant I've noticed in my contact with mental health services: avoidance. The resources are stretched beyond the strength of their elastic and something feels like it's about to snap. Perhaps it will be me.

I try not to make eye contact with the guy beside me. I sense that if I do, he'll draw me into conversation with him, and that's the last thing I can cope with. Before this appointment, I hadn't left my house in over a month. I had to take time off work to hide inside the safe doors of my home. The only person I saw during that time was my girlfriend, and that's only because she lives with me. I know she's getting tired of me. She looks at me with eyes filled with pity more than admiration now. She's stuck around for a long time: four years so far. That's longer than any of my relatives have wanted to spend with me in my adult life. I haven't seen my parents in months. They live five minutes from my front door, but they don't need the drama in their lives, they say. They're entitled to enjoy their retirement without the disruption of my crises. If only I could pull myself together, maybe they'd want to see me. I know I should be having them over for Sunday dinners, doing odd jobs around their house, now that I'm an adult, making myself useful to them. But I'm not useful; I'm too disturbed to be useful, and emotionally, I'll never be an adult.

I tried to have myself committed a few years ago. I was seeing things when I was out, walking around – things that no one else seemed to see. The faces of passers-by were the faces of the devil. The flames of hell roasted my feet with my every step. I was too terrified to open my eyes in the morning – every day the visions were getting worse. So, one day, when it all got too much, I decided to walk to the emergency room alone. No point in alerting anyone to my plans – I was alone in my own mind anyway. It doesn't matter how many hundreds of people might fill a room; I was the only one occupying the reality inside my head. I cried so hard I couldn't see where I was walking, and I was too unwell to care who saw me do it. Everything was so blurred I could have walked into oncoming traffic and not even noticed until it was too late.

I got to the hospital and walked into the room. Everyone in the waiting area had perceivable injuries: broken bones, limps, bleeding wounds. I looked like I was in as good health as the staff on shift. I knew before I spoke to them that no one would believe me, and I was right.

"How can I help you?" the secretary said, from behind her protective screen.

"I'm seeing things."

"What do you mean, you're seeing things?"

"Like, visions."

"So, what should I say is wrong with you?"

"I don't know."

"I need something to type into my form."

"Can't you just type that?"

"No – I have to fit you into a box for treatment."

"Ok, well, you could put that I'm depressed."

"Can't you go to your GP with this?"

"No, I've already been to them – they don't know what to do."

"So, what do you want us to do?"

"I guess I need to see a specialist."

"Can't you get a referral?"

"I'm losing my mind – please - help me."

She reluctantly typed up something on her computer.

"Take a seat."

I shuffled over to the only seat I could see without occupied seats next to it. I might have to sit in that room for hours and I had to stop myself losing control. I needed to remove myself from people. They were like sharp moving objects, out to do me harm. I couldn't see their features anymore. I needed space, or I'd walk out and miss this one important chance. I put my head in my hands, closed my eyes and tried to transport myself to another place.

Hours later, and by the time every one of my nerves had been shredded apart, my name was called. I picked myself up from my seat. An end to suffering was in sight. I was going to see an expert and they would know what to do. I'd probably be moved to the inpatients ward; I might have been one of the only people who wanted that outcome from their hospital visit. That's how bad the alternative was.

A doctor waved me over and led me down the corridor without saying a word. I reached a room and he told me to sit on the bed. It seemed pointless; I didn't need to lie down.

"Well, what can I do for you?" he asked, taking a chair and observing me from the far side of the room.

"I'm losing my mind."

"What do you mean?"

"I feel like I'm going crazy."

"But what is specifically happening?"

I couldn't attempt to put it into words. I'd hoped he would intuitively understand. He didn't.

"What do you want the outcome of today to be?"

I couldn't understand why he was talking about it like he was my careers teacher and we were discussing my future goals. This wasn't a place I would have visited without real reason to do so. I expected him to tell me they were over-booked, to come back in a quieter season when there was less competition for a free room.

"I think I need to go into hospital."

"What for?"

"I need help."

"Ok, I don't know what to do with you – I'll get an ambulance and send you over for assessment with the mental health team – is that what you want?"

"Yes, please."

My muscles slackened. I was safe, safe from myself; for then.

An hour later, an ambulance arrived, and a paramedic wheeled me outside. It felt unnecessary. There was nothing wrong with my legs. But no one seemed to know what to do with you unless there was. He grabbed me by the arm and helped me inside. I sat in a seat and made small talk with him and his workmate. I knew they were wondering why I needed an ambulance at all, but I couldn't turn off the act I'd got so used to putting on to convince everyone I was ok.

We arrived at the hospital and they stood back to let me climb out of the doors myself, satisfied by then that there was nothing much wrong with me. I was led down another long corridor. It mirrored every single one I'd seen in a hospital in my life. Corridors that led you to bad news always looked alike. I was left in a room where I waited alone, wondering if anyone would ever join me. The building felt unmanned; spookily still, apart from the occasional holler of one of the inpatients. It wasn't much different than a fictionalised mental institution I'd seen on TV. It had a gothic exterior, was miles away from any other building, so remote there wasn't even a streetlight in sight, and it felt like we'd reverted to the days of no central heating. If the place had any, they weren't making use of it. Had my mind been less sick, I would have run out the door and never looked back, but I needed help, no matter where I had to stay to get it. It was life or death. If I didn't get help soon, that voice and the visions were going to drive me to an edge from which I could never return.

Finally, after the longest of waits, a doctor strolled into the room.

"Sorry to keep you waiting…"

He tailed off, without attempting to explain why. I was starting to learn that the health service could treat you however they wanted to; no one was going to hold them accountable for their actions. No one was even in the same region of the hospital to oversee them. I suddenly felt like I had walked into a dungeon, a nightmarish place that gave the appearance of being a treatment centre when it was anything but.

"What's your name?"

"Pierce Jones."

He lazily scratched it onto his paper.

"Why are you here?"

"I went to A&E and they sent me over here."

"What for?"

"For help."

"What's wrong?"

"I feel like I'm losing my mind."

"You're not losing your mind."

"I feel like I am."

"You're not. I need you to be specific – what symptoms brought you here?"

"I can hear a voice."

"Voices or a voice?"

"A voice."

"Usually with Schizophrenia, you can hear more than one."

"Well, I can hear one."

"Are you sure it isn't just a misinterpretation of events?"

"What do you mean?"

"Like you think it's a voice, but it isn't really."

"No, it's a voice. I recognise it like a real person as soon as I hear it."

He looked at me disbelievingly and sat, leaning forwards in his seat, his chin on his fist.

"Listen, do you really want to stay here?"

He said it below his breath, like he was offering me a hit of something illegal. I looked up, and as I did, I saw a face in the doorway, pressed against the glass. It was like an apparition and I couldn't tell if it was real or if my mind was playing tricks on me again. The doctor followed my eyes to the window in the door.

"That's just Lesley – one of our patients. That's what I mean. You aren't like the people in here."

"I need help."

"Well, I think staying here would do you more harm than good. You might need help, but I'm not the one to help you."

"So, what am I meant to do?"

"Go home and get some rest. Things will look brighter in the morning."

I stood up and wandered back into the hallway. I was disoriented and couldn't separate hallucinations from true sightings, but there was nothing to do but go home. I called Molly and told her I was getting a taxi. I didn't know where on Earth I was. The name of the hospital wasn't one I'd ever heard of before, like it was one of society's shameful secrets. I didn't know which side of the city I was on and hoped a taxi company would have a better idea. Otherwise, I sensed I'd be stranded there until morning.

I got lucky - if you could call it that - and got home an hour later. Molly was waiting up when I got in. The day was gone; it had been sunny for Belfast when I'd gone into hospital and now the night was the deepest tone of black. Molly looked se-vere when I got there. She was getting more and more annoyed with my vague answers to questions I didn't know the answers to myself. She thought I was keeping something from her - that there was someone else. I couldn't bear to tell her there was someone else: this unwelcome companion I carried around with me every day. They had yet to be introduced. If I could pretend to be normal for long enough, maybe I'd become that way and the topic would never have to be broached.

Aside from my secret, we led a normal existence. We had both graduated from university and had stuck around in the South of the city while we looked for graduates' jobs. I had picked one up quickly: a call centre job - a post anyone could have filled. That's what I needed: something to supply a dependable pay-check with dependable duties on a day to day basis. There were enough of us lined up at desks in the centre that I hoped my mental health problems would be lost amidst the masses.

Everyone seemed to do the same things every day: sign in on the phones, talk to a few memorably difficult customers, a few forgettable kinder ones. They made trips to the toilet, to the smoking area, to the vending machines: anything to get some respite from their ringing phones. My anxiety was making my job untenable. Every time the phone rang, I started shaking and couldn't remember the rehearsed speech I'd had to give on the line. I paint myself as the oddity of the office, but everyone seemed oblivious of my issues. I've got used to putting on a face that covered all the disorder behind it. I've had a lifetime to practice it. My girlfriend works a different shift to me; she is still sleeping when I leave the house for work. It suits me well since mornings are my lowest point of the day. I couldn't feign soundness of mind at that hour, nor could I discuss it, even with her. I don't like discussing my hidden terrors with those close to me; once I unleash them into the physical world, I might never be able to plaster over them with convincing sanity again.

I start the day with coffee and empty moments before it's time to log on at nine. Every day is the same as the last. I walk ten blocks to my office, swipe my security pass and enter. It isn't what I had planned for my life. I'd wanted to play music but singing sporadically at gigs wasn't enough to fund the groceries, never mind the rent and monthly expenses. I still thought about songs when I was bored in work – playing around with lyrics and key changes. Music is the only thing that stops the shrill screeches of the monster in my mind. That's one thing I've discovered: if the volume of the music I'm listening to exceeds that of the voice, I can drown it out for a little while.

You probably want to know what the voice talks about, how he has had enough conversational material to fill so many years. He's not very diverse when it comes to topical choices; he likes to rehash the same ones over and over: suicidal suggestions, spelling out my inadequacies, dishing out his opinions on everything I hold dear, and never in a positive way. Every time I think about the tone of his voice, and his words that chip away at my personality, I feel weary. I just keep hoping one day he'll stop talking and I'll know what it is to have peace.

Anyway, when I got home that night, Molly wasn't pleased to see me. She didn't bother getting up from the sofa with her usual barrage of questions. She'd got used to never getting a satisfactory answer from me and frankly, I was glad she'd given up. That look of disappointment and suspicion on her face filled me with self-disgust. All I wanted was to make her happy, happier than I was capable of being, but I was failing. She'd stopped reacting to my unexplained arrivals. I wondered if that meant that she had already mentally exited the relationship. How long would it be until her feet followed suit? I looked at her, with her eyes glued to her book, wondering if they were really absorbing the lines of print that they traced, or if she was merely looking for an excuse to avoid looking me in the eye.

"How was your day?" I asked.

"Ok," she shrugged. "I went for dinner with some friends. Didn't think you'd want to come."

"Oh, how come?"

"You've turned down every one of my invitations in the last two months."

"Oh, I'm sorry."

"It doesn't matter. I've just decided to get on with my own stuff."

I wanted to tell her that I wanted her to be the one person I'd disclose all my abnormality to, but I couldn't bring myself to do it. If I did, she might decide I was a freak and the relationship would be cut off in one cruel chop. I'd do anything to extend it for as long as I could. I let Molly go to bed and didn't follow her. At that moment, I made a choice: I was going to behave normally, whether I felt it or not. I couldn't afford to lose the things I would if I sought treatment. I'd lived twenty-four years unaided. Surely, I could endure another twenty-four?

My plan to ignore my mental state lasted a couple more years. The pressure inside me was mounting. I was struggling to hold onto my job, to keep going in each day, to sit like a dummy behind that screen, my fingers tapping the keys without thought. My existence was useless. No one really knew me, not even my own girlfriend. The mask I wore to be accepted socially was so firmly glued to my face I didn't know how to remove it even when I was alone. It was like a hamster running on a wheel continuously, never stopping for food and drink, never stopping until its worn body collapsed with the wheel still spinning. That wheel was my world; it kept going despite my suffering. Every morning when I woke up, I was dismayed to find it still churning me round and round in its senseless cycle.

I kept smiling, kept making small talk with my colleagues, making superficial connections with my girlfriend. Until one day, I snapped. I walked out of work, leaving a room of confused faces whispering behind me. I hadn't explained my exit. I just stood up from my desk, set down my headset and logged off my computer for the last time. I left, leaving everyone wondering what was wrong. They'd probably put it down to a heated exchange on the phone, an intolerance to the blandness of the job. Really, it was both of those things and more. Not only were the phone call and the job futile, my existence was.

I got to the bus stop and headed straight home. I turned up my music and nodded my head, looking at my knees. Maybe if I looked absorbed in my music no one would see that I was crying onto my grey suit trousers. I looked at them with loathing.

I was losing all the features I'd had that had made my personality different; I had become one of the masses, one of the ones that will do anything not to stand out. I couldn't pretend anymore. I couldn't pretend to myself, to my boss, to the lady sitting next to me on the bus seat. I got to my feet and waited for her to get up. She thought the next stop was mine, but I just relocated to another bench on the bus with no other occupants. I was crowded and the voice was becoming audible again.

"You should have thrown yourself under the bus, not got onto it – you don't even have the courage to do that. Why don't you do it now? It isn't too late. Just wait next to the carriageway and put yourself out of your misery. You know it's the only answer."

I put my head in my hands, hoping it would relent long enough for me to get back to the safe isolation of my house. If I just made it inside, I promised myself I'd never have to leave again. I wasn't thinking of the logistics of that - just the fact that it was the only goal I had to see through to its end. It was my last chance of survival. The bus journey was only fifteen minutes. What passed too quickly every morning on the way to work was suddenly dragging beyond belief. With each stop, the gangway filled up with new characters. They were like sneering clowns in the sad performance that was my life. I couldn't endure it any longer. I beat my way through those nameless figures and got off at the next stop. I looked around. I still had a mile to walk, but at least I could do it without a busload of passengers staring in my face. There were no more elements I couldn't control: no traffic lights, no tailbacks; just my feet and my choice of walking pace.

When I got home, I was relieved Molly wasn't in. I still wasn't ready to admit that my mind had defeated me. Not to her, at least. Molly was a person of high achievement. She had just been promoted in her job at a restaurant. Her salary was double what mine was. She never seemed to make any human errors. It was a tough measuring stick to stand next to, daily. Her success had become a reference point for my failings. I walked in the door, went straight to bed, and cried into my pillow until it was like a saturated sponge. The tears were coming in a deluge. Almost three years of contained feelings and they were coming out so strongly at once it was debilitating. I didn't think I'd ever find the strength to get up from that bed again, even if I needed water, even if I needed the bathroom. I'd rather die there than get up and face up to life again. That day, that was how I felt, and that's what led me to nearly be dead.

CHAPTER TWO

I woke up in a strange bed. It was one with sheets so clean they were almost crispy and an indefinable hum that made relaxation impossible. There was a curtain drawn around the bed, tubes in my arms and a mask over my mouth. I was delirious, but it was a scene so plain it couldn't be misinterpreted: I was in hospital. It took a few moments to remember why I was there, to be disappointed that I was there. I had attempted to end my life, but obviously I hadn't succeeded. That thought didn't give me any relief, just a more pronounced feeling of failure. I couldn't sit up to reach the straw on the bedside table. My mouth felt as dry as an envelope seal awaiting saliva. It was only at that moment that I realised Molly was sitting beside me. She was in the one chair next to the bedside, visibly worried and unaware of the fact I'd come around. I was surprised to see her there. I thought she'd shy away from anything that involved painful emotions. She didn't talk openly about her own, but maybe that was because I didn't share mine with her. We lived in an emotionally icy atmosphere. It was all a farce. It was time to be real with her. The matter at hand didn't leave me with a vast array of other options.

"Hey," I croaked.

I could hear my voice clearly inside my mind, but physically, it seemed to lag behind.

"You're awake," she gasped.

She looked at me, flushed and I noticed her tear-stained face.

"I guess I am," I said.

I checked the walls of the room for a clock, but then I realised the time didn't matter. I didn't know the day, the date, the month, and I didn't need to. Time was unimportant now that I was on holiday from any timed obligations.

Molly seemed to make sense of my disorientation.

"It's 4pm, Thursday. You collapsed yesterday. You didn't leave a note or anything. I didn't know what had happened. Why didn't you say something?"

"I didn't know what I wanted to say. It wasn't something that was planned out."

"I had no idea you were depressed. You could have been dead, and I never would have known why."

She cried and pressed both her hands around mine, like a clamp.

"I'm sorry – I didn't know what you'd think. I felt like it was weakness – that you'd think I was weaker than you."

"I don't think that. Depression is serious. My sister had it. She had to be hospitalised."

"I didn't know that."

"You never mentioned it."

"I was scared to bring it up."

My voice was coming back, but physically, I still felt drugged. Every organ seemed to hurt, like the severest of hangovers, and everything in the room felt far away, no matter how close it was. It felt like if I closed my eyes and let sleep envelop me, I might still be able to reconnect with the other realm I had almost entered. But now that Molly knew, I couldn't leave her alone to deal with that. I'd assumed she'd be unaffected by it all. She hadn't seemed to notice much about me lately. She was always out socialising with her friends. Every day of the week, she seemed to have an event lined up for the minute her shift finished. We rarely ate together, and I was often asleep before she got home. I'd thought she'd be glad to remove me from the inconvenient position I took up on her social calendar. But here she was: the only person that had cared enough to show up. I was sure my parents had been informed by then. I already knew what their response would be: shame, denial, burying their heads. Suicide to their generation was a word that carried so much dishonour. They were churchgoers. They believed in doing the "right thing," even when it felt wrong to me. Following the lines of the good book was more important to them than offering compassion when an unwanted circumstance arose.

Molly kept her hand pressed to mine. It was hot and clammy. Why had I worried about trusting her? I'd misread the entire situation. When I'd met Molly, I'd thought she was a sensitive, musical type. She dressed well, like she put a lot of thought into the little details. She wore well-fitting jeans, her tops were always vibrant, not something you'd find without searching far and wide. She had lips that looked like a bow: a perfect red pout. Someone with those lips couldn't be unfeeling, they couldn't be shallow. She looked like a passionate person, which was what had initially drawn me to her. But observing the way she lived her life had changed that view. Molly never missed a day of work and she was never subjected to the fluctuations of her moods. She was so level, I'd decided without asking that she didn't understand me.

"You can talk to me, Pierce. Promise me you won't try this again – you have to tell me before it gets to this point."

"It's hard to put into words."

"I know, but just tell me what you can, and I'll try and listen."

I smiled at her. Her support wasn't enough to make me want to be part of this world, but it felt a little less harsh than it had a day earlier.

"Do you know when I'm getting out?"

Molly shook her head. "We'll have to wait and talk to the doctor."

A short while later, the doctor emerged. She checked all my vitals and seemed satisfied with them.

"Do you know how horrible it is to overdose on Paracetamol?"

"No."

"You could have survived and destroyed your liver."

I felt like I was a child being scolded by an adult for something that I'd done for valid reasons that they failed to see from their adult viewpoint. She unplugged me from everything that was physically keeping me there and went to look for the on-site counsellor.

"We'll need to sign you off before you go. You aren't going to try this again, are you?"

"No," I said. I didn't know whether it was true or not; it just seemed like what she wanted to hear. I couldn't control how close to the edge the voice drove me.

"You're only twenty-seven years old. Whatever reason you had for doing it wasn't big enough."

I nodded and waited until she left the room.

"Let's go."

"No, Pierce, you have to wait for the counsellor."

"What for? So they can make me promise not to do it again?"

I got out of bed and Molly followed me out of the ward.

"Let's just go home. These people don't have anything to offer me."

"Well, you need to talk to someone."

"Ok, I'll make an appointment with the GP."

"Ok," she said, following me with hesitance until she realised that I appeared completely fine.

Two weeks later, I tried it again.

CHAPTER THREE

That gnawing voice wouldn't stop hassling me. It didn't matter how much I closed myself away from society, cut myself off from human contact; there was no escaping him. He pestered me until one day, I stepped out my bedroom window. It wasn't very high up and I didn't do more than injure my leg, but it was enough to put me on suicide watch. Molly accompanied me to the hospital. I'd planned on just letting it go again, but she made me wait for the counsellor this time.

The lady walked into the room in her severe way. Her sharp heels clicked on the floor, like further stabs of sound to my mind. She looked neither empathetic nor approachable, but I had no choice but to entertain her.

"We're referring you to mental health services, Pierce. You'll be sent over there today."

"Ok," I tried to hide the surprise in my voice. I'd thought they'd consider me a less serious case; one who was only at risk of hurting himself, not of leaving the world any time soon.

"we'll get an ambulance to take you over there."

I followed Molly into the rear of the van. Thankfully, the paramedics on duty weren't the ones I had met before. I hoped the place they were sending me to wouldn't be the same as last time. I didn't have the patience left for another ineffectual appointment.

I was glad to see that the exterior to the building didn't resemble the one I'd visited before: no gothic style turrets, no faulty lighting, no eerie quietness. It was a modern place with staff bustling about their business. It felt like there was life about the place: a good thing when death was all you had on your mind. The lights were bright without being painful and the air didn't have that heady hospital odour I'd got so used to smelling. The scene almost made me hopeful that they would be able to help me.

I told the receptionist I'd arrived, and we took our seats amidst Belfast's other undesirables. I wondered if I'd be classified crazy if I completed a questionnaire. It was funny to think that was a possibility. I'd always thought if you were mentally ill, you'd feel much less of a normal guy than I did. I didn't look intimidating, at least, I didn't think so. I had a bit of a baby face and kind eyes, I'd been told. I didn't fantasise about reprehensible things or stand out as the one weirdo at a social gathering. But here I was, needing professional help, and not feeling ungrateful to be there.

"Pierce Jones," a lady called.

I got to my feet and tried to smile. Was I supposed to smile, or would that not help my case? Maybe if I looked happy to be there, she'd think I had no reason to be. I brushed my hair back from my face, thinking of the impression I was making. It felt like I was going to a job interview. I tried to stand up straighter, but I'd got too used to walking around in a permanent slouch. I always carried the weight of a million woes wound around my neck.

"Take a seat, Pierce," she said. She looked questioningly at Molly. Maybe she wasn't meant to be there.

"This is my girlfriend, Molly."

"Would you mind waiting outside, Molly? We just worry that patients won't feel they can be truly honest with us if there is another listening ear."

"Sure," said Molly.

She looked a little rebuffed but walked away.

I instantly became more nervous. The situation was exponentially more intimidating without a familiar face encouraging me along. I took a seat and tried to sit normally, but I was giving every move I made too much thought. My anxiety was taking over, and the shakes began.

The lady didn't seem to notice.

"I'm Bronagh. I'm a mental health nurse here. Welcome to community mental health."

"Thanks."

"Well, how did you get referred to us?"

"I attempted suicide a couple of times recently."

She examined me with caring eyes.

"Well, let's have a wee chat about your mental health history and we'll try and get a better picture of what's going on here."

"Ok."

She picked up a pen that looked like it was running low on ink. They all did; there had obviously been a magnitude of notes taken in that little box room. I had absolute faith in them; I'd finally made it through to the specialists – they would know the answers I'd failed to find myself.

"How old are you, Pierce?"

"Twenty-seven."

"And are the problems you've been having recent?"

"No, I've had them as long as I can remember, but I'd say they've come to a head recently."

"Ok, so what are the main things you struggle with?"

"Depression, anxiety, hearing a voice."

"What do you mean, a voice?"

"Like a man's voice."

"That's unusual. Usually there are several voices. Do you hear any others?"

"No."

"Are you sure that it's a voice or could it just be a misinterpretation of events?"

"It sounds like a man's voice and I can hear it speaking."

"Ok."

She typed something onto her computer screen. I tried to read whatever it was without looking nosy. Whatever she was recording was in a shorthand I couldn't understand: the doctors' own personal code I couldn't crack. I hoped they'd have more luck cracking mine.

"Do you ever have any visions, Pierce?"

"Yes."

"What like?"

"They're usually like nightmares – demons, weapons, things that are out to harm me."

"Ok, so we don't know if they are real visions or just representations of your fears."

"Well, I can see them."

"Like in a dream?"

"No, like you're sitting in front of me right now."

"Ok, we'll send you over for a scan to rule out anything physical that could be the cause of it."

"What like?"

"Like epilepsy or damage to the brain."

"I'm going to transfer you to community mental health and get you a CPN. Then you'll have someone to call when you need help."

"Ok."

I must have looked like I found that insubstantial.

"Do you feel like you're likely to attempt suicide again?"

"No."

What else could I say? If I admitted it was still a temptation for me, she might send me back to hospital, where no one took me seriously.

"Give me a minute, I'll go and discuss this with the team and see what we can do today."

"Thanks."

I scanned the room for something that gave the room a personable feel to it, like it was occupied by humans with unique characters. It was all unimaginably bland and featureless. Maybe they had to keep each room looking sterile and blank, so it didn't agitate any of the patients, or bring up negative associations for them.

I sat for what felt like over an hour, worrying about Molly waiting outside. I'd ruined her whole day. I'd never intended to do that. I'd planned to slip away, with her barely noticing my exit. I didn't feel important enough to have such an effect on others, whether I was there or not, but the fact I'd wasted Molly's time bothered me. People say suicide is selfish. Maybe the act is, but not the intention behind it. I never wanted to cause Molly an ounce of discomfort, I just wanted to simplify her life, to allow her a better chance at contentment. How can you be contented when you're living under the same roof as someone so haunted and troubled by things?

The nurse finally returned to the room.

"We're going to give you a prescription today, Pierce. You can take the note to your GP after this and pick it up. I've requested that you be placed under the care of Tim Hanlon. He is one of the primary mental health team members. He's a psychiatrist with years of experience. He really knows his stuff. I think you'll find your experience with him positive."

"What's he like?" I asked.

"You'll get on well with him. He's an older member of the team, very witty, dry sense of humour. I think you'll enjoy his company, but he'll also have a lot of valuable advice for you."

"Sounds great."

"He's always highly sought-after. You're just lucky he's recently dropped one of his case-load, so he has room for a new patient."

My timing was lucky, I had to admit. A sense of brand-new opportunity suddenly seemed to blossom about me. With the right guide, I hoped things might start to look up, but maybe that was too much to hope for.

CHAPTER FOUR

I first met Tim two weeks later, with 500mg of antipsychotics in my system and a new feeling of sluggishness. I felt less agitated, but more receptive to whatever advice came my way. I decided that would be a point in my favour; I'd been told about the common resistance of patients to mental health treatment, but I couldn't have been in a more passive state. I'd do whatever was suggested to me; things could only improve from there, supposing I put the suicide notion to bed.

I was sitting in the waiting area, staring into space. I half-noticed the other patients walking the vending machines, making trips to the toilet, staving off panic attacks. I looked around the room at all the posters for group therapy: art, music, sport, every activity under the sun - not one of them I wanted to attend. I didn't expect that spending time around the mentally unwell would work wonders on my mental state. I'd leave that to the professionals - to the ones that knew what they were talking about. They had studied their subject in depth, likely having gone into it with a pure passion for it. I'd heard rave reviews from the GP about my psychiatrist. It turned out they were good friends; they played football together at the weekends, they'd gone to university together. Everyone who knew Tim Hanlon thought he was the most accomplished of advocates for mental health. His methods were supposed to be innovative, modern, experimental – a new approach I was dying to learn. Maybe I'd be a successful member of society by the time he was done with me. I had the highest of hopes for him; he would be the saviour I needed – I was sure of that. And that's why I was so disappointed when I met him.

CHAPTER FIVE

"Pierce," a lanky figure appeared in the doorway with the announcement of my name. I got up and walked towards him. He was towering over me. At five foot ten, I'm not a small guy, but this man was the tallest of structures: long-limbed, lean, his mind so high it seemed unreachable.

"Alright," he said, loosely holding my hand in his own.

His handshake was as lifeless as his eyes, and I felt an instant dislike for him. But I was hardly capable of sketching out an accurate character profile; I was barely what could be classed sane, and I knew one introduction wasn't enough to form a true impression of him. I followed Tim into a corridor, the colour of which I associated with sickness. The hallways felt haunted by the mental disturbances of every patient that had passed through them. An open-minded person might have described me as intuitive, but a rational one would have called my intuition paranoia instead. I could feel the frets of a thousand souls making a channel through my body and playing with my nerves. I walked into Tim's bleak office. It overlooked a busy junction that the inner view of two trees didn't manage to mask.

"Well," he said, slouching in his seat.

He didn't bother to smile, and I wondered why he was hailed

in his profession as the solution to all strife.

"I had a look at your file."

He seemed to smirk at me, but maybe the light just made his face seem to contemptuously brighten. Maybe he wore a neutral expression and I was just reading too much into everything in my current frame of mind.

I nodded, waiting for him to say more.

"The first thing I think we should do is reduce your medication."

"Why?"

"You're on 500mg of Quetiapine?"

"Yeah. They said that was my starting dose – they might put it up later."

He shook his head abruptly.

"Medication is not a fix-all. It shouldn't be abused. If you rely on it to make you well, you'll never take responsibility for your own problems."

"Ok."

"Let's reduce the medication to 100mg and see how that goes."

He scribbled barely legibly on his pad and tore the page off.

"Give this to your GP today and we'll get your medication lowered as soon as we can. Has anyone talked about a diagnosis with you?"

"No, there have been suggestions of schizophrenia, but nothing concrete yet."

He made a sound like he was blowing out a particularly stubborn flame on a birthday candle.

"That's not what I think – but we'll give it some time and see what we observe."

He kept using "we," like I was fully involved in my own treatment and he wasn't coming up with all his ideas independently from me.

"What do you think is wrong?" I asked.

"I think it's acute stress. Bad coping mechanisms, most likely. We need to break the pattern."

"Ok, what about the hallucinations?"

"Pierce, I only have a ten-minute slot per patient. I'm sure you noticed the waiting area out there. Any questions you have, write down and we'll deal with them next time."

He pulled out a folded piece of cardboard, like the mental health team's very own business card.

"I'll make another appointment with you for two weeks from now. Is Monday the twenty-seventh at eleven ok?"

It wouldn't be, if I was back at work, but it suddenly felt increasingly unlikely that I was going to make it back to my desk any time soon. I hoped they'd hold the position for me; it was so easily refillable - any breathing being could have done it.

"Thanks," I said.

I wasn't sure whether I was thankful or not; I felt disorientated more than I felt any other sensation. I walked out to the grey waiting room. He followed me out and called the next patient before saying goodbye. He was obviously inundated, so inundated he didn't have real time for any of us. But I knew I had a propensity for negative thinking, and I needed to stop making assumptions about people's intentions without giving them a chance to show who they were first.

The colourlessness of the waiting room dissolved as soon as I opened the door. It was like in *The Wizard of Oz*, when Dorothy enters Oz, and everything is suddenly bathed in vibrant colour. I was glad to see the world's colour again. Mental health buildings had a special tone of grey I'd never seen so densely packed into one place before.

I walked to the bus stop around the corner. I was in the city, but instantly aware of nature after the dearth of it at the clinic. The blackbirds were twizzling, the small patches of greenery stood out to my eyes, and the place seemed bountiful with wildlife, despite being one of the most deprived parts of town. I felt like my mind was running away with itself, shifting its chemistry in anticipation of its lowered dose of medication. I had to prepare myself for the worst; for feeling my worst again.

I stepped on board the bus, and as soon as I did, I wished I'd walked the three miles. It felt like the ventilation system had shut down and we were stuck in a sauna behind impenetrable glass. It was hard to know whether it was due to my mental state, or the conditions of public transport. My brain felt like it was contracting, reducing in size, but still holding the same number of thoughts. They were swelling inside it until the membrane couldn't hold the pressure back anymore and they flooded my body. But that's what they say about getting help isn't it? About counselling, about medication? You always feel worse before you can feel better. You can't just improve by one unit per day; you decrease by five, then go up four, and then go back down to minus numbers again.

The bus came to a halt and I realised it was my stop. I got up and joined the queue disembarking. All of us living in the one area, all leading different lives, probably none of them as dysfunctional as mine. I went home via the doctor's surgery. The receptionist knew me well by then. We always exchanged a few pleasantries – she seemed to intuitively understand my struggles. Her eyes enlarged a little when she read Tim's note. Maybe my initial reaction hadn't been without cause, but Tim was known for his unorthodox methods of treatment that were famed in mental health circles. I had to step out in faith, even if it looked like I was stepping off a ledge above a ten-storey fall into traffic.

"It'll be ready at three tomorrow, Pierce," she said. "Are you ok?"

"I think so, yeah. Hope you have a good day."

I took my time walking home. There was no reason to rush anywhere anymore. I was out of commission; nowhere near well enough to go back to work, to do tasks like the weekly food shop, to engage in any social activities. I was, quite simply, walking home to bed, again, and again, and again. I hoped Molly would be out when I got home. I didn't want to explain myself. She'd want to know every detail of my appointment that day and I was feeling too deflated to discuss it.

I got indoors and the phone rang. My mother; she only phoned me when she wanted to remind me of a familial obligation: a birthday, a funeral, a payment due.

"Hello Pierce."

"Hi, Mum."

"I'm just ringing to remind you it's your dad's birthday on Friday."

"Ok."

"Have you got anything for him yet?"

"No, I haven't had a chance to get anything."

"It would be nice if you could make the effort to remember these things."

I felt like launching into a tirade of all the things it would be nice if she did too, but I held myself back. The relationship was strained enough without me putting it under further duress.

"Are you going to call over on Friday?"

"I hadn't planned to, but I will if you want."

"I thought you would have wanted to."

"Ok, I will, Mum. I have to go. I'll see you on Friday."

"What time are you coming at?"

"I don't know yet."

"Suit yourself, Pierce – you always do."

I hung up and felt like my self-worth falling even further. That was something I couldn't handle the thought of, never mind the execution of: picking out a present. That meant a trip to town, busy crowds and their rush hour manners. I'd have to do it; I was already in my parents' bad books. I didn't want to be labelled the selfish child again, even though I was a grown man. In my parents' minds, my sister was elevated with the angels and I was digging around underground with the devil. I needed to redress the balance. Maybe it would be a chance to show them I could be the son they'd only met in daydreams. I'd think about that tomorrow; now I was doing nothing but breathing the scent of my sheets and allowing sleep to give me a glimpse of death's peacefulness. I sat down on the bed, easing my shoes off. They were tied in a double knot and I didn't have the energy to untie even one of them. I lay down, face first, into the pillow and cried myself to sleep, letting my pillow absorb the sobs.

When I woke up again, it felt like years had passed. My dreams had been like a blanket of black. I couldn't remember a thing, but I felt rested. I climbed out from under the covers and tried to work out the time; it was dark. But it was winter – it was always dark. It was dark when I woke up and dark when I got out of work. Everything was enveloped in navy light; a light that didn't give me an ounce of hope for a brighter day.

• •

Molly got home a while later and I realised it was night-time. I was getting a bad comedown from my drugs – one so bad I'd never have imagined you could get from anything legal. I was sweating and shivering, fighting back vomit, my legs were in a state of agitation. I couldn't link words together to make a sentence to try to explain myself. I just looked like I'd lost the run of myself and was suffering the consequences of a night of serious overindulgence.

"What's wrong?" Molly asked.

Maybe she could sense it; I could smell my own sickness in the air, like the sign of something rancid hidden below the floorboards.

"I don't know," I mumbled.

I had returned to my spot on the bed, balled up like a useless tissue: a piece of waste with nowhere to go but decomposition.

"Sweat's dripping off you. Are you sick?"

I shook my head.

"I don't know what's going on Pierce, but you're seeing a doctor and you seem even worse."

I shook my head more violently; I couldn't allow her to suggest my only chance of living a normal life wasn't working. Tim was my get-out-of-death-free card, and if I put him back to the bottom of the pile, I had nowhere else to turn.

"My medication… changed. It's just that."

"Ok, well, maybe you should get some sleep."

I didn't have the heart to tell her I'd done nothing but that all day. I felt like I was taking up the earthly space of someone far more valuable than I was. Molly deserved a guy with drive, someone who was taking steps towards a future; I was struggling to stay in the present. Maybe it was time to do her the greatest favour I could think of – to finish the relationship and allow her the chance to meet someone else. I thought about her big, soulful eyes filling up with tears, the pained look of rejection on her face – it was heart-breaking even in my mind's eye. But it would be a quick pain – pain in order to make her life richer. I thought about it while I stayed glued to the spot. I couldn't sleep, but I couldn't move an inch. My body ached like I had the flu, but my mind was as wakeful as ever.

That night, I felt Molly's body mould itself into the mattress, but I couldn't make a connection with her. My brain was still active, my hands paralysed. I wanted to reach out for her hand, but I couldn't. She slept beside me, her back rising and falling, her breaths slow and soothing. I was envious of her ability to switch off, to get a break from living. But maybe her version of living didn't require as much from her as mine did. Maybe being restful wasn't the same rarity to her that it was to me. My mind churned with everything. It felt like the thoughts of every member of the human race were whirring around in my mind. I needed to offload some of it, but there was nowhere I could deposit it to. I looked at the sheen of her hair in the room. Her blonde hair was so bright you could see the colour of it even in a full room of darkness. But the roots were as dark as the unlit room; she wasn't as straightforward or naïve as I thought she was. She had more strength than me, and when I did what I had to do the following day, I knew she'd take it well.

CHAPTER SIX

Molly went to her mum's house the next day. She didn't put up much of a fight when I suggested we separate our lives. She seemed resigned to it, like she'd thought of the idea herself but had been too afraid to bring it up when I was in such a fragile state. I knew before she left the house that she'd meet someone before the week was out. She had already mourned the loss of the intimacy we had once had. I hadn't shared an important thought with her since our early dating days. It was for the best, for both of us. Without the distraction of a girlfriend, now I could focus my attention on treatment and getting well enough to lead a "normal" life.

By the time my next appointment came around, my withdrawal symptoms were gone. But in exchange, I had received a new dose of paranoia and delusions. It was hard to see my way through it to the truth. When were people staring me down and when were they just looking, glassy-eyed, in my direction? When were they making harsh judgements about me and when were they thinking of something else that was causing them irritation? I felt like my thoughts could be heard in the waiting room, broadcast over the sound system to every eager ear. I kept trying to apply rationale to the situation, to convince myself those thoughts had no foundations, but it wasn't that easy to dismantle them. They felt as real to me as the work rotas pinned to the office wall.

Tim's voice snapped me out of my thinking. It had a firmness to it that made me pull myself together. I got up and followed him back to the same room. I couldn't remember the layout of the place even having been there once before. Every doorway mirrored the last and the sameness of it was disorientating. Maybe that was by design – to stop you seeing yourself as an individual with fresh problems; we were all one and the same – trapped in the same negative thinking, needing the same advice offered up in a freshly photocopied health service booklet.

I hesitated about which seat to take. There were three in the room and I didn't want to accidentally sit in Tim's. He had a presence that told you not to overstep boundaries with him, so I waited for him to tell me what to do.

"Take a seat," he said, gesturing to the chair opposite him.

"Well, how have things been?" he asked.

He sat back in his seat and looked at his notepad, his pen poised above it, ready for my disclosures.

"Not good."

"What do you mean?"

"Things have been worse."

"And why do you think that is?"

"I think it's since my medication was decreased."

"Nonsense."

I looked at him, confused.

"Medication being decreased isn't going to make you worse – it's only if you're convinced you need it to get better."

"Well, I have been having more hallucinations and feeling paranoid since it was lowered."

"That's normal and will soon pass. I think we need to get you involved in something."

"What like?"

"Well, you're not working at the minute, are you?"

"Well, I have a job, but I haven't been going to it."

"If you aren't able to go back, we need to get you involved in something purposeful."

"But I don't feel up to it."

"Why not?"

"I struggled to get here. I had to get a taxi because I couldn't face the people on the bus. The waiting room nearly tipped me over the edge."

"You need to get these thoughts in check. You can't avoid life just because you're worried about other people."

I felt completely misinterpreted, like he had shut down every means of understanding me.

"I don't choose the thoughts - I can't stop thinking they're real. Everyone's eyes are boring into my own. I think they can hear what I'm thinking and that they're out to get me. It's terrifying."

He looked blankly at me.

"Well, if we get you involved in something with people with similar mindsets, it will be less daunting. We have a walking group that meets once a week, a group of sufferers who meet for group therapy and go on trips together, classes you can take."

It all sounded nightmarish, but I'd go along with anything if it meant things got better.

"Why don't you go to the walking group? Getting some fresh air would help and you'd get the chance to talk to people with similar issues."

I felt like a sheep being herded into a pen with other sheep, bleating the same sad song. I'd spent my life trying to become one of the other animals – the ones with a more cheerful tune to sing. Now the latch on the gate was secured, and I knew I wasn't going elsewhere any time soon. I had to prove that I wasn't mentally ill first – to myself, to Tim, to the world.

CHAPTER SEVEN

That Tuesday, I joined the walking group. We met on the Greenway at a local park. Everyone was wearing running gear and I was still in my boots, my jeans and my Black Sabbath T-shirt. I looked a bit misplaced, but that only made plain how I was already feeling. Everyone hung around, like paint drips waiting for an artist to do something with them, waiting for the facilitator to arrive.

"Right, everyone," came a shrill voice, "Sorry I'm late, the traffic was terrible."

I couldn't help wondering how the traffic we'd come through could differ so much from hers, with us all moving around in the one city. It was hard to believe she cared about any of us.

"What's your name?" she asked me.

"Pierce."

"Ok, everyone, this is Pierce, he is going to join us, so give him a warm welcome."

Everyone looked at their feet and shifted around uncomfortably. It looked like they wanted me there just as much as I wanted to be there. That moment, the rain began. It came down in a steady stream, collecting with the water in the park pond. The sky was grim, and the clouds seemed to ripple, like a threat of thunder.

"We'd better get moving before we get soaked," said the facilitator. "I'm Anne, by the way."

"Nice to meet you."

A girl with red hair sidled up next to me. The hood on her raincoat was up, the drawstring tightened, but I could still see her velvety locks poking out of the sides of it. They looked untethered, like they had a life force of their own.

"Hi," she said, shyly.

"Hi."

"I'm Kate."

"I'm Pierce."

"I just started coming here a couple of weeks ago. Wasn't really my decision – I was talked into it."

"Same here."

"It's not bad, gets you out of the house. Do you work?"

"Yeah but I've been off recently. Do you?"

"No, I can't do that," she laughed, like it was a ludicrous suggestion.

For a second, I wondered if my current setup could become a permanent way of living. What if I was never well enough to go back to the office? What would I do? How could I support myself? My mind was racing away from me like a helpless passenger at high speed. I tried to focus on the moment I was in. It was a real strain, but I tried to make conversation.

Kate had a pretty face, but one that seemed to have prematurely aged. She had young eyes and healthy hair, but deep lines under her eyes and on her forehead. She took a roll-up from her bag and lit in while we walked. I smoked sometimes too, but she looked like the type that struggled to get from bedtime to morning without smoking. She didn't offer me one and I sensed she was one of the self-focussed kinds of smokers, but she seemed so open it was hard to believe she could be anything but kind.

We walked in a loop around the park pond. It was a couple of miles in total. For the volume of trees in the place, they didn't seem to give any umbrella effect against the rain. We were all drenched; my feet felt frozen inside my shoes and every step I took made a squelch between my sock and my insoles. I was ready for the outing to be over, so I could tick the box saying I'd done it, and retreat to my house. Tim couldn't hold me accountable for evading treatment if I did what he'd advised me to.

"What's your diagnosis?" Kate asked. "Sorry if I'm being nosy."

She said it like a disclaimer, so I wouldn't take offense, rather than because she regretted being so forward. From the first second, I noticed how she looked me directly in the eye and didn't appear embarrassed in the slightest. She seemed comfortable with her own diagnosis, whatever it was.

"I don't have one yet. What's yours?"

"BPD."

"BPD?"

"Borderline Personality Disorder. Are you on any medication?"

"Yeah, an antipsychotic."

"Oh, I'm not on that. I'm on antidepressants."

It felt like she'd got out a measuring stick to measure which of us was the craziest, but it was strangely comforting talking to her. She felt familiar to me, like a piece of myself I hadn't accessed since childhood. The strands of her hair that hung out the front of her hood were saturated and straggly. She had a combination of knowingness and lostness about her. I knew right then that we were going to be friends.

CHAPTER EIGHT

The next day, Kate invited herself over to my house. There was no getting to know each other period – Kate was all in from the first moment. We only lived half a mile apart, so it made sense for us to get to know each another. I didn't feel up to venturing further afield than that, so it suited me just fine. The doorbell rang earlier than I'd expected. I'd got myself ready, but I hadn't done a thing in the house. It was beginning to look like a student house; the dishes and laundry were accumulating and there was nothing left to make the place look homely. Anything like that had been removed by Molly. I wondered where she was now. We hadn't spoken since. I doubted we'd speak again. I hoped she would stay single long enough for me to get well. Then I'd be worthy of her company again.

I opened the front door and let Kate into the hallway. She took her backpack off and set it down. I wondered what she carried around with her. It seemed to be bulging with supplies. She looked like she could be an artist, a photographer, a sculptor. You wouldn't know what was in her bag; it intrigued me.

"Would you like a cup of tea?"

"Yes, please. Look at you – all domesticated."

"You haven't seen the state of the kitchen," I said with a laugh.

"Well, for a single guy, it's not that bad. My flat is pretty bad too."

"It is?"

"Yeah, I keep it clean, but it's still a dump."

"How come?"

"Damp, old carpets – it's a rental – the landlord doesn't look after the place. He doesn't want to spend the money on it. It's better than my last house though."

"How come?"

I started walking into the kitchen and she followed close behind me.

"Dodgy area."

I looked at the kettle and saw it was half full, flicking the switch on.

"Don't you refresh it?" she said. "I always do."

"Oh, ok," I said.

Kate grabbed the kettle, emptied the water out and rinsed it out several times before turning it back on. I wondered if she had obsessive tendencies, and if they might manifest in other ways.

"Would you like a biscuit?"

"No thanks, I'm funny with food."

I didn't know what she meant but was afraid to ask in case she had an eating disorder. She wasn't painfully thin, but she somehow looked malnourished. She reminded me a little of a wartime child – off-colour, bags under her eyes, a general tone of ill health.

I shouldn't have made any judgements on her appearance. I wondered what my own was like. I'd barely glanced in a mirror in weeks. I doubted I'd manage to get a hairbrush through my hair without resistance. She was looking at me fondly.

"You don't really smile, do you?"

"I don't know, we're not talking about anything funny."

"Just an observation – I didn't mean anything bad by it. Don't be offended."

"I'm not."

I wasn't, but I suddenly wondered if I should be. I passed her a cup of tea and she inspected the contents. I led her into the living room, and we sat down next to each other. She sat at the far end of the sofa.

"I get the impression you don't like physical closeness," she said.

"What makes you say that?"

"Just a vibe I'm getting."

I shrugged. I was feeling a little uneasy, like I was being psychoanalysed. But that was just part of her condition – she couldn't help doing it. I was the same – I couldn't help being who I was: not being a smiley person, not emitting a welcoming glow.

"So, how are you finding mental health services?" she asked, taking a sip from her tea.

"Is it strong enough?" I asked.

"It's ok. I like builders' tea – so strong it's like sucking on a teabag."

I laughed. She gave me a coy little smile.

"You looked lovely there – you always suppress your smiles. But you just laughed in such an unrestrained way. You should do it more often."

She told me every detail of her life for the next hour. Finally, I reached my hand out to offer to take her cup from her. I was happy to have visitors, but there was a clear time limit on it for me.

She jerked her head back.

"Do you want me to go?"

"No, I'm just tired."

"Ok, if you want me to go, I'll go."

"It's not that."

"No, I get it."

"Don't be offended."

"I can't help it. It's just the way I am."

"We can meet up again."

"How about tomorrow afternoon?"

"I can't, I have a party to go to."

"Whose?"

"My dad's."

"Ok, the next day?"

"Yeah, I'll ring you."

I closed the door behind her and felt a mixture of relief at meeting someone who knew what it was to wear my shoes, but simultaneously fearful that they might step right into mine.

CHAPTER NINE

My dad's birthday was the most awkward event I'd ever attended. My parents seemed to have accrued a whole new circle of friends and relatives since we'd last seen each other. The house was filled with distant cousins I couldn't have picked out of a line up. I sat on my own at the table. The only exchange I'd had with my parents was a greeting of "happy birthday" and a donation of gifts to the presents pile. I wondered why they'd wanted me there at all. But maybe my perception of everything was still skewed. I couldn't rely on my senses to assess the social temperature of a situation.

I sat at the table, drinking wine and knowing it was a bad idea while I did it. There was nowhere to put myself. I sat at my childhood dining table and felt like I hadn't earned the right to be there. Every one of my actions had been a major disappointment to my parents, even though I felt like I hadn't done anything significantly good or bad with my life. The wine was acrid, but I choked it down anyway.

My mum approached me, shooting a disparaging look at my glass.

"Don't overdo it, Pierce, leave some for the guests."

"I'm not, I've just had one glass."

"Ok, well, slow down. You don't want to let your dad down."

"Why did you invite me here?"

I suddenly felt emboldened by the drop of alcohol in my system.

"Because you're a part of the family, whether you choose to be or not."

"Celia isn't here."

"Celia has a family of her own to attend to. They're coming down later."

She was still the golden child, while I was the distressed, cheap metal one. Age couldn't change that, circumstance or effort; my character was chiselled in stone. I just had to put the afternoon in and get home.

My mum served up platters of party food and I offered to help. She and two of her friends had an efficient system going and they didn't seem to want any disruptions to it. I sat next to my dad as soon as a seat came free. He was, quite rightly, the pivot of the party, and I hadn't had a chance to say more than two words to him.

"Hope you're having a good birthday, Dad."

"Thanks, son. How's work?"

"I've taken some time off?"

"Oh? Why's that?"

"I haven't been well."

"You seem back to your normal self now. I'd make sure you don't lose that job – your mother and I can't afford to keep you."

"I didn't ask you to."

"Well, sooner or later, you need to start taking responsibility for your life, behaving like an adult. How's that girl you were dating?"

"We broke up."

"Probably for the best – she seemed a bit of a wild one, with

55

that bleach in her hair and those flamboyant clothes."

"She's a good person."

"It's time to get your life on track – you're still living like a teenager."

What he said chimed with my own feelings ringing deep inside me. I wasn't a fully formed adult, a man – I was an overgrown child with the emotional capacity of a twelve-year old boy. Nevertheless, I was angry with him. Angry about his lack of encouragement, angry about his flippant comments that had laid out my fate long before I'd made any attempt at a future. It was time to go home. I'd put my face in long enough I couldn't be accused of non-attendance, not long enough to repair our severed relationship.

"I have to head, Dad. I'll call and see you soon. Hope you had a great birthday."

He turned away from me, his silence louder than any pronouncement of displeasure could be.

My mum met my early departure with similar disapproval, but she still ticked the boxes of social graces. She wrapped a piece of birthday cake in a napkin for me and forced it into my hand. I didn't bother to make another arrangement – she'd likely come up with excuses until the next calendared event.

On my walk to the bus, the pain of missing Molly suddenly came through. I hadn't given it a huge amount of thought, so preoccupied I'd been with everything else. But that night was like a cavernous hole, waiting to be filled by the first thought I didn't want to have. And sure enough, Molly appeared first. At least it was preferable to the alternative: the voice I never wanted to hear from. I saw the outline of her face, real but enhanced, like her best features were outlined by the pen marks of memory. She was smiling in my mind's eye, more so since our separation. She looked as carefree as she had that first night when I'd met her. I thought about the details of her I still loved until the bus pulled up and loud reality interrupted my fantasies. The bus was filled with a representative of every one of the city's people: the loud, the quiet, the impatient, the easy-going, the polite, the rude. I stood in the gangway with a few others. My ears were ringing with the volume of chatter and the screech of the bus's brakes. It stopped at every one of its sign-posted stops, filling up more and more, until I got off. I'd walk home rather than standing chest to face with a stranger. Three miles, but my feet were filled with endless energy, my mind was, sadly, just as active. Molly returned to my thoughts right away, and I ached for her, even though I knew our break-up was the best gift I could have given her. Just because I wanted her to be happy didn't mean I wanted to be sad, and I stayed submerged in those feelings until I reached the familiar door of our house. Behind it were so many memories I never wanted to forget, but that I didn't want to remember at that particular moment. I turned the lights on and looked around at the blankness of the rooms, awaiting a woman's touch. She had taken every decorative item with her and the place looked like it had been stripped of all its soul.

I lay down on the sofa and closed my eyes, dreaming about the scent of her and the comfort of her voice. I was disturbed by a knock at the door. I had a feeling I knew who it was: my friend with the wavy hair and the unhealthy disposition – the last thing I needed. But I opened the door anyway; something about me sensed that she wouldn't stop, whether it be at knock one, or knock one hundred.

I opened the door with caution as I raised my eyes to look her in the face. It wasn't her. It was Molly – her deep eyes drawing me in, like I was sinking into their safety.

"Hi Pierce, sorry to call over unannounced."

"It's ok – I was just thinking about you – come in."

She followed me into the living room and sat down next to me on the sofa. She perched on the edge of it like she was in a waiting room – not somewhere she had laid her head countless times. I waited for her to speak first. I had no idea why she was there, and I was scared to open my mouth in case it allowed an outpour of emotion I couldn't hold back.

"Pierce, I miss you – I don't want to break up."

"I miss you too."

"I just don't know what to do when you won't talk to me – I'm open with you and I need you to be the same way with me."

Her eyes scanned the room.

"It looks so different here now – like I was never here."

"I can feel you in every room, every day. It feels empty."

"It's because you don't own any knick-knacks," she smiled.

"It's not just that. I want you to live here – it's not the same."

"Ok, I'll move back in. But I need you to try to talk to me about what you're thinking – I can't keep guessing."

"I'll try."

She leaned back on the sofa into my arms and we were reunited again. I had to pull my life together quickly – if not for myself, then for her.

CHAPTER TEN

The next week I had an appointment with Tim.

"Well, Pierce, what's new?" he asked.

He had a casual way of leaning back in his seat that made me feel like he wasn't taking me seriously. But my opinion of him hardly mattered; the quality of his treatment had been clinically proven.

"I went to the walking group you told me to go to."

"And?"

"It was ok, I got talking to a girl there."

"What was her name?"

"Kate."

"Oh, she is a good person to know."

"How come?"

"She's been through treatment and is coming out the other side. She's got a lot of wisdom to offer."

"That wasn't how she struck me."

He gave me a contemptuous look and I backed down.

"I hope you'll keep going – you look fresher this week."

"Well, my girlfriend and I got back together."

"Do you think that's a good idea?"

"What do you mean?"

"Is it a good idea to bring someone back into your life who could interfere with the success of your treatment?"

"Why would she do that?"

"You can't just focus on getting better if you're prioritising someone else."

"I feel happier when we're together."

"That's co-dependency. That's not happiness. Happiness is two stable individuals coming together and having an equal relationship - and you are anything but that."

I knew I was frowning and that I was eyeing the door, willing the appointment to end so I could take control of my own decisions again. He tapped his pen against his page and the rhythm of it somehow made me more tense.

"I'm going to suggest you put your relationship on hold until you're further into treatment – but I can't tell you what to do – I'll leave the decision up to you. Have things stabilised since you had your medication reduced?"

"No – they've got worse."

"We need to challenge that attitude of yours. We'll work on that. I'll keep your medication at its current level until you adjust to it and then we'll talk about removing it."

"You're going to take it away completely?"

"Well, that's the ideal – being able to manage your condition without intervention."

I hadn't managed it to date and wondered how on Earth it would be feasible under the same health conditions.

"Why do you want that?"

"I want to encourage you to be independent, Pierce. You've got a working diagnosis at the moment of…"

He paused and rifled through the pages in front of him.

"Schizophrenia. But I see no evidence of that. We'd like to eventually remove that."

"Why?"

"We want you living independently in the community. We're inundated here – the more people we can get leading stable lives the better."

"But can't we try that on medication?"

"Why waste government funds on something unnecessary? I'll look into where you can be referred on to when we are finished here – maybe we can get you some CBT or something."

"What's that?"

"Cognitive Behavioural Therapy – it's all about changing your feelings through changing your thinking."

"But that's not what's wrong with me – I see and hear things that aren't there."

"You think you do – that's what we can work on."

I was getting angry - worked up to the point I felt like demolishing his office, but I sat still with my rage, trying to stop it coursing through me.

He lifted his eyebrows. "I think we need to squeeze in an extra few sessions."

"That would be great." I managed to keep up the act, but it was killing me.

"Come and see me this time next week, and you can't tell anyone this – but here is my private phone number – if you're really stuck, just ring it."

"Thanks," I said, gripping the piece of paper. I'd never held something so valuable in my palm before – a direct line to help.

My anger melted away, and I put my coat on.

"I'll see you next week."

"Pierce?"

"Yeah?"

"Just try and trust what I'm doing here – you'll see how it will work in a little while."

And it was at that point that I decided to let go and put my trust in him. His smile was too sincere to be anything else.

CHAPTER ELEVEN

Molly got me a surprise gift, and I had to turn it down: tickets to go away for two days the following week. I felt bad turning it down, but she left me no other choice.

"I'm sorry – I'd love to go, but I've got an appointment then."

"Can't you change it?"

"No, he might not give me another one."

"You're letting this guy dictate what you do with your life."

I felt resentful of her remark. It was easy for her to say something so dismissive when she wasn't living the reality I was. Things had spiked upwards in a positive direction between us, like a second honeymoon period, but then the graph line had plunged back to zero. I couldn't stop Tim's wise words circulating in my head – maybe it was too much, trying to juggle a relationship whilst I was in treatment, living with someone else, filling my time with their needs and wants rather than attending to my own. Still, I knew if we broke up again, that would finish it for good. I'd have to coast along, distancing myself from becoming too romantically involved until Tim gave me the go ahead to have a relationship.

I knew Molly didn't understand me. I was intrigued by her; enough that I hadn't grown bored of her in the years we'd known each other. But we didn't have a soulmate connection; she didn't understand my darkest thoughts and I wasn't aware of whether she even had any in her head. She had two moods I noticed – contentment and light irritation at the things I didn't do that any normal boyfriend would have, and should have gone along with. It was nearing Valentine's Day, but I couldn't face a filled-up restaurant. We would have to do something low-key at home instead. It wasn't Tim that was dictating the terms of my life; it was my own mental deficiency.

I used up the day as wastefully as I could. I was desperate for it to end. It was only in sleep that the pain ceased. I thought about my options again. The city was heaving with them: traffic, buildings, bridges, trains: a million quick exits without time for a second thought. I pulled the piece of paper from my pocket. It already looked aged, like when you've opened and closed a note more times than the paper was made to endure. Etched on it was my only emergency contact; the man who had the answers to save me. That was the solution: I needed to rely on the person whose aim it was to rebuild my life.

I dialled his number and waited anxiously for it to connect. Each ring made me doubt the truth of his offer. But he did pick up. It was a Saturday, so I knew he was off duty.

"Hello?"

"It's Pierce."

He breathed into the phone. It was a sigh that expressed the opposite of surprise. Maybe he knew when he handed me the paper that I'd use it that week.

"I need help."

"What's happening Pierce?"

"I'm losing it."

"You're not losing it."

"I am."

"It might feel like that, but you're not."

"I need my medication put up."

"No, you don't. You need willpower. You're like an addict in withdrawal. You have to convince yourself you don't need it."

"But I do need it."

Not only did he hold the answers to my survival, he held the power of the pen over the prescription pad.

"Look, I'll give you a home visit, so we can discuss this."

"You can do that?"

"Technically not outside work hours, but I want to help you, Pierce. Give me your address and I'll be over in an hour."

When I got home, I still had forty minutes to wait. Time was moving indescribably slowly, like scenes building to a grand reveal, but one that never comes. I sat on the sofa, catatonic, a cigarette in my hand. I didn't have the energy to tap the ash over a tray and I knew if Molly was there, she'd scold me for being so careless. But her shift was a long way from ending. She was unreachable to me, her phone on silent at the bottom of her bag, probably. I stared into space and turned on some music to fill the disturbing silence. The singing voice seemed to echo my pain, crying out in the quiet room.

There was a knock at the door, and it made me jump. The fact I'd been waiting for it somehow made it no less startling. I got up and walked to the door, looking through the peephole. Tim was standing in his typical slouch outside the door, hands in pockets, neutral expression. I opened the door and fought the urge to cling to him, hoping to absorb some of his self-assurance. He had a quality that made it seem that even the worst of situations would be ok in the end.

"Pierce," he dragged out.

"Come in," I said, opening the door right up.

He followed me into the living room, observing our surroundings without a notable reaction. It was hard to tell whether my mode of existence was something that deserved his disapproval. Tim's approval was important because it meant that you were getting better. He was the medical measure of whether you were progressing or deteriorating.

Tim sat down opposite me and took out some paper and a pen.

"So, tell me what's going on?"

"It's hard to put into words, I feel like everything is getting out of control and I'm afraid of time."

"You're afraid of time? That doesn't make any sense."

"It feels so long and empty."

"Ok, are you still seeing or hearing things?"

"Yes."

"We need to strip back your support system."

"What do you mean?"

"Remove anyone that isn't helping you from it."

"Like who?"

"Well, you've clearly deteriorated since you've been with your girlfriend."

"Why do you say that?"

"I can see it. I have a more objective view of it. I'm not emotionally invested like you are."

I looked doubtfully at my shoes. I didn't want to look him in the eye in case he used it to coerce me into doing what I didn't want to do. I'd already let Molly down once – I couldn't bear to do it again.

"You look ill, Pierce. Your complexion is pasty, you've a noticeable tremor, you aren't taking care of your appearance. We need to get you back to how you were before this woman destabilised you."

"Why do you think it's her?"

"You know it is. You just don't want to see it. Love is deceptive. It makes you believe things are good for you that cause you the most harm. I need you to do something if you want me to help you."

"What?"

"Commit to treatment. Put it first and put everything else on the back burner. It's the only way you'll progress."

He pulled a booklet out of his shirt pocket.

"We have a whole programme of activities you need to get involved in. Most of our patients that are doing well in treatment are actively involved in them. You are responsible for getting your own help."

He left the programme sitting on the table and got to his feet.

"I'm going to increase your medication slightly," he said.

"You are?" my voice sounded more surprised than I'd intended it to.

"Yes, just until you get more supports in place, but that is up to you. When we next meet, I hope I'll be able to decrease it."

He scrawled a note on his pad and tore it off, handing it to me.

"Go get your fix, Pierce."

"Thank you," I said. I felt like begging him for the highest dose available, but I fought the desire to do it. I couldn't afford to have him retract his generous offer.

As soon as Tim left, the emptiness hit me again. The house felt as hollow as if it had a hundred rooms rather than half a dozen. The air filling the place felt toxic, like it emphasised the fact the only stifling company I had was my own. I picked up the pamphlet and started looking at my options.

CHAPTER TWELVE

The next week, with more medication in my system and marginally fewer problems, I headed out to a social gathering of "my" people. I belonged to a different calibre of social group. I couldn't mix with those with their heads screwed on. I was too different to deserve that. I needed to stick to my own kind: a species haunted by self-hatred and dysfunctional behaviours. If I surrounded myself with what made sense to me, I told myself, the world would make greater sense too.

I walked into a meeting room at the clinic. It had been set up for the sake of scrapbooking: a few tables pushed together giving the illusion that we're all in everything together. I sat down timidly and waited while the facilitator passed notebooks around the group. There were supplies in the middle of the table. Everyone looked uncomfortable – more because of the skin they were in than any environmental factors. I picked up some patterned papers and felt a little ridiculous selecting one as a background; they were all pastel florals, like something resembling my long-dead grandmother's curtains.

Kate walked into the room. I was surprised to see her there. I didn't know why. I'd been told she was an active participant in all areas of treatment. She always seemed to have her life together, with her slow and deliberate way of speaking and her intense eye contact. She unveiled her arms from her coat. They were bandaged up: the full length of both forearms. There is generally only one reason to be wearing a dressing like that, and the sight of it upset me. She sat down at the table in a morose kind of silence, her scarf still wrapped tightly around her neck, like she had no intention of staying.

"Glad you could join us ...," the facilitator beamed.

Twelve nervy pairs of eyes observed her from a safe distance, like they were waiting for something to kick off.

"Mm hm," she replied.

She stayed stationary in her chair, her hands resting on her knee.

"Ok, everyone. This is designed to aid relaxation so just make your scrapbook however you like. This isn't a competition. We aren't testing you on your scrapbooking skills."

There was a chorus of awkward laughter from the table and then everyone put their heads down. Not a person in the room seemed open or willing to talk to me. Maybe that was detrimental to treatment anyway. I looked across at Kate whose eyes seemed to pass through me to whatever hung on the wall behind me. She was looking at me straight on, but wasn't seeing anything.

I looked from my book to the window and back again. The activity wasn't abhorrent to me, but the atmosphere was. I kept to myself and filled a few pages. At the end of the session, I got to my feet, expecting Kate to follow me to the door and accompany me home. But she didn't budge from her seat and remained there, trancelike. I didn't know what to do, so I walked out.

That night, while I lay in a state of insomnia, I felt haunted by the image from earlier that day. I absorbed bad feelings like a sponge does water. I felt infected by Kate's angst, like it was a contagious disease that was embedding itself in my system. I had to get up and phone her. It didn't matter what time it was or what Molly made of the situation. She was in such a peaceful sleep she didn't even stir when I got up from the bed.

I walked into the living room and closed the door behind me. I felt guilty doing it, like I was trying to hide something. I looked at the clock on the fireplace: 1am. It was likely a wasted phone call, but I had to at least attempt to make it.

"Yeah," a voice said, groggily into the phone.

For how sleep-filled it sounded, she had picked up awfully quickly.

"It's me - Pierce."

"What do you want?"

"I'm checking you're ok. I was thinking about earlier and I couldn't stop worrying."

"Why?"

"Your arms. Are you self-harming?"

"Why?"

"Do you need to talk to someone?"

"Who?"

"I thought you said you could talk to Tim about this?"

"Can I meet you tomorrow? I need to discuss something important with you."

"Sure. Want to come over for coffee tomorrow about eleven?"

"Yeah."

She disconnected the call without saying bye, and curiosity about what could have been said kept me up for the remainder of the night.

CHAPTER THIRTEEN

Molly left for work. We worked round each other like tenants of the same flat, back on different schedules. Now that she was on day duty, I was on night shift. The promises I'd made her were coming undone. It was easier to commit to becoming a better version of myself in fantasy than it was in plain old life.

I folded the sheets over and climbed out of bed. I didn't bother making it anymore; I knew it would never be long until I was settling into its sheets again. The flat was getting grimy, thanks to Molly's absence and my inertia, but still, I couldn't find the motivation to make it better. The hour was advancing towards midday quicker than I wanted it to, and I needed to get dressed. I sat down on the sofa, unfed, just about dressed, smoking, waiting for the buzz of doom to come at the door. The hand whisked its way around the clock until eleven was gone, and my tobacco was too. I saw Kate pass by the window and got up from my seat, composing myself as much as I could. My anxiety had kicked in; I could feel it rising inside me as I approached the door. As Kate got closer, I felt a tug at my soul, like we were spiritually connected, but not necessarily in a positive way.

She knocked the door and I opened it, looking her in the face. Her skin was red and raised from too many tears and the touch of too many abrasive tissues. She looked emotionally spent and I couldn't find the right words to say, so I just stepped back to let her in. Her energy seemed to sweep through the hallway, and I followed her into my own home. She was relaxed there, as confident as if it had been her own. I sat on the sofa next to her, observing her as she shrugged off her coat and showed me the bandages that hadn't succeeded in holding back all the blood.

"Are you ok?" I asked.

"Are we ever ok?"

"Good point."

"Do you have any fags?"

"I just ran out. We can walk to the shop if you want?"

"I can't face anyone today. It took everything in me just to walk over here."

I nodded, searching for something to say.

"So, what was it you wanted to talk about?"

"It's about Tim."

"What about him?"

"I think something is going on."

"What?"

I looked at her pupils. They were dilated.

"We have to stick together."

I couldn't help wondering if she was delusional. It sounded like the kind of behaviour I displayed when I was off medication and left to battle my own mind.

"What do you mean?"

"The mental health team – they're trying to get us."

"Why would they do that?"

"Power."

"... when was the last time you slept?"

"You don't believe me."

"It's not that."

She pulled her coat on brusquely, not bothering with the buttons and flipping her hood up.

"I have to go."

"I didn't mean to upset you."

She refused to look me in the eye and busied herself with buckling her backpack. She had a violent energy about her that made sure I knew not to intervene. I stayed in my seat when she walked out. When the door slammed, I flinched. I couldn't even sustain a healthy relationship with the people that were just like me.

• •

When I left to go to my appointment with Tim, I felt like I was betraying Molly. She was unaware I was going, but it felt like I was sneaking around behind her back with her nemesis. Maybe that thought was just a sign that Tim was right about her. I knew I shouldn't feel like my treatment was impacted by knowing her.

The day was clear, and the blue sky was long like colour block on a stretched canvas. The whole city was awake and cheery. The weather had no bearing on my mood. I was feeling nauseous from the overload of thoughts in my head. The voice was loud that day. It was reminding me of my inadequacies, and I couldn't even see out of it to see the day around me. It always bothers me when people talk about depression, or mental health issues and others say to stop and look around – what do you have to be down about? It's like asking why a widow is grieving on a hot summer's day. The heat didn't do me any favours – it just made the walk harder as I struggled to put one foot in front of the other enough times to reach the clinic.

As always, the clinic was engulfed in greyness. Its own little personal raincloud was hovering above it and walking inside felt right to me that day. The sun continued to mock me in the distance, and I was glad of the grey walls for once. They felt respectfully sombre. I was the only person in the waiting area. I guessed everyone had taken a holiday from their problems to enjoy the heatwave. Thankfully, that meant I didn't have to wait long. Tim came out in his languid way. He reminded me of a slow-moving reptile – one that was too smart to do anything with perceptibility.

"Pierce," he nodded.

"Tim," I said back.

It was like we were friends acknowledging each other in the pub. But he was going to supply me with something of much more use to me than a pint and a pat on the back. I followed him into his office. It was like a pocket of sunlight – a suntrap inside. Pierce's notes were strewn everywhere. There were so many of them it didn't even feel like confidentiality was compromised because of it. His messiness didn't surprise me – he was cavalier about things, but that didn't mean he was inept at his job. On the contrary, maybe messiness was conducive to good work. His attention was focussed on what mattered, and in that minute, I knew that was me.

"Pierce, how have things been?"

"Not great, my girlfriend hasn't been happy with me."

"What is she doing now?"

"She booked a surprise trip for us and I turned her down."

Tim nodded like there was nothing surprising about that.

"I didn't want to miss this appointment."

"I think "want" is the wrong word choice."

"What do you mean?"

"You couldn't miss it. You need it. You need to think about why she'd do that."

"Why?"

"Why is she trying to take you away from treatment? Doesn't she know how important it is?"

"I guess not."

"She's not thinking of you. It's clear she doesn't understand."

"She thinks you're a bad influence on me."

Tim looked affronted. His eyebrows rose and he looked at me sternly.

"I've warned you about this girl, Pierce, but you aren't following my advice. You need to distance yourself from her or she's going to ruin your life."

"I fell out with Kate."

"You've had an eventful week."

His pupils enlarged and shrank, quicker than a camera flash.

"What happened with Kate?"

"I can't really talk about it."

"If you aren't transparent with me, how can I help you?"

"She just thought I didn't believe her stories."

"You've been making a bit of a nuisance of yourself this week, haven't you?"

I didn't know what to say to that – it just felt like the truth.

"I'm going to suggest you work out a way to extract yourself from your girlfriend's life."

"I can't break up with her again."

Tim looked at me like I didn't have any options left. It was his choice or my ruin.

"I'm taking you off your medication, Pierce."

"No, please don't," I begged.

"You need to stop depending on it."

He scribbled out a note for the GP and I felt tempted to throw it in the bin on my way out, but I couldn't - Tim never missed a thing.

CHAPTER FOURTEEN

"**H**elp me!" I yelled.

Kate jumped awake. She never stirred easily, which highlighted just how loud I must have been.

"Help!" I shouted. I made a protective helmet out of my hands and placed them over my head.

"What?" she asked.

"Can you feel it?"

"Feel what, Pierce?"

"The knives."

"The knives?"

"Yeah, get out,"

I shoved her out of bed, and she stumbled to the ground. I didn't feel bad about it because it was necessary. When you're saving someone's life you don't have time to consider treating them delicately.

She looked at me, horrified.

"Why are you pushing me over?"

"Get out."

I forced her under the doorframe. It was the only place the

blades weren't falling.

"Where are they coming from?"

"Pierce, are you dreaming? You aren't making any sense."

I rubbed my arms. They were punctured all over and blood was gushing down my forearms. I was scared to look under my clothes to see what other damage could have been done. I was in enough pain to know it could end up being fatal. We had to get out – but to get to the front door we'd have to face the shower of knives again. I decided it was worth a few more stab marks to get out of there for good.

"Let's go," I shouted.

"Where?" said Kate. She didn't look panicked in the least – just confused and worried.

"Anywhere that isn't raining knives."

They were falling through the air so fast, all I could see was the gleam of the metal

"I don't know what you're talking about, Pierce," said Molly. She looked frustrated, like when you're trying to explain a concept too advanced for children to a group of unrelenting child questioners.

"Just come with me," I pleaded.

"It's the middle of the night, Pierce. I don't fancy going for a walk in my pyjamas with the drunks and the stray dogs."

"Maybe the front porch is ok," I said.

The knives were slowing down, but I could still feel the ache of all my injuries. Molly had marks all over her too, but she didn't look like she'd even noticed them.

"Pierce, what are you seeing?"

"Knives, everywhere, falling on us. Can't you feel it?"

Molly shook her head.

"Pierce, you're imagining it."

"I'm not," I said. It was too real to be something imaginary. I was offended Molly would even suggest it was.

"Come here," she pulled me by the arm into the bathroom.

I could still feel every individual knife slicing me. There were so many incisions I couldn't focus on the pain of one. She sat me on the bathroom floor and poured water straight from the tap all over a hand towel. She used it as a compress on my forehead.

"You're burning up," she said. "Do you feel sick?"

"No," I said. "I'm scared."

I felt weak admitting that to her, but she just looked at me with concern.

"I think you're hallucinating Pierce."

I wanted to persuade her that I wasn't, but it was useless. She didn't seem to see or feel what I could. In that moment, I knew no matter how good she was to me, she'd never get me.

CHAPTER FIFTEEN

I was alone in Tim's office, waiting for him to return from the photocopier. He'd gone to print off a list of scheduled activities to keep me busy. I had a feeling a lecture was coming my way, and I wasn't in the emotional state to handle it. Sure enough, once Tim was back in his swivel chair and he'd handed over the goods, his face dropped.

"I'm not happy with your progress so far, Pierce."

"I agree."

"Do you feel better?"

"No, not since I stopped taking medication. Do you think that's what it is?"

"No," said Tim, shortly.

"What do you think it is?"

"Lack of willpower."

"Mine?"

"Yeah, look at your life, Pierce. You're not working, your girlfriend has moved out, you've fallen out with the one friend I introduced you to."

"You wanted my girlfriend to move out."

"Yeah, but I didn't want you to sit festering afterwards. It was meant to be a quick cut and a positive shift. You're just moping."

"I can't help it. I'm depressed."

"That's defeatist talk. Do you think I got the status I have by allowing patients away with that?"

It was like tough love for the mentally tortured, and I didn't understand how he could be so cruel.

"You aren't helping me."

"Excuse me?" said Tim. He visibly moved back in his chair, straightening his shoulders. "You aren't helping yourself. Don't use me as an excuse for your own feebleness."

I got up from my chair. I didn't have the energy to argue with him, and I didn't feel like surrendering to his policies that day. All I knew was that life was less worth living than it had been when I'd first set foot in his office. Maybe that was a coincidence. Maybe that was my fault. All I knew was that I couldn't take it.

"Wait," said Tim. "Don't go yet."

"Why?"

"I need to ask you something."

"Ok?"

"Didn't you do your degree in accountancy?"

"Yeah, how did you know that?"

"I had it in your notes."

"Why do you ask?"

"Didn't you work in a call centre when you first came here?"

"Yeah."

"There you go."

"There I go, what?

"Pierce, you can't sit around doing nothing for the rest of your life. What a waste of your degree. Why did you spend all that time and money on your studies if you were going to just give up?"

"I can't do it."

I walked out the door. It felt like the last person in the world, whose job it was to understand me, couldn't.

CHAPTER SIXTEEN

I bumped into Kate that week. It was odd considering we both avoided spending time in public settings and I'd only ventured out because my option was that, or to starve. She looked different. Her hair was more tousled than usual, like the waves had been better cared for. She was wearing a full face of makeup and I couldn't decide if she looked improved by it, or the opposite.

"Hi Kate," I said.

I was tentative about it, in case she exploded right there on the shop floor. She looked distracted – like her friendship with me was the last worry on her mind.

"Are you ok?"

"Oh… Pierce," she said.

"Are you ok?"

"I don't know the meaning of that word."

"I rarely feel ok either."

"Well, don't waste time on niceties with me. You know me better than that."

"Do I? I thought we weren't speaking anymore."

"I'm just disappointed – that's all. I thought you'd believe whatever I told you."

"It isn't up to us to question the professionals."

She turned her blazing eyes to look straight into mine.

"Can we see each other again?" I asked.

"Why?" she said, defensively.

"I've missed you."

"You have?" She said. Her friendly temperature seemed to warm up.

I nodded. "Should we just give treatment a real chance?"

"Have you seen Tim since we last spoke?"

"Yeah, have you?"

"No – I didn't show up for our last appointment. He left me a voicemail saying if I did it again, he was removing me from his list."

"Are you going to go back?"

"I guess," she trailed off. "Are you back together with your girlfriend?"

"Why do you ask?"

"I saw you together last week."

"Where?"

Kate just shook her head like that was information she wasn't willing to give up. I felt uneasy, knowing she could know the intimate details of my life without asking me.

"We broke up again."

"Oh," her face brightened. "What happened?"

"I told her it wasn't working – she doesn't get me."

"I know," said Kate, closing the space between us. She reached out and gave me a consolatory rub on the arm.

Then, she withdrew her hand and her eyes seemed to get far away from me without moving their position. Her face might have been painted on, but she was in a hell of her own and I knew it without having to ask.

CHAPTER SEVENTEEN

Kate

I'm going to Tim's house today. I've been a few times before, for personalised treatment. I haven't told anyone where I'm going to – it's our secret. Tim might not be allowed to have patients over to his house, but I know I'm important to him. I guess he thinks it's worth the risk of getting caught. Tim's able to give me the kind of undivided attention I'm desperate for. My upbringing wasn't good – maybe that's why I'm here in the first place. Tim says I'm incapable of forming healthy attachments. I always seem to sabotage them, by getting so intense the other person can't cope with me.

My last friend hurt me immeasurably. We had the instant type of connection I have with Pierce. That's the thing that always draws me in. I don't care if our tastes aren't aligned, or if the person is cold, or even cruel; I'll do anything for that kind of connection. I have it with few, but I have it with Tim, and I have it with Pierce.

Anyway, the last friend to betray me was a girl called Lily. She made me important, and in the end, she pushed me away. We had met through church, when I used to go. She was a stable type – the kind of person whose head is so firmly set on their shoulders it makes yours feel like it's wobbling like a nodding dog in motion. Since we were both running late for the service, we were slotted into a back bench in the room. The singing was underway, and we smiled at each other as the lady next to us sang loudly and unselfconsciously, though tone deaf. We communicated through the service with glances and smiles and saved our opportunity to talk until the end. I could tell she was as eager to talk to me as I was to talk to her. My sexuality is fluid – like the rest of my personality; I show a preference for men, but sometimes I can feel attracted to women too. It depends on someone's personality and the connection we have more than their looks. I just had a feeling from that first encounter that Lily and I would have a special kind of closeness, but I think I misread the situation. She looked at me, the way I imagine old ballroom dancers peered from behind their fans at suitors. She was curious, but standoffish in equal measure.

"I'm Kate," I said, outstretching my hand.

She placed hers in mine and I remembered the saying "cold hands, warm heart." She must have had a very warm heart because her hands were as cold as ice burns. She gripped my hand loosely and I pressed my palm to hers. She smiled at me.

"I'll have to go," she said. She moved towards me apologetically, like she was asking me to move out of her way.

"Do you come here every week?" I asked.

"No, I'm a sporadic church goer."

"Same here."

I knew she was about to walk out of my life, and I panicked.

"Would you like to meet for coffee sometime?" I asked.

"Yes," she said, standing still. She didn't reach for her phone or look hurried about getting my phone number.

"Let me get your number," I said.

I pulled my phone from my pocket and took her number. I liked her name – it was delicate and sounded like someone who'd be open and receptive to me. That was what I needed. My childhood had been like the material of horror fiction. I grew up in England and I'd moved to Northern Ireland to escape it all. Both my parents were what I now know is defined as abusive – I was just afraid of them. When I was little, that was what was normal to me. As soon as I turned eighteen, I had the bravery to get on a boat and refuse to come back. I knew that I hadn't advanced much emotionally, but at least distance-wise I was safe. My mother was a controlling woman. So much so, I still found it hard to lead my own life without looking for advice from the outside. But at the same time, I had to develop an intimacy with someone. There was something a little bit bossy about Lily – nothing she said – more of a vibe I got from her. I liked that about her. She looked soft and motherly, but also like she wouldn't put up with anyone's nonsense. She'd be a hard woman to keep happy, but that was what I was used to.

"I'll phone you tonight," I said, smiling.

I followed her outside. I had no reason to hang around after the service either. I hadn't met another person in the few times I'd been there that had bothered to make conversation with me. I couldn't understand why everyone stayed well back, like I had an odour that they couldn't stand. It must have been the way I looked, because how can anyone judge you before you've even uttered a word?

"Whereabouts do you live?" I asked Lily.

"Oh, about a mile from here," she said.

"Want me to walk you home?"

"No, thanks, I have to go to the shops anyway. Talk to you later."

When I phoned Lily that night, she didn't answer. I thought that was the end of it – another friendship that had fallen apart before it had even had a chance to gain momentum. But then she returned my call. Maybe I was likeable after all. Maybe I could make a real friend and experience the enjoyment that I usually only saw other people having from afar.

"Hi Kate, sorry I missed your call. I was in the bath."

"No problem. How was the rest of your day?"

"Quiet. I just got some shopping done and came home."

"Do you live alone?"

"Yeah, do you?"

"Yeah, it gets lonely sometimes."

"I don't really get lonely."

"Do you have many friends?"

"Yeah I have a group of female friends – we spend a lot of time together."

"Oh."

I took that as a personal sleight. It was hard to not see other people as a threat. Any time my parents had had guests when I was a child, I'd seen a side to them I never had the luck to experience at any other time. Their bad temperedness cleared up and their vibrant, entertaining sides came out. When their friends were there, the atmosphere was less tense, but I got none of the attention. I always thought that they came and claimed the love my parents had never had for me.

"Would you like to meet up for coffee some day?" Lily asked.

Her proposal surprised me – I'd assumed she didn't have time for any new company. But I still jumped at the chance for companionship. Even if you're what the world labels "abnormal," that doesn't remove your human need for a connection. It was finally here – the moment I'd waited for since arriving in

Northern Ireland: I was going to have a friend.

Two months later, Lily stopped talking to me. She threatened to phone the police if I contacted her again. I thought she was misinterpreting my behaviour. She'd gone quiet for a week, so I'd phoned her a few times to see what was wrong. I'd ended up crying at her front door, and someone had got the police to come out. Lily had come to mean everything to me, and I was terrified of that being taken away. In my small world, a day felt the length of a month. I had no work, no company, no diversions – just waiting, looking at the face of my phone, waiting for love. That was when I realised the love that I received would always be conditional. But I would have been happier with that than with nothing.

When I got into Tim's house, I thought about that short-lived friendship. At least I knew Tim wouldn't abandon me. I might have had irrational periods of not trusting him, but that was inevitable coming from the background I did. If I looked back over the time I'd been in his care, he had never shut me off from him. He was like a treatment tap that never turned off.

I rang the doorbell and waited for him to answer. I'd never been to his house before, but I knew he lived across the street from Pierce. I'd never tell Pierce that, of course. He had no idea and I had to protect Tim's privacy. He lived in the upstairs of a house. It had been converted into two separate flats. I'd expected Tim to live somewhere more affluent. I'd thought his job would have allowed him to have a better lifestyle. But he just lived ordinarily. That made me trust him a little more. Sometimes, you have to see the full context of someone's life to feel like you know who they are. He was inviting me into his most cherished place, and I felt guilty for ever suspecting him of malpractice. All the blinds were tilted, so you could see outside, but no one outside could see in. It was a private place. I could see Pierce's house from the living room window, under a streetlight, but the angle meant he couldn't see us. I had to make sure no one saw me with Tim in my free time, or he'd get in trouble – he might even lose his job.

Tim invited me to sit down with a wave of the hand. I perched on the edge of his sofa. The room was decorated in dark tones that gave it the feel of a Victorian boudoir. It was a relaxing environment to visit. There was even a chaise longue, positioned next to a desk, making me wonder if he regularly conducted private appointments there.

"Would you like a cup of tea?" Tim asked.

"Yes, please," I said.

"Do you take milk?"

"Yes, thanks."

Tim walked out of the room and left me alone with the ticking clock and the black screen of the TV. I couldn't help wondering what he watched on it. I felt the urge to snoop, but I didn't have the opportunity for it. Tim returned quicker than I expected with our tea.

He encouraged me to make myself comfortable enough to unburden myself of what I had to say. I felt like he could already read what I was thinking. I thought back to our first meeting together. It was nearing the one-year anniversary of when I'd started treatment. I didn't have many occasions worth marking, but that was one of them.

From the minute I met Tim, he was so self-possessed. His confidence had immediately put me at ease.

"Hello Kate… it is Kate isn't it?"

"Yeah, no one calls me Katherine. How did you know that?"

"Your reputation proceeds you," he said with a grin.

"What do you mean?"

"I've heard around town about a relationship you had with a girl – Lily?"

"Yeah, we were friends for a while. What did you hear?"

"That you were harassing her."

"What?"

"Apparently you turned up on her doorstep when she wouldn't speak to you. We will deal with this in treatment."

"Deal with what?"

"Appropriate social behaviour. Tell me, Kate, do you have many friends?"

"No, she was the only one."

"Not surprising. We'll get you sorted out. What medication are you on?"

I listed the mixture of medication I was on. It sounded like a long list when you said it aloud.

"We need to increase those dosages," said Tim.

"I thought I was already on a high dose."

Tim shook his head. "Not high enough for the problems we're dealing with here."

"What do you think is wrong with me?"

"Where do I start?" smiled Tim.

There was something condescending about the way he looked at me. But I'd been told so many times, people with my disorder saw emotion in an expressionless face. That was why I'd got myself into such bother in the past. I'd reacted when there was nothing to react to.

"I think we need to expand your social circle. We run a walking group every week. They meet in Victoria Park and do a circuit while you get a chance to meet fellow sufferers."

"Oh, I don't know if I'd have the confidence to talk to anyone."

"Everyone is similarly disordered – you'll find someone."

Tim didn't ask me many questions – he looked pressed for time. He scribbled a note to the doctor to increase my medication, ripped it off the pad and handed it to me as he stood up. He reached for the door handle and escorted me into the corridor. It was time to go.

I came back to the present moment and thought about the comment he'd made about Lily. I'd wondered since how he'd come to find that out. I had to ask him about it, even if it seemed irrelevant now, even if it was a year-delayed response.

"Tim?"

"Yeah?"

"You know Lily?"

"Lily?"

"The friend I used to have."

"Yeah."

"How did you find out about our friendship?"

"I was in the pub one evening and there was a group of people your age laughing about it at the next table. Your name stood out to me because I'd seen it on my list of new patients that week. A girl was telling them about you and how you'd stalked Lily. They said you were damaged, and they knew you, just from walking around town."

"I don't know anyone in this town."

"Some people walk around in their worries with their heads to the ground. Other people look around so they can gossip about someone else's."

I sat for a long while, feeling betrayed. I'd known Lily's bossy side, but I'd never supposed her to be a gossip. I'd thought what had happened between us was sacred – not open for discussion all over town. I stayed quiet, but inside, I was hysterical.

"You can't worry about what everyone says about you," said Tim. "There isn't a person on Earth who escapes other people's

93

judgement."

Tim polished his bald head with the palm of his hand, contemplatively.

"Do you know why I suggested you coming here?" he asked.

I shook my head.

"I think you're special, Kate. You're one of my favourite patients. I'm interested in what you have to say. I want to study your behaviour and make sense of it so I can help you."

"I don't know where to start."

"Just be yourself and I'll figure out the rest."

I finished my tea and Tim invited me to recline on the chaise longue. It looked like a typical therapy chair and laying there made me feel like a lying cliché. Tim didn't bother taking notes; he just looked me directly in the eye, waiting for my revelations.

"You're 28, aren't you Kate?" he asked.

"Yes."

"Do you smoke heavily?"

"Yeah, it's the only thing that keeps me sane."

"You can tell – your face is heavily lined."

"I think that's more to do with stress than anything else."

"Tell me about your childhood."

"I haven't told many people about it."

"All the more reason to open up to me."

I lay there, staring at the ceiling and opening myself up to him, like the interior of a damaged flower. He was the bee, hungry for pollen, and it felt like something natural that had to happen.

CHAPTER EIGHTEEN

Pierce

I t had been two weeks since I'd left the house, and no one had checked in on me. I couldn't get up the courage to open the door. It felt like the only way to stay safe was to stay away from people. I guess times like that show you who really cares. The only people to contact me were Tim and Kate. The paranoia was so strong I didn't want to tell the truth to anyone. I was stuck in my head with that damn voice – making me miserable in any way it could. I couldn't hear much of myself inside my mind anymore. He was taking over and even the pitch of his voice was unbearable. It was so deep it hurt to listen to, like the lowest notes on a piano. It had no tune – just menace. He was pestering me to get out of life – to end it in every conceivable way. He gave me suggestions I hadn't thought of before, that I don't even want to acknowledge on paper.

The phone rang repeatedly, and I couldn't bear to lift it. Tim left me several voicemails, but I couldn't speak. The words were all jumbling together in my mind until they didn't make sense anymore. I just had concepts – no sentences left, like a slideshow of disturbing pictures that kept me awake all night. Everything was rushing inside. There was a knock at the door. It sounded violent and I couldn't tell if it was loud or if my mind was just amplifying it. I knew it was Kate. Who else could it be? I still didn't answer. I couldn't trust anyone. I couldn't face questioning. Any question became like an interrogation to me when I wasn't feeling good.

Kate was persistent. She didn't just knock, give up and go away. She stood there for about half an hour, knocking and then shouting.

"I know you're in there, Pierce. Why are you ignoring me? I need to talk to you."

Her pleas usually would have worn me down, but I was feeling too paranoid to let anyone talk me round. She was growing more and more upset, but I couldn't move. I stayed silent, hoping she'd decide that I was out. I thought about calling the police, just to have her removed for that moment, but I knew she'd never forgive me for that. I knew I was being irrational, but I felt afraid. Whether I was more afraid of Tim, Kate or myself, I couldn't decide.

CHAPTER NINETEEN

"**K**ate's in hospital."

"What, why?" I asked.

I'd been called in for a check-up, but Tim had assured me there was nothing urgent about it. I guess he'd just downplayed whatever had happened to make sure I turned up.

"She attempted suicide."

"What? What did she do?"

"She cut herself. There was a lot of blood, but she's stable."

"Do you know why?"

"That's why I brought you in, Pierce. It was because of you."

"What? Why?"

"She left a note saying that you were her last friend and that you'd shut her out too – that she'd called at your house to talk to you and you had ignored her. She'd needed someone to calm her down, and instead you made it worse."

"That's awful – I never meant to do that to her."

Tim looked at me like he didn't believe me.

"Not everything is about you, Pierce. You need to think about other people too. She's another patient – she's fragile."

"Well, why did you encourage us to become friends?"

"I thought it would be a positive thing for both of you – but you've created more problems for her."

"How did they find her?"

Her neighbour reported sobs to the police – was worried there was a break-in or domestic dispute because it was so loud. They sent out an ambulance too – assumed there would be serious injuries. Good job they did."

"Did she phone you?" Tim asked.

"A couple of times, yeah. I just thought she wanted to hang out."

"It just shows you the importance of every one of your actions."

"You think this is my fault?"

"Who else's fault could it be, Pierce?"

Emotion flared up inside me. I couldn't cope with the responsibility of that on top of everything else. But Tim was right – Kate had always been there for me and I had abandoned her, knowing it was her worst fear.

"Can I visit her?"

"No, she's not having visitors at the moment – they've moved her to a psychiatric ward."

"I have to talk to her."

"No – you need to work on yourself. I think it would be best if you cut contact for now."

"But what if it happens again?"

"She's safe now, especially now she can't see you. Get your coat, Pierce."

"Why?"

"I'm taking you somewhere."

"Where?"

"Stop asking questions – just follow me to the car."

We walked through the reception area and no one gave us a second glance – Pierce had his own set of rules in the workplace, and I'd never seen anyone dare to question them. He walked out the double doors and wasn't a bit subtle about it. I guess his reputation allowed him to come and go freely within working hours. I followed him to his car and was surprised it wasn't flashier. He seemed like someone to drive an expensive automobile with every new feature and to drive it with arrogant speed. But his car was a modest model. I climbed in and felt right at home. It had Tim's scent. He had a potent scent – not unpleasant – just distinctive. I could see how he could be intoxicating to the opposite sex. He was someone who stayed with you long after he had left. I wondered again about his private life. I knew so little about it I couldn't help feeling curious. He played classical music in the background as we drove, and I had no idea where we were going. It wasn't a direction I typically took. We sat in silence. I'd never experienced an awkward silence with Tim. He was too self-assured to ever appear nervous or lost for words. When he was quiet, it was always a choice. The weather darkened as we drove. Ten minutes into the journey, he became more animated and took me under his notice again.

"I'm taking you somewhere I think will make an impression on you, Pierce."

"Where?"

"You'll see soon. I want you to think about the last year and how you've spent it – what you've achieved."

"I haven't achieved anything – in fact, I've done the opposite."

"So, you'd agree that you're stuck in stasis?"

"What do you want me to say?"

"I don't want you to say anything, Pierce – this is about your opinion."

"Is it?"

It felt like my opinion was being squashed so flat there was nothing left of it, but I couldn't see anything objectively. I knew whatever point Tim had to make was important enough to take him outside his daily diameter. The rain was beating down so heavily now that the wipers weren't making any difference. There wasn't anything to see but trees and concrete anyway.

"Of course it is - you can't just let life happen to you – you have to take charge of it."

"I don't know what you mean."

"You need to stop giving up on everything. People who give up always lose."

I returned to silence and waited until he pulled into a carpark. We appeared to be the only ones there, the only ones mad enough to be there in torrential rain.

"Where are we going?" I asked.

"We're going for a walk."

"Now?"

"Yeah, a little rain never killed anyone, Pierce."

We got out of the car and made a dash for the cover of the trees. We were beside the river and the water was running with a vengeance. I followed Pierce along the towpath. He walked purposefully, like he was walking to a specific destination.

"What's your first thought?" asked Tim.

"That there would be 364 better days a year for a walk," I laughed.

Tim cracked a smile. His smiles were like bursts of the purest sunshine caught between clouds.

It was dark but the place seemed to light up for a mere moment. Then his face closed down again and he had that look of neutrality that was his most used expression. We walked in breathless silence for a few minutes until Pierce came to a stop at the waterside.

"Did you ever hear about Paul McHugh?"

"Who?"

"He drowned here three years ago, right in this spot."

"What happened?"

"Suicide."

Tim's face darkened for a minute.

"Did you know him?"

"He was my patient."

"Oh."

"You remind me of him."

"I do?"

"Same lifestyle, same lack of direction, same defeatist attitude."

"What was he like?"

"He was a good guy – he just didn't think he could do anything. He was always asking me to increase his medication, but I could see that wasn't the answer. He probably realised that as he was jumping, but by then it was too late."

I wondered how Tim could speculate about such things in the face of suicide. How could he think it was more important that the guy realised he was right than that he had decided to live?

Tim pointed to a little dedication masked by long grass. It had a photograph of a guy about my age, maybe younger. He was smiling in the photo and gave every appearance of being healthy. There were a couple of wilted bouquets lying next to it and a plaque stating nothing that gave any clues about his personality.

"Loved son, brother and boyfriend, took his own life here at the age of 22. Always in our hearts."

I felt sorry for him, that even in death he didn't seem to be noticed as unique. He was just a number selected from a catalogue of pre-written plaques.

"Do you think anyone visits it?" I asked.

"They must if there are flowers here, but not in a long while. He's probably one of those ones where, once the shock wears off, he's forgotten amidst the grass. There's no reason to come here other than to visit this. It's not convenient or inviting."

"I know…"

"You don't want to end up here do you, Pierce?"

I shook my head, but I could think of worse fates; at least Paul was at peace. That was more than I could hope for.

"Why did you bring me here?"

"I wanted it to hit home that if you don't make changes, you'll end up in the same place."

I had never thought of the river as a suicide spot before. It felt like ideas were being introduced into my head that had never existed there before. And like ideas with a drive behind them become reality, I wondered if the same could happen to me.

CHAPTER TWENTY

Tim

K ate is a cold creature. She gives every appearance of being warm – touching your arm as she talks, looking you straight in the eyes, filling silence with chatter. But I know the truth behind the social construct. She is just a sad being.

The first things I noticed about her when she walked into my office were how beautiful she is and how damaged she is. She has that kind of natural beauty that could get her good things if she had the self-esteem to accompany it, but she doesn't. She looks at you with wide eyes that seek your approval and it shows she's open to your criticism too.

I'm the most lauded psychiatrist in the country. It's a small place, but you can count the highly skilled specialists on one hand, which makes my job all the more important. I'm spending my days saving lives – so many mentally-messed up people rely on me. When I was little, I knew I was special. That fact was substantiated by the fact that I was an only child. My parents told me when they had me, they realised how unique I was, and I guess they lost all incentive to further procreate. They think I'm highly sensitive, but I can just read them like a bold print book. They were my first tool to practice the skills I needed for my job. Sometimes I don't know how I came from them. They are ordinary and unexceptional. They don't know the meaning of the word "manipulative." They are so simple they only see one possible meaning to everything. I guess I just see everything in a more intricate way. It allows me to understand the machinations of people's brains without understanding why they behave how they do. I'm not impaired by feelings the way they are.

That's why I have no respect for these creatures who come into my care. All that matters to me is public opinion. As long as I'm thought well of by the top people, that's all that affects my happiness.

The first time Kate sat down in front of me, she burst into tears. She was so hysterical I could barely understand what she was trying to say. I'd be willing to bet if you asked her, she'd claim she was cool and collected when she came in. No - I think she thought she'd finally reached a place of refuge where she could offload her worries, but all I was doing was storing up information. When someone confides in me, that's what I do. I have no sympathy for them, but I have a good memory, and it serves me well. I can remember everything she ever told me, without checking my notes. Maybe it's because I have a personal interest in it – in knowing these things that give me the upper hand.

I think my neighbours probably feel sorry for me – those who don't know who I am, at least. They just see a single man returning to a single-bedroomed flat every night. They probably assume that I'm lonely, but I don't know the sensation of loneliness. I come home every day of the week, relieved to be removed from others' company. I face an office-full of fools every day – patients and workers. The only good thing about that is that it makes me the god of the place. No one can question my techniques when they don't have the comprehension skills to understand them.

I'm good at getting straight to the heart of a person and using it to my advantage. I could tell that Kate was a hollow person when I met her. I knew she came from a bad background and had been used and abused by her family. She's like a succubus – someone so starved of attention that they'll take it from any source. I'm happy to give it to her – at least if it helps my agenda. I had everything mapped out in my mind from day one. She would be one of my targets. I like to select a target every few years. I can't do it more regularly than that because it would become too obvious to the police. They're good to me, and don't need them sniffing around for evidence and drudging up old cases that were never questioned before. But I need to drive certain patients to the ultimate destruction. It gives me renewed energy, knowing that I can influence people so much.

I have an emptiness inside. I don't tell anyone about it. But I can tell you, detached reader, because we'll never meet. You can admire my techniques from afar without becoming a danger to me. I get easily bored. I don't get sad, or regretful or sentimental about things. I just need easy entertainment, like most people need to quickly switch to a new TV series when the one they're watching ends. But I need to make a project out of a person and watch them writhe under my heat lamp instead.

I finished off one of my patients a few years ago. His name was Paul McHugh. He was a pathetic person; no one would have ever doubted that he'd committed suicide. I didn't murder him – I just encouraged him to do what needed to be done. Now I need a larger project – I need to prove my power again. Once something is completed, the ecstasy I get from it drains away until I'm back where I started – empty and bored. I could find smaller ways to feed my needs, but the effects wouldn't last as long. Within days I'd be looking for another fix. At least my job enables me to do the work I need to do, unhindered.

You're probably wondering what makes me select a patient as a target. I usually search for someone who is falling apart on the outside but who must have an inner strength holding them together. I like to break that apart. It gives me the best feeling of power, knowing I can break someone who has managed to remain unbreakable until we meet.

I knew I wanted to target Kate, but the day that Pierce walked into my office was the day that the whole plan came together in my head, and I knew exactly what it was I wanted to do.

CHAPTER TWENTY-ONE

Pierce

Tim and I stood at the water's edge for a long time. He remained in contemplative silence and I didn't interrupt it. He was probably having another burst of mournfulness, a feeling of guilt for not being able to save that soul. I couldn't even pretend to understand how hard that must have been for him, so I just respected his silence. The only sound was the gushing of the river. It was so loud you couldn't hear the falling of the heavy rain. My head was rushing just as loudly, like the pressure of everything was bringing me down like decompression. I felt horribly depressed, infected by the mood in the air. I'm sensitive to environments. If I know that something negative has happened somewhere, I seem to absorb the negativity like it's gaseous.

Tim stood for a long time, his elbow on the railing, his chin on his hand. If I didn't know the reason, it would have looked like he was an excellent actor. It looked like a haunting scene from a movie – one that would stay with viewers for generations past its release date. He had such a strong jaw and sharp features that combined to make a jarring image in your mind. He was like something iconic – one of those people you only meet once in your lifetime.

When I got home, I forgot that Molly wouldn't be there. She'd left a month earlier, but I was so used to her rhythms that mine were still in time with hers. I could smell her when I walked in the door, but it was just the potency of my imagination. The place was enshrouded in darkness and I turned on a few lights. There was something about the house that unsettled me, like it hadn't been home to me that morning. I could feel the presence of someone there. I couldn't hear anything; but there is always a change in the air when a room becomes occupied. I looked around the house, keeping my distance from every part of it that I was scared to explore. My sanity was draining away like overspent money and I had to get some sleep. I wedged a chair under my door so no one could come in. I lay for most of the night with my eyes squeezed shut, but sleep eluded me.

I finally found it in the early hours, as daylight was setting in, but I was woken by my phone ringing. I squinted as I looked at the screen. It was a withheld number, but I knew it was Tim. I answered groggily.

"Why do you sound like you're just getting up?" he asked. "Do you know what time it is, Pierce?"

"No."

"11am."

"I couldn't sleep last night."

"So, you're making up for it by wasting the day?"

I didn't say anything.

"I need you to come into the clinic today."

"Why?"

"I need to make a referral for some tests to be done."

"What kind of tests?"

"Just come here, Pierce. Get ready and come straight down."

It took me a long time to extract myself from bed. All the energy had left my body and I couldn't see or think straight. My eyes weren't working properly – I had the vision of someone with concussion. My sheets badly needed changed, but I didn't have the were-withal to do it. I needed a cleaner– not for reasons of extravagance – just to cover the basics. But if I got one, I knew it would just strengthen Tim's case against me. I was a lazy underachiever. He was right about that. My body hurt in every nerve. It felt like I'd been hit by a bus the previous day, shaken it off and returned home, trying to convince myself nothing was wrong. Everything was wrong. I walked over to the mirror that hung on the bedroom wall. It looked like I was suffering from something terminal. There was no colour in my face, and none in my eyes either. I'd once had bright blue eyes, but they seemed to have no definite colour now. I perched on the end of the bed, trying to gather the energy I needed to step into the shower. I loathed myself. I was tired of being stuck in my own body. I thought about other people and all I could see was their immense value. I had none. I felt sick – like I was suffering from the most persistent of hangovers, but I hadn't even had a sip of the jolly juice. I was experiencing the aftermath without the fun that justified it. I kept counting to ten, trying to get up, but when I made it to ten, I hadn't gained any energy. I did that for so long I could have counted out forty-five minutes.

Finally, I used both hands to press my weight against the bed and I got up. I wasn't standing straight, I was so slouched over I was nearly doubled over, but it was enough to get me to the shower. I climbed into the bath, stood under the water and let it run off me. I couldn't even wash myself properly. I needed help. The water beat loudly off the curve of the bath and I wished I could drain down the plughole like the used water. I stood for a long time, letting the water hit me and run back off. Then I forced myself to get dressed. I pulled on the first T-shirt and jeans within reach and skipped brushing my hair and eating breakfast. I stepped out of the house and stood on the worn-away welcome mat, trying to remember if I'd forgotten anything, or everything. I had my keys and I had my phone – that was all that was needed. I wondered what Tim was so eager to tell me and I felt shaky. Had they created new testing for mental illness? What if it told me I had something severe? What if it told me I had nothing at all? That all the problems I had daily were my imagination? I couldn't face that thought. I didn't bother with the bus and walked to the appointment. It took much longer than it did on an average day - my aches were holding me back. The streets were empty, and I was glad of that. I couldn't have coped with meeting people's eyes, crisscrossing paths with people who tried to go left when I went right. I felt stalked by everyone, and I didn't know why. I didn't notice anything while I walked; nothing except for my pains and my feet moving. Finally, at what felt like the closing scene of an apocalyptic film, I arrived there.

The place was deserted. The usually rammed carpark was deathly quiet and there was one lone car there: Tim's. Had he closed the clinic for the purpose of our meeting? Was he allowed to do that? What would all the other people praying for help do that day? My head was swimming with responsibilities – not just my own, but other people's responsibilities to themselves. I stood still on the spot, working up the courage to open the door. I didn't feel confident enough to comport myself in conversation with anyone that day, especially if that person was Tim.

CHAPTER TWENTY-TWO

Kate

I went back to Tim's tonight. I was last in his flat a week ago. I didn't want to go so often I scared him away. It was beginning to feel like he was the only person that understood me. He's so good looking, like one of those men who looks striking in black and white. He always seems sensible – sensible and calm, but when he smiles, it's like watching the first joy after a long period of mourning.

I sat down in the seat I'd sat in the last time. His furniture was comfortable even though it was crammed into the confines of his office/living room. At his great height, he seemed too big for his home – like someone ready to move onto better things. It was odd that he lived so modestly when I knew his wages allowed him to live luxuriously. The fact he didn't have expensive taste made me feel closer to him – like he was just one of "us."

"You look tired today, Kate, did anything happen?"

"I've just been struggling the last few days."

"What with?"

"I don't know."

"Why don't you lie down – it might help you to relax."

"Ok."

I spread myself out, but it didn't seem to have any effect on my tenseness.

"What's been happening since I last saw you?"

"Nothing."

"Nothing at all – are you sure?"

"I've just been feeling really sad for no reason."

"There is always a reason."

"There isn't."

"Even if you don't think there is, there always is."

"I've just been feeling alone. It was my mum's birthday this week."

"Did you speak to her?"

"No, I just know the date. She's dead anyway."

"Oh, I didn't know that."

"Yeah, my dad is still in their old house, but she died a few years ago."

"How did she die?"

"Alcoholism."

"Oh, that's not a good sign."

"Why?"

"It's often genetic."

"I don't drink."

"That's probably for the best."

Tim sad quietly, staring at me, like he was waiting for me to reveal more. I didn't know where to start or what to say.

He was watching me intensely, and I started to wonder if it could be possible that he had feelings for me that went beyond professional responsibility. He closed the gap between us and reached out to touch my hair. He did it in a paternal way and it didn't feel inappropriate. I'd never had that kind of gentleness from my own parents, so I lapped it up like an attention-hungry dog.

"You're just lost, aren't you?" he said.

"Yeah. What should I do?"

"You're doing the right things – you've managed to stay out of hospital for a few weeks now."

"Doesn't mean I won't end up back there."

"Why?"

"Life always disappoints me."

"Doesn't it disappoint everyone? It's all about your attitude."

"I try to keep going, but nothing seems to improve."

"Maybe you aren't meant to strive to do more than you can."

"What do you mean?"

"A job would be too much for you, Kate. I don't think you could cope well with being surrounded by lots of people either. You don't like to socialise."

I'd always thought I'd enjoyed chatting to people, when they gave me the time of day, at least. I loved hearing stories and making a connection, however superficial. It reminded me that not everyone in the world was like my parents. But maybe Pierce was right – maybe I needed to separate myself from everyone. I hadn't had much social interaction lately. I could only focus my attentions on one person at a time. I hadn't seen Pierce since before I'd ended up in hospital. I didn't want to admit to him that I had weakened to that point, in case he gave up all hope of recovery.

"Have you seen Pierce recently?" asked Tim.

It was uncanny how he seemed to read my thoughts at the exact moment I was having them. I shook my head.

"Not since I got out of hospital."

"Probably for the best."

"Why?"

"He doesn't want to see you."

"He told you that?"

"Yes, I had an appointment with him yesterday."

"Why doesn't he?"

"He thinks you're a bad influence. You know, Kate, when I met Pierce, I thought you'd form a healthy relationship, but you don't seem to be able to do that. I might end up being the only friend you have left."

"But we aren't friends."

Tim reached out and placed his hand on my knee.

"Aren't we?"

Before I could process what was happening, he leant in and kissed me. I needed it too much to complain. Tim continued to kiss me and interlaced his fingers with mine. His kiss felt personal, like he meant it.

When he stopped, I didn't know what to say.

"You know, Kate, we'd better not tell anyone about this – you could get in a lot of trouble for coming onto your doctor."

"I did?"

I ran through the scene in my head and was sure I hadn't started it, but if that's what Tim said happened, that's what must have happened. I couldn't trust my own impulses. But his lips against mine had felt right, so I didn't regret it. Keeping silent about it was a small price to pay in exchange for physical contact with the person I respected most in the world.

Tim leaned back in his chair and seemed remote again, like he was deep in thoughts he never planned to share with me.

"You should probably go now, Kate."

"Why?"

"I just don't want you to pose a threat to my status."

"I promise I won't tell anyone."

"Really?"

"I've done it before, haven't I? Kept secrets about bad things, and this isn't a bad thing."

"Ok, if you do tell anyone, you'll get into more trouble than me."

I nodded gravely. I knew it was like playing with knives, but the feeling of belonging, with someone, to someone, was worth it.

CHAPTER TWENTY-THREE

Pierce

"I'm going to refer you for testing, Pierce."

"What kind of testing?"

"To eliminate anything physical."

"What like?"

"Epilepsy, structural defects. I just want to cover all bases, so it's in your notes I've done all I can to rule those out."

"What do I have to get done?"

"A scan of the brain. It won't be too invasive."

The fact that the tests would be held in a different place worried me more than the tests themselves. I never went anywhere new anymore. I stuck to the small circuit of places I knew. I wished I could ask Tim to go with me, but I sensed he wouldn't. Maybe I could ask Kate instead. I hadn't talked to her since before she was admitted. I was scared to ask how she was. It was my fault she'd done it, after all. But when fear of losing someone overcomes fear of how they'll react, you manage to acquire the courage to reach out. That's what I planned to do – to phone Kate as soon as I got home.

"Have you spoken to Kate?" Tim asked.

His ability to chime in when appropriate made me feel like he could read my every thought.

"No, I was thinking about it."

"So why haven't you?"

"You told me not to."

"Oh, so for once, you're following my advice?" smirked Tim.

I nodded and pulled my coat on. Hopefully he'd take the hint.

"You're leaving now?"

"I need to get back."

"What for? To talk to the voices in your house?" he smiled.

I didn't laugh.

"I'm only joking, Pierce. Lighten up."

I walked out of the office, feeling as humourless as I did useless.

CHAPTER TWENTY-FOUR

Pierce

I went to the hospital with Kate by my side. She was the only person that I knew I could depend on to come to my appointment with me. Getting on the bus alone had been more than I could bear. I couldn't cope with anyone noticing me - even momentarily taking note of my existence. Kate knew what that felt like and I didn't have to waste time explaining it to her. We sat on the bus and she held my hand, whispering to me to keep looking at the ground. As long as I kept my eyes to the ground, I could be anywhere I wanted to be. The noise was echoing in my ears and I could hear fragments of conversation coming at us from all sides. Everything people were discussing was trivial – the weather, the news that day that would be forgotten for the news the next day, the week's work gossip. It reminded me of life's pointlessness. I couldn't understand how everyone was satisfied with that level of conversation. I wished with all my might that I could change into someone satisfiable.

We got off the bus and I followed Kate to the hospital. She'd been there before, and she knew the drill. She'd assured me that it was an in-and-out procedure and that an hour later, I'd see how insignificant it all was. I hoped Tim wouldn't turn up unannounced. He could always sense when I was doing something I shouldn't. I was sure I could smell his scent in the air – like it was coming from Kate. My paranoid thoughts were taking over and I felt like no matter where I went in life, Tim was always watching me. Logically, I knew he was behind his desk, but he seemed to pervade everything.

The hospital had that sick smell about it, created by ointment and illness. It made my anxiety rise and I walked quickly to try and get it over with. We came to the reception desk and the receptionist took her time rounding up her conversation with her colleagues before she acknowledged us. Everyone who attended that hospital suffered and everyone who worked there apparently suffered just as severely, from boredom.

"My name is Pierce Jones – I have a scan at 2pm."

"Yes, I have your name here. Take a seat."

We sat on the stiff metal chairs and waited for the sound of my name. Kate was more vibrant that day. She was talking incessantly and watching everything around us.

"I love people-watching," she said.

"I can't do it today," I replied, without looking up.

"Pierce Jones," a lady called.

I got up and followed her into the room.

"Do you want me to come in?" Kate called.

I shook my head and aimed for a smile. I didn't want her, or anyone I knew, to see me in such a submissive state. I was already receding so far into the background, after all my failures, I was becoming only a trace of who I'd previously been.

I was conveyed into the cat scan, pulled through and out the other end. I was still intact, but I'd still be happy to return to my safe, small radius. Kate was right - It was uneventful and weeks later, I got my results on the phone. The next time I saw Tim, he brought them up on the screen in front of us.

"All clear – so it's all in the mind, Pierce."

"What do you mean?"

"It's psychological."

"You think I'm imagining it?"

"I know you are."

I shook my head. I wanted to defend myself, but I didn't have the strength left. I was growing wearier with every appointment. Two weeks was making a hell of a lot of difference to the person I was. Maybe Tim was right about me – I wasn't getting better, but it was because of my own failings – not something outside my control.

"I'm enrolling you in a treatment programme I'm starting soon," said Tim.

"What is it?" I asked, sceptical.

"A group therapy session – it'll be once a week. We meet up and everyone can discuss their problems and get objective advice from each other."

"I don't know if I want anyone to know my problems."

"Everyone already does."

"What?"

"You can tell you've got problems just by looking at you, Pierce."

Tim gave me a smarmy, but somehow charming smile. His eyes seemed to flash when he said something that took me down a notch.

CHAPTER TWENTY-FIVE

Pierce

I walked into the room and the temperature was as cool as the atmosphere was. There was a circle of chairs in the centre of the room and every member of it was staring at Tim. I inserted myself into the circle and I saw a familiar face: Kate's. She looked away from me, like we didn't know each other and her refusal to make eye contact upset me. What had I done since the previous week? How had I let her down? Was she angry I'd needed her to come with me to the hospital?

I didn't know any of the other faces in the room, but they all represented the same thing. Pierce was like a zealous pastor at the centre of the group. Seeing him in a group setting seemed to enhance his personality. His aura carried all around the room and everyone hung on his every word. People who have an impact always speak slowly and deliberately, I realised. Maybe that was why everything he said sounded so considered and important – I supposed he'd sound the same discussing last night's dinner or the TV schedule.

No one was making any attempt to speak. I thought about taking the lead, but Pierce didn't look like he wanted to be interrupted – he was having his moment. I could see how much at home he was in his job. It gave him a stage to share his expertise. He rubbed his scalp with his palm while he spoke. It was like he was trying to draw attention to his baldness, like he was confident about the features most people are insecure about. I wanted that kind of confidence. Maybe I needed to stop battling him and surrender to his will. He pulled a swivel chair into the centre of the group and shuffled his notes.

"Does anyone know why I brought you here?" he asked.

No one replied.

"As a sounding board. You have no objectivity about your conditions when you don't have input from outsiders. You are going to work together to break bad thinking patterns and we'll monitor your progress over the next few weeks. I thought we could start the session by going around the circle and naming one thing we don't like about ourselves and that we'd like to fix by the last session."

I could think of so many features of mine I despised. Singling one out sounded challenging. From my patchy sideburns to my patchy memory, there was little I could think that didn't displease me. I sensed everyone in the room was the same way, or they wouldn't have been there in the first place.

Kate stuck her hand up in the air.

"I have one."

"Go ahead, Kate."

"I hate that I'm easily influenced."

"in what context?"

"With men, in relationships, everywhere."

"I'd have to agree with that – you're impressionable. But I wouldn't name that as a negative trait," said Pierce. "Let me give you an example – Kate, we'll discuss you since you've volunteered."

"Ok," said Kate.

It felt like he could have asked her to convert to satanism and carry out heinous acts and she'd still reply with an "ok" in the same tone.

"Kate and I have noted in treatment that she can be clingy and intense, isn't that right, Kate?"
Kate nodded and looked at the floor.

"But we are working on that – and we are working on removing the toxic influences from her life."
Pierce shot me a look, but I knew the timing could have been a coincidence.

"I'm feeling better already, Tim."

"See? I promised you would. I know you had your doubts."

"Yeah," said Kate, faintly. She looked like a whisper of the person she used to be.

It was discouraging to see that deterioration in such a short space of time. But maybe she was in the same position I was – being broken down to be rebuilt into a healthier person.

Tim cleared his throat and took his gaze away from her. She followed it as it moved to the next person, like she was pining after it. Tim's attention was the most beautiful thing until he moved it onto someone else and you were left feeling like you'd ceased to matter. The next candidate was a plain looking guy – someone with no real personality to him. Tim gave him a warm smile.

"Well, Neil. What do you want to share?"

"I can't think of anything."

"I think you're right – I've seen major improvements in you – well done."

"Your treatment has saved me," he said, blankly.

He looked like someone so bland he couldn't have a strong

emotion or reaction to anything. Tim looked pleased with him.

"This is what we're aiming for," said Tim, gesturing to Neil. "Someone who is compliant with treatment and takes the advice given. My methods aren't praised for no reason."

Tim rubbed his stubble and raised his eyebrows, like his confidence was rising with each passing second.

"I asked Neil to come along as an example to everyone else – he's done so well in treatment he is even going to be volunteering as a mentor."

Tim looked at me and his expression became like one belonging to a different face.

"Pierce, what would you like to share?"

"I guess... I get frustrated."

"Would you like to elaborate?"

Everyone was looking at me with globular eyes.

"I don't believe I'm getting better – but I try to."

"You're resistant to treatment. This has been a problem. Let's pick this apart and see what we can take from it," said Tim.

He got to his feet and grabbed a marker pen, drawing a table on the whiteboard.

"Let's make a list of the common impediments to treatment," he said.

"What like?"

"Attitude towards medication for one thing."

He scribbled it on the board without okaying it with me first and the pen made a horrible squeak as he wrote.

All the windows were open, and I felt chilled to the bone. A ride-on lawnmower passed by the window, drowning out the volume of Tim's voice.

"Would someone shut those windows?" he said, irritably.

"I'll do it," said Kate, jumping to her feet.

"Why are they cutting the grass at this time of the day?" asked Tim. I wasn't sure if he was talking to himself or to us. "They could cut it any time, and they choose to do it while I'm running this session."

The final window was closed tight, and the sounds of life outside were muted.

"That's better," he said.

"So, attitude towards medication. What else?"

"I don't know," I said.

Not only could I not think of an answer to his question; I couldn't think of anything – clear or otherwise. I was losing my train of thought like cards once in sequence dropped in a disordered pile. Kate still wouldn't look at me and that was upsetting me more than Tim's subject of choice.

"What about... shirks responsibility – you don't want to work."

"I wouldn't put it like that."

"That's the most honest way to put it, isn't it, Pierce? How long have you been out of work for now?"

"A few months. There are others here that don't work."

"That's because they can't – you make the choice not to."

"I don't."

"Denial is another problem – being unable to self-assess. And isolating yourself."

"I thought you wanted me to "

"Only because of your negative influence on others."

I was sure Tim shot Kate a wink, but it could have been a trick of the light. The sunlight made a block of rippling light across his face. It obscured his eyes so you couldn't see the real intention behind his smile.

"I'm sure Tim won't mind me telling you that he recently broke up with his live-in girlfriend, and that he destroyed a recent friendship."

I was starting to feel like Tim had a lower opinion of me than I did of myself, but I just saw my own self-hatred reflected to me in every face I looked at. A picture of my character had been drawn before we'd even got talking. I wished there was a point of comparison in the room – someone I could compare myself to, illness-wise, but no one seemed eager to share.

The voice appeared in my head. His low, emotionless voice spoke to me, coming into a crescendo.

"You're useless – even your doctor has no faith in you. It's your fault – he's happy with the progress of the patient before you. He isn't a negative person. You're the problem."

I was getting lower and lower, sitting there, slumped in my seat. My body was following my feelings and I couldn't hold myself up straight anymore. Everyone was staring at me like I was a class project – something to dissect that none of class wanted to get too close to, but that they couldn't draw their eyes away from. A girl coughed uncomfortably and looked at her hands.

"Do you have anything else you'd like to add at the moment, Pierce?"

I shook my head.

"We should move onto the next person, but I'll keep these points on the board, in case any of you want to note them down for reference."

A guy with ginger hair and white, freckly skin stuck his hand up. He had a broad Belfast accent and a friendly tone.

"Is there something you're proud of?" he asked me.

I sat for a long time and then shook my head. I couldn't think of one redeeming quality. The energy was draining from my body, like the conversation was a hoover to my self-worth. I went silent and waited for the focus to be moved to the next person.

"Well, Carly," said Tim. "What would you like to add?"

"I find it difficult to keep stable relationships," the next girl said.

She didn't look particularly engaged in the session and her eyes were glazed.

"But your medication is helping with that," said Tim.

I looked at him and he gave me a quick glance.

"Yeah, but that was your call – that wasn't me."

"Thank you," said Tim, growing happily red in the face.

"You really know what you're talking about," continued the girl. "Everyone should trust this man," she said, proudly to the room. "I just want to take this opportunity to praise Tim's work," she said, getting to her feet. "A round of applause for Tim. He's turned so many lives around," she said, leading everyone in applause.

I clapped mechanically, but I didn't understand what she was talking about. Maybe I was just too damaged to benefit from his treatment. It felt like life was rounding up and it was nearly check-out time. I was trying to find one last flicker of hope, but it was dying down like embers in a fire beyond revival.

Tim got to his feet and beamed at everyone. It felt like the only two people he didn't beam at were Kate and myself, but maybe I was getting into that paranoid state of mind again.

CHAPTER TWENTY-SIX

Pierce

"**K**ate!" I called after her as she walked towards the double doors.

She didn't turn around.

I called her name a few more times and then realised there was no chance she hadn't heard me.

Someone reached out for my arm. I looked round and it was Tim.

"What do you think you're doing?" he asked.

"What do you mean?"

"Didn't I warn you to stay away from Kate?"

"Yeah, I haven't been seeing her."

"I know you got her to take you to the hospital last week."

"How did you know that?"

"She told me. She says you're harassing her. If you go near her again, I'll call the police."

"What? What did she say?"

"I can't disclose those details, but you should be ashamed of your actions," he said.

"I didn't do anything."

"I can't help you anymore, Pierce. We'll finish up treatment and then I'll discharge you."

"No, I need your help."

"I can't help you – it's hopeless."

"It's not – I'll stay away from Kate. Please…"

I didn't know why I was begging for his help, but I just knew in that moment I couldn't cope with the last person I needed turning their back on me.

"No," he said, "I need to get back to the clinic."

My head started spinning and I couldn't see the entrance. I walked outside in a hurry and stopped inches short of a reversing vehicle. The driver blared the horn and everyone in the carpark looked at me. I knew they'd labelled me the difficult one in the group. I couldn't stand being stared at like that. I was blinded by misery and walked blindly to the gates.

I walked home in the same state. I couldn't see anyone around me, I couldn't spot any obstacles - I knew I must have bumped into countless people, but I couldn't see their reactions, I couldn't hear what they were saying, I couldn't tell if they even noticed me. I was going home, but I didn't know why I was going there so quickly. What would I do once I got there? I'd be left alone with the same empty time. I didn't have anyone I could phone. I didn't have anyone I could see. I didn't have anywhere else to go. My thinking was lost to the point I couldn't prepare a piece of toast or work a remote control. The basics were slipping away, and they'd been all I'd had within my grasp. I was lost in the world – I could see how people ended up homeless in sleeping bags, on side streets, starving. I couldn't cope with the simplest things – how would I pay a bill, how would I feed myself, how would I keep waking up every day? As I walked home, I was already hatching a plan that would be the resolution to every worry.

CHAPTER TWENTY-SEVEN

Pierce

A t home, I phoned Tim repeatedly. He didn't pick up until the fifth time. By then I was in a frenzy and I needed to talk to him more than I needed my next breath.

"Please, don't cut me off," I pleaded.

I was beyond the point of being able to mind sounding pathetic – I was begging for my life.

"Why would I work with you when you do the opposite to what I tell you? You fight me at every turn."

"I won't. I'll do whatever you say."

"I need to see proof of that."

"What kind of proof? I'll do whatever you want – just don't leave me on my own."

I was like an animal clawing savagely at the door of the house they'd been banished from.

"Ok – I'll consider it – but I need you to do one exercise."

"What is it?"

"I need you to write a list of all your flaws – get really honest with yourself. If you can manage to do that, I'll meet you on Thursday. Come to my office at 11am with the list."

My stubbornness about composing such a thing had vanished. I would do whatever it took to stay under Tim's care.

CHAPTER TWENTY-EIGHT

Tim

I have to get revenge on Pierce. Since the first time I saw his face, I knew that would be my aim in life. His obliviousness angers me – it does more than that – it sends me into a hateful rage. I lie awake, thinking about him. He is a stubborn one – but I can see him disintegrating a little more at each appointment. That gives me hope that my methods are working. Don't get me wrong, I know what I'm doing. I deserve the praise I get as a psychiatrist. When I want to, I employ my methods for good. But that alone doesn't satisfy my need for authority. Watching people being discharged from my care and going on to lead normal lives doesn't give me a sense of satisfaction. Yes, I enjoy the awards that periodically come my way, but I need more. I need human proof. My ugliest emotion is envy. It's one thing I can't stand about myself. Putting that aside, I'd say I'm nearing perfection. The only way to get rid of the envy is to get rid of the source of it. You might wonder why I'm so envious of Pierce. He lives directly in my line of view and watching his life from afar has sickened me for many months. I'd been toying with the idea of murdering him in a different way. I know no one would suspect me of such a thing, so my chances of getting caught would have been slim. But that isn't as much fun. I want to see him gradually falling apart before the final act. I want to see him do it to himself.

Every day, he walked up and down my street, parading his girlfriend around town. He didn't even look grateful for what he had. She was better looking than him – one of the sexiest women I've ever seen. I know she would have been dying over me in my younger years, but now I know I'm past my prime. My charm more than compensates for it, but I knew I couldn't tear her away from him, even if I tried. The way she looks at him enrages me. She's rapt – hanging on his every word, and he doesn't deserve it. He doesn't even seem to notice. It never occurred to me he might be depressed – I just thought he was arrogant. But I couldn't believe my luck when he walked into my office. What were the chances that he would have psychiatric problems and happen to be paired up with me? It was like a gift from the gods. I would have been ungracious to turn it down. I got a letter of his one day and that's how I first found out his name. I delivered the letter in person so I could have an excuse to be invited in, but he answered the door, taking the letter with a quick "thanks." He was neither smiley nor friendly. That made me dislike him more. But mostly, I was irritated that he'd had the audacity to take a favour from me without returning one. If I do something for someone, I expect them to provide me with compensation for it. I deserved to look at the interior of their house and be given a cup of tea, but it wasn't offered to me. I guessed his girlfriend was out. I had to know her name.

"Your name is Pierce Jones?"

"Yeah."

"That's good, I'm glad I got the right house."

"You have a partner too, don't you?"

"Yeah."

"What's her name?"

"Molly."

It disappointed me that that was her name. I'd built her up like a goddess in my mind and she should have been renamed something more appropriate – Eurelia, Orphea, Lisandra. Molly sounded like it should belong to someone ordinary, and she wasn't that. Maybe if I could get Pierce out of the picture, I could snap her up. But how could I present myself as her support? I needed to make myself into a crutch she couldn't let go of. Once I accomplished the whole thing, I knew my self-belief would quadruple. With that amount of power, I could only imagine the things I would be capable of. When happiness is illusive, you have to find your kicks where you can. The thing is – I know no matter what I do, I'll grow bored with it. The trick is to keep moving from one chaotic scenario to the next. Stopping is the worst thing you can do. Time to reflect isn't something I need. I want to keep myself safe – safe from introspection.

I waited for a few more minutes on Pierce's doorstep. He still didn't extend an invitation to me. He seemed like he was in a strange mood. I hadn't believed men to be moody until that encounter with him. Women were usually the ones who lost the run of themselves, but I could tell by looking at him, he was mentally weak.

That is one of the attributes of an important psychiatrist: identifying mental illness where it hasn't yet been uncovered. I finally realised I'd have to work harder if I wanted access to the inside of their house. So, I went home and returned to the research at my desk. I had the perfect desk-position for full view of their lives. I sat behind the tilted blinds watching them and eating my meal for one.

CHAPTER TWENTY-NINE

Kate

I'm unravelling. I have the same feeling I had when I first arrived on Northern Irish soil - lost, agitated, terrified. I've fallen into a pattern of going to Tim's house. It's become a weekly event – but I don't know how to survive in-between times. I've nothing to work towards. Tim says we need to focus on my treatment before I even think about venturing into any social arena. I've given up the walking group now. I had to – to avoid Pierce. Tim gave me clear instructions the last time I saw him: avoid Pierce or he'd cut me off from treatment. He was angry – the only time I'd seen him angry with me. I know that's because he's developing feelings for me and he wants what's best for me. Any suspicions I had about Tim were delusional. I think back to that time and can't believe my own stupidity. How could I ever have challenged his methods? They are miraculous.

When Tim warned me off Pierce, he gave me good reason to avoid him. I hadn't realised that he was a dangerous person – a predator of sorts. Tim confided in me everything he knew about him – how his life had been perfect on paper. He'd had a valuable degree, a home of his own, a steady wage and a girlfriend that adored him. He'd thrown all but the house away. Being in his vicinity was like being on the site where a torpedo lands – you weren't going to escape unscathed. If it hadn't come from Tim's mouth, I would have found his assertions hard to believe. They didn't add up with the image of Pierce I had in my head. How could he be so calculated? How could he play off the feelings of the mentally ill?

"He's on a path to destruction – and if you continue following him, he'll take you there too."

"I don't know how to cut from him," I said, sadly.

"Why not?"

"I'm attached to him."

"It's unhealthy."

"I'm still attached. It's not that easy to just walk away."

"You need to, for your own safety."

"I don't know if I can."

"You can – just stop all contact – don't allow him to make eye contact with you when you see him in group."

"If you believe all this about him, why are you treating him?"

"I don't have a choice."

It was hard to believe that Tim would do anything because he felt obligated to. He gave an aura of being above instruction. He sat back in his chair putting one ankle on the other knee. He looked at me with that special look that can entice me to do anything.

"Are you going to follow my advice, Kate?"

"Ok."

As soon as I agreed to that, his demeanour changed from one of impatience to one of acceptance. He looked at me lustily and I wished I'd had the courage to cover up more. People always assume because you have skin on show that you're sure of yourself. For me, that couldn't be further from the truth – it's a distraction from all the inner tenderness I don't want to reveal. Tim looked like he had an appreciation for it, even though he said otherwise.

"You should cover yourself up a bit more, Kate. You're making yourself into a target."

"I don't see how."

"Your body is perfect. I know you have insecurities about your face, but your body is perfect."

He looked me from top to toe and I felt exposed. But maybe it was ok to feel exposed by Tim. Maybe that was the key to success. He reached out and glazed my form with his hand. He was barely touching me – just enough to feel my outline. For some reason, it didn't feel sexual – it just felt like a natural touch. Tim wanted to know me – to know me inside and out. He wanted to know every component that made me tick, including everything of my physical form. I lay back on the bed and let him explore me with his hands while he prodded me for answers on every subject he wished. I could only speak openly – I knew no other way.

CHAPTER THIRTY

Pierce

I arrived at Tim's office with my completed list of personal failures. It was easier to compose than I'd imagined. I'd wondered how I was going to go about it – but the words flowed as soon as my pen touched the page. I was writing in an unconscious way, like I was offloading my problems onto the paper. Tim would be proud when he saw how real I'd got with myself.

The paper was crumpled when I got to the office. I'd been carrying it in a clammy hand for half an hour. I was afraid to put it in my pocket, in case I lost it and had to repeat the same exercise again. It had been gruelling, even though it wasn't hard to come up with any negatives. Dreaming up negatives just seems to breed more negativity. I was feeling the lowest I'd felt about myself in a long time, and that was saying something.

I sat down in the waiting room and wished no one could see my face. I felt ugly and embarrassed to be alive. I'd made so little of my existence. I thought about all the people leading significant lives – helping others, making money, growing. I was never going to improve. I was like an unfinished project abandoned in a paper bin.

"Pierce," Tim called me.

He gave me a smile – the kind where the lips move mechanically, but nothing seems to light up. He looked tired, like he'd been through a long day. I never took the time to stop and think how the job must be affecting him. You couldn't spend your life in a clinic like that and not be impacted by it. I sat down in my usual seat and Tim filed away some papers in his desk.

"Well," he said, looking at the list that shook in my hand. "Did you complete the exercise I asked you to do?"

"I did," I said.

I gripped the paper tightly – there was something about opening it up to him that felt like letting a cut bleed freely in shark-infested waters.

I handed it over, reluctantly.

"Let's have a look," said Tim. He put his glasses on. He only ever did that when he was paying attention to something particularly important.

His face had a glow to it as he read the list.

"This is revelatory, Pierce."

"Why?"

"You've never been this open about your failings before. When you see the full assembly of them, you realise how far you are from living a normal life."

"Yeah, there are quite a lot."

"I'm not going to make you read over them again – that would be cruel, but I'm going to keep this for future reference," he said.

He put it in the drawer before I had time to argue. At least he was bound by confidentiality and it couldn't go further than us.

"I need you to complete another exercise now."

"What is it?"

"Draft the notes you would have written had you committed suicide. We need to pick apart your reasons for trying it – imagine what you would say as your closing words."

It didn't sound like an idea that would take me out of a dark place, but I'd promised to do what I was told. I couldn't risk being kicked off treatment for good.

"I meant to say – I don't think you should come back to the group."

"Why?"

"I was thinking about it and I don't think I's beneficial having you there – to you or to anyone else."

I nodded slowly, afraid to challenge him.

"After the last session, a few of the others came to talk to me in private. They said it was triggering for them. I can't destabilise the rest of my patients for your sake."

"I didn't mean to do that."

"Well, everyone was appalled by your lack of direction, Pierce. These people are trying to get their lives on track and listening to you failing to do so doesn't motivate them."

I thought about Kate and how she'd ignored me during the session. That had been my last opportunity to see her, even if she didn't acknowledge me. I wondered if Tim would ever agree to let us see each other again. I'd become more attached to her than I'd realised, and it felt like she'd been the last friend I'd had left. I told Tim about that, but he didn't want to hear it.

"People pass in and out of your life, Pierce – to teach you lessons. No one stays for good. Stop clinging to things that aren't yours."

I felt ill every time I thought about the past – I idealised it and thought I'd never manage to succeed again, and I was right.

CHAPTER THIRTY-ONE

Pierce

There was a knock at the door. It was a gentle one. Sometimes if you listen closely enough, a knock is enough to identify someone. Everyone has their characteristic knock – shy or brutal, bland or interesting – it's like their personality summarised in a second. I knew the knock like I knew the sound of my own voice. It was Molly. I took my time walking to the door, trying to compose myself. I paused at the mirror and looked at my aged face. There was nothing a few seconds could do to salvage it. Getting my hopes up is something I should have learnt not to do, but I could feel myself getting excited at the prospect of her presence.

"Hi," she said, looking at me with clear eyes.

They lacked agenda; that was something that stood out to me in that moment. They just saw me, without trying to manipulate me. I tried to hold onto that thought, but it was already crumbling away. I wanted to be sociable and put my best self forward, but it didn't feel possible. Constructing a sentence was more than I could cope with. I stepped back to let Molly know she was welcome to come in. She placed her hand on my arm and looked deeply concerned.

"What's wrong, Pierce? You don't seem like yourself."

I just shook my head; it was beyond explanation.

"Would you like a cup of tea?" I asked.

"I'll make it," she said, walking to the kitchen and getting out our two favourite cups, like she'd never left.

She put the kettle on to boil, and she didn't bother changing the water or commenting on the state of the house. She didn't seem to even notice – she just noticed me. I remembered the delicious feeling of her attention again, and I felt more than a pang of longing. I watched her wring out the tea bags with a spoon. She topped up our teacups with milk and carried them into the living room.

"You sit down, you look exhausted," she said.

I nodded.

"What's wrong?" she asked me.

I squeezed my eyes shut. I hoped she'd think I was just struggling with a headache, and not struggling to hold back tears.

"You can tell me, Pierce."

"I don't know," I said, and it was true – I couldn't qualify what was happening to me. I just knew I felt worse that day than on any other day on Earth.

"Are you still seeing Tim?"

"Yes."

"This is because of him, Pierce. You've got so much worse since the last time I saw you."

"It's not."

"It is – you weren't like this before you met him. I can see the change – it's immense."

I shook my head. I wouldn't allow anyone to question his

methods – they were the last filament that connected me to the world.

"I need to help you, Pierce – what should I do?"

"I don't know."

"Should we report him?"

"No," I said. I felt threatened by her suggestion. "Why did you come over?"

"I wanted to see if you were ok. I think about you every day."

"You do?"

"Yeah, I feel so bad for leaving you to cope with everything alone."

"You didn't – it was my choice."

"Well, you still need a friend."

"I have friends."

"That's great, but where are they?"

"I don't know. It's complicated."

"Pierce – you look like you haven't washed in weeks, your eyes look sunken in – are you getting any sleep?"

"It's all I do."

I couldn't face talking about myself anymore.

"How are things with you?" I asked.

"Good – I'm still working away. I've been seeing someone for a while."

"Oh, who?"

"You don't know him."

"Is he like me?"

"Not remotely."

She looked sad as she said it.

"You were always my first choice, Pierce – but you didn't want me."

"That's not why. I'm glad you've met someone – you deserve it."

"So do you."

I shook my head.

"I'm too broken to have a relationship," I said.

"I don't think anyone is."

She put her hand on top of mine and her palm was warm against it.

"What can I do, Pierce?"

Molly waited for a long while as I tried to figure out the answer to that question.

"Nothing."

"Are you sure?"

"Yeah – I think it would be better if you left."

"If that's what you want, Pierce."

"I do."

I didn't, but I'd never admit to that. Sometimes the best way to love someone is to let them get free of you.

CHAPTER THIRTY-TWO

Kate

I know Tim is trying to keep me away from Pierce. I've been growing increasingly suspicious of him lately. I had a striking realisation about him last night when I went to his flat. When I walked inside, there was something that unsettled me – a familiar scent.

My mother had never perfumed the air in our house. It always smelled stale and like a window hadn't been opened in months. It smelled identical in Tim's house. Everything looked disordered, and it made me feel unsafe. But I knew I was overdramatising things. It was just a house that needed airing. That couldn't hurt me. Tim was nowhere to be seen, so I walked into his office. We'd made an appointment for 7pm. He just left the door unlocked for me – I knew his home well enough by then to let myself in.

When I walked into the office, Tim was sitting with his back turned to me, looking out the window.

"What are you watching?" I asked.

"I just saw someone I know."

"Was it Pierce?"

"Yes, what makes you say that?"

"I know he lives on this street."

"Oh, I didn't know that – what are the chances of that?"

"Yeah, you can't get away from anything in this country. Your work follows you home."

Tim looked at me, as if to say I was a demonstration of that. He didn't seem happy to see me. Maybe he'd had a draining week and the last thing he needed was another appointment.

"We don't have to talk if you don't want to," I said.

"Well, why else are you here?" he asked.

I shrugged.

"Lie down, Kate – make yourself comfortable. I'll get my notebook."

"Ok."

"Why don't you tell me some more details about your childhood? You never go into any detail about it."

"Why should I? It's over now."

"No, it isn't – you're living the effects of it every day, aren't you?" Pierce smiled at me.

His smile looked sick to me – like he was taking pleasure in my misery. But I didn't have enough confidence to walk out because of it.

The word "co-dependent" resounded in my head. Tim had told me so many times that I was – he was the expert. I knew it was just a kind way of calling me clingy. But Tim never seemed to mind my clinginess – he acted like it satisfied something in him.

"My mum was a cruel woman – my dad was never there."

"Ok – what do you mean by cruel?"

"She used to put me through things – things children don't deserve."

Like?"

"Like if I didn't do what she wanted, she'd physically punish me."

"What are you afraid of, Kate?"

"Water."

"Why water?"

"She used to get angry and hold my head under the water when she washed my hair."

"Is that why you rarely wash your hair?" he asked, still smiling.

Again, his smile made me uncomfortable, but I wasn't able to confront him.

"I do wash it – but only ever standing up. I can't put it near deeper water – can't go in the sea, can't go swimming."

"That's restrictive. You need to face those fears, or you'll always have them."

"What do you mean?"

"You need to stop running from your childhood – or you'll be traumatised forever... Why don't we work on that together now?"

"Work on what? The water thing?"

I didn't know exactly what he meant, but the word "water" was enough to send me into a panic.

"Follow me," he said.

He ran me a bath and instructed me to get into it. It'd help me release my demons, he said. I hadn't lain in a bath my entire adult life. As soon as my toe touched the water, I felt a panic attack taking hold. I couldn't breathe, I couldn't think, I couldn't say anything except "I'm going to die."

"You aren't going to die, Kate. Don't be so ridiculous."

"It feels like it. I can't do this."

I hated standing there in front of him, undressed and exposed. He looked me up and down, not necessarily in a sexual manner but in a way that made me feel predated upon.

"The rest of your body isn't what I expected it to be."

I didn't answer him.

"It's less young and pert – more lopsided and loose-fleshed."

"Why?"

"I'm not saying that's a bad thing – you just aren't how I imagined you in my head."

I felt strange thinking about him imagining me without clothes on while I was disclosing the most personal things I'd told anyone. Wasn't that malpractice? But Tim had the type of character that wouldn't allow him any wrongdoing. Why would he toy with his career so carelessly after working so hard to get where he was?

"Once you're lying down, you'll feel more at ease."

I slid into the water. It felt like slipping into silk. I looked around the room and realised how much it looked like home. There was nothing decorative that marked it as a home. It was characterless – like a bathroom in a hostel. My mum had never gone in for good scents and adornment. That wasn't what she focussed her attentions on. I felt like Tim must have known her. The situation was too close to what I'd experienced. How did he know? Had he researched me? Or was it just textbook parental abuse? Maybe every one of his clients had the same triggers and he knew how to tackle them.

"Close your eyes and just return to that last moment in your mind."

"My mum was sitting beside me while I was having a bath. She didn't talk to me. She was sitting in uncomfortable silence. I could tell something had annoyed her. Even if it wasn't me, it was going to be me."

"How was she behaving?"

"Irascible. Like she was just keeping the lid on her rage, but she'd choose when to let it off."

"That must have made you anxious."

"It did," I said, tears starting down my face.

"It's ok – you're in a safe place. Then what happened?"

"She started to wash my hair – but she was being too rough. I didn't like it."

"What way rough?"

"She was scrubbing my scalp, violently. I told her it hurt, and she got angry. She pushed my head under the water," I said.

I was shaking thinking of it. The water didn't feel pleasant to me – it felt like the squeaky kind of friction between skin and silk. I wanted to jump out, but Tim encouraged me to stay put. He came to my side and stroked my hair. It wasn't gentle and I tried to get up. He rubbed my forehead with his hand, like he was soothing me to sleep and then held my face down. I gasped, intaking water. How was this happening again? I couldn't see anything – I could just feel his thick hand holding me down. His hands were large and strong – like huge paddles. I'd noticed their strength before, but never imagined him using it against me. He let go and I came to the surface, gasping, choking. He let go and backed away.

It took me a while to get my breath and to cough up the water that had gone into my lungs.

"Why did you do that?" I said, between coughs.

"I thought if we recreated the scenario, it would help you deal with it as an adult."

"Why would you try to hurt me?"

Tim didn't answer me. Bad people never tell you the true whys of what they do.

I got out of the bath and climbed, dripping into my clothes.

"Where are you going?"

"I have to go, I'll talk to you tomorrow," I said.

Anything to placate him so I could make it home alive. In that moment, I believed that I'd never talk to him again.

He watched me, smiling while I pulled my clothes on.

"I thought you were more graceful than this. I'd always pictured you taking you clothes on and off sensually, not ripping them on and off like a restrictive bandage."

He gave me a fond smile, to counteract the bitterness of his words. I knew those tactics – I'd lived them in England for twenty-five years. I knew I needed to get out of there. I'd made it onto a boat before and started over in a new country – I could make it a mile down the road and manage to stay away from him. It was nothing in comparison.

"Why are you in such a hurry?" he asked.

He genuinely didn't seem to understand why. That was the first hint of doubt I'd seen in him. Maybe he instinctively knew I was backing away.

"Thank you for your help – I see what you were trying to do," I lied. "I'm feeling better already."
My breathing still felt uneven and I could feel the weight of the water in my lungs from minutes before. I'd never been so sure I was going to die before, and at the hands of someone so responsible.

CHAPTER THIRTY-THREE

Tim

My plan is developing beautifully. I've tried to keep Kate and Pierce apart. There are too many moments where I see a sign of recognition in her eyes – like the start of her suspecting something. I'd encouraged their friendship because I'd known it would enhance their co-dependency. Kate needed someone to cling to, and Pierce needed to stay out of such relationships. But I know he wouldn't say no, in the name of politeness. I thought if I managed to create a connection between them, it might aid me in my plan to kill them both. If I could stage a suicide pact, it saved me half the trouble, but I could still work the situation from a distance. I'd start their relationship intensely. I wouldn't even have to work at that – that's the way they go about forming relationships – at least Kate does. Pierce is isolated and after losing his girlfriend, he would have gone along with anything to rid himself of his loneliness. Loneliness – I still don't understand the concept of it. I spend most of my free time alone, and I've never felt the need for company. I get enough of it in work, and even then, the company only serves to feed my craving for control.

I hoped once I got them attached to one another, I could create a situation that allowed me to instruct them to stay away from each other. I can wear them down better singly, and the pressure of it will build until a final meeting leads them to simultaneously end their lives. I'm confident of that. I know how faultless my plans are. There might be slight variables – but they never cause people to wander from the end goal. I like to sit back, watching the whole thing coming together like an artist finally seeing a picture forming out of all their individual brushstrokes.

I can see that Pierce is weakening. I've had to work harder on Kate. I'd thought she'd be the more fragile of the two, but I was wrong. She's better at going through hell – she's had a lifetime of practice at it, I suppose. I recreated a traumatic scene she described taking place with her mother. I hadn't known about that in advance – I'd just seen the opportunity present itself. Not everything I do is calculated – sometimes it all just falls together, and I get surprised along the way. Kate left my flat abruptly after that. I could tell it had affected her, even if she didn't talk about it. She would have been less likely to talk about it if it had, in fact. But I always get the feeling she's trying to stay in my flat until I suggest she just stay over. She hates to be alone with herself. I have a feeling she is going to reach out to Pierce soon, but I'm going to try to hold her off a little longer. I'll make an apologetic phone call later. I still have some work I need to do on Pierce.

I waited a couple of hours and then I phoned Kate's number. I withheld the number to be sure she'd pick up. As the dial tone sounded, I tried to remember every instance I'd heard someone sounding contrite. That's what I have to do, since I've never felt the emotions myself. I watch films and real-life people comporting themselves in ways and reacting to situations how I know I "should." Then, I make note of them.

Kate answered the phone. Her voice sounded weaker – like she was a younger person than she'd been just hours before.

"Kate…" I said. "I needed to check you were ok."

Nothing.

"I was so worried about you after earlier. I tried a new method with you that I hoped would cause a breakthrough. But I can tell it didn't work and I'm so disappointed – I never meant to frighten you. That's the last thing I would want. You mean a lot to me – Kate. Not just as a patient, but as a person. You're special and I don't want to do anything to destroy that."

"Thanks. I'm still shaken up."

"That is understandable. Sometimes reverse psychology works – I've had lots of success with it in the past. But obviously it wasn't appropriate in this case – it just brought everything back – and I'm terribly sorry it did that."

"It's ok."

I could hear her voice warming up a little, so I could take my word count down. I only bothered with excessive wordiness when I was trying to win someone over. Otherwise, it was a waste of energy.

"I mean it. I deeply regret it."

"I know – I know you'd never do anything to intentionally harm me, Tim. You just aren't that kind of person. I just wasn't ready for that – it wasn't your fault. It's my fault – I'm sensitive to that."

"Understandably."

"I understand what you were trying to do."

"I'm glad."

I'd got her back as a devoted patient. I could tell from the tone of her voice. She might have had the beginnings of distrust in her mind, but she was reverting to old habits: making other people's behaviour ok for them, apologising for her existence.

"Can I come to your office for the next appointment?"

"Of course. I won't bring you back to my house until you're comfortable."

There was a long pause. For a second, I was worried I was losing her. But then she said, brightly, "see you this Thursday?"

"Of course – I promise it'll be entirely different."

CHAPTER THIRTY-FOUR

Pierce

I started drafting my first suicide letter. I didn't understand the point of the exercise – maybe Tim would get me to challenge every one of my reasons for considering it once he had them on paper. It was hard to think what to say. I had plenty of reasons I'd considered it in the past, but they felt too personal to name. But I wasn't publicly announcing them – it would just be between myself and Tim – like a sick secret. I felt cowardly writing something I wasn't going to immediately follow through on – I don't like playing at things and never accomplishing them. But there must have been some value in doing it – I'd promised to trust Tim with my life, so I could trust him with my hypothetical death too.

I sat down in the study I hadn't used since I'd last done anything productive. It felt like a long time ago. I was wasting years of life, sitting around in my own space. It was hard to write the letter in a way that didn't sound contrived.

I've decided I want to take the easy way out. Too much has been lost to attempt to salvage it. Please tell Molly and my family that I loved them.

Pierce Jones.

It looked too short, but I had nothing else to say. I knew Tim would want more, but I didn't know what. I'd have to ask him to elaborate at the next appointment. I knew if he was disappointed with my efforts, he'd make it clear.

I tried to write something better, but the words weren't flowing, so I just crumpled them up and threw them in the bin. I went to bed - I couldn't think of one thing to do with my time, and I was learning the dangers of empty time and too many thoughts.

At the next appointment, I walked in with my one pathetic piece of paper. I hadn't thought of anything more. I wondered how I'd ever worked at a job. I couldn't even come up with ideas about myself.

Tim seemed different that day – less interested in what I had to say and more concerned with how he looked. He kept looking at his reflection in the mirror and fixing his collar. Maybe he had something else happening that day I didn't know about. I didn't like to ask. He treated me like we were friends – brutally honest friends, but I knew the boundary was still up, to keep me out of his personal life. He looked good and smelled strongly of cologne – like he was getting ready to go on a date. There was a vitality about him that added another dimension to his hypnotic presence.

"Did you want to see the note?"

"Oh, yeah, let me see it."

I handed him the single piece of paper.

"Didn't we agree you were going to draft several versions?"

"I don't get why."

"For comparison, and to pick apart the issues."

"Don't we know the issues?"

"Are you challenging me again, Pierce?"

"No," I said, and shut up.

"I need you to draft several versions – in detail – by the next appointment," he said, sternly.

A member of staff passed through the room.

"Sorry to interrupt," she said. I didn't recognise her – she must have been new there. She was young and put together. She was wearing office wear that was just short of appropriate length. Tim gave her a charming smile.

"No need for apologies," he said.

"Dr Hanlon, I just need to pick up a prescription request pad. Do you have a spare one?"

"Don't call me Dr Hanlon – it makes me feel old. Call me Tim," he beamed.

I couldn't imagine Tim with a partner – he seemed above all that – like romantic love was too basic for the likes of him. But I could see something flash in his eyes that told me he was interested in her. She was young, just into the profession – probably a receptionist or something. She looked about my age, but in better shape. She seemed overly nice and a little bit gullible. I was sure Tim would look after her though – he loved to have someone to take under his wing.

She took the pad from his hand and his glazed hers.

"Excuse me," he said. But it was too slow to be accidental. It felt like the world was conspiring against me. Everything was intersecting at a sickening speed. Everyone I met was connected in multiple ways. We were all living lives too close to each other and I felt a sensation only slightly less serious than suffocation.

"Don't worry," she smiled. "I'll let you get back to your work."

She turned to give him a last look and a mascara-heavy flutter. It was like a stereotypical office scene in a film – ones that always end in affairs. But I couldn't imagine Tim using his work to gain access to anyone – especially someone so much younger than him. He always had the moral high ground, no matter how he behaved – that was his defence.

CHAPTER THIRTY-FIVE

Tim

Everything is coming together like story parts forming a whole at the finale. I can see Pierce weakening. Kate is lapping up my words again and now I have a new project too – a different kind of one. She can give me the type of attention that's lacking. She seems sweet and unspoiled. She's probably a virgin and unaware of bad intentions. To young women, older men – particularly older men in impressive positions - are just mature, steady - everything men their age aren't. Even if that isn't the case, we've had plenty of time to polish that act. I know I could convince anyone of anything. In a way, these simpletons who come into the office straight out of university are too easy. I don't have to turn up the charm too high – the challenge doesn't last long, but I still get some adoration in the process. I've had a lot of admiration in my career lately, but not enough in my personal life. I need a diversion – a little hobby for my dull moments. Sara was that to me. As soon as I saw her, I was drawn in by her freshness. You can tell she hasn't been through much in life. She's classically good-looking, but a little inexperienced to realise the power she could wield with that. She's like most people I meet

– she wants validation. She probably has low self-esteem and needs someone to reassure her she's ok. I can be that person, at least for a little while, until the novelty wears off. The novelty always wears off, but that doesn't take the fun out of it. If I can get admiration from several different sources, it feeds my needs better than putting all my attention in one place. I want to reach the point of ultimate perfection. I might have certain areas covered, but the best way to achieve that is to have professional power mixed with romantic control – what a concoction.

So, when I saw Sara stroll out on her lunch break, I asked her if she needed someone to show her the ropes. Who better than me? She was probably shocked I was able to free up the time to give her that. It just proves to her what a good, generous guy I am. I'd take her to a nearby café and we'd have a "business meeting." I'd talk through the basics of how the clinic is run – nothing too deep of course. Why would I share anything of value with someone who hasn't earned it? She has a menial role – taking phone calls and shuffling papers at the front desk. But if she likes me, she'll act like a buffer between myself and the difficult patients, and that is important.

Sara is the image of the kind of woman I see on my arm in my mind. I like to fantasise about walking down the street with a young, ten-out-of-ten woman next to me. I care little about her brains, as long as she is attached enough to me that I can manipulate things in my favour. I love the look of envy I get from other men when a good-looking woman is beside me. I know she'll never measure up to me, but that makes it more satisfying. When I can make a covetable woman feel less than me, that's what boosts my confidence. I play out the fantasies of what we will become, until the boredom sets in, at least. Then I'll probably cheat on her with one of her acquaintances – denying the whole thing, of course.

The thought of Kate walking into my office and seeing the girl at the desk excites me. I know how insecure she is – she'll know she has caught my attention. The best scenario would be if a competition began between them to hold onto my attention. That's what I dream of on empty nights. The thought of such situations is enough to tide me over until I get my next fix of excitement. I know I have several coming soon, and I can hardly contain myself – it's going to be magical.

CHAPTER THIRTY-SIX

Kate

T im phoned me. I hadn't expected to hear from him again. I'd planned on refusing the call if it did come through, but he'd withheld his number. He's too smart for me. On one level, I know what he's doing. On another, I don't want to see it. The memory of that night has been flashing in my mind all day and all night. I think other thoughts and dream other dreams, but they are always spoiled by it. It's funny how a few seconds has the power to change your life forever. I thought I was getting stronger – but that set me right back. I'll still go to see Tim. I can't avoid it when I'm feeling like this. Who else do I have to turn to? I'm not allowed to see Pierce. If we were caught together again, I know Tim would refuse us both treatment and where would we turn then?

When I spoke to Tim on the phone, he sounded more regretful than anyone I'd met before. Surely that was a sign of a good heart? He'd just been trying a new technique – one that had gone a little too far. If he doesn't experiment now and again on patients, how can he develop his methods? One part of me tells me that's true. The other part screams with discomfort but doesn't try to tell me anything as an intelligible thought. So, I go with the former.

You can't help loving Tim. I think falling in love with him is just a part of treatment. I'm sure even the men idolise him. He's someone to aspire to when you can't remember the defining features of yourself. That's what mental illness is like – it strips away every piece of your personality until you can't remember who you were, who you should be and what you could have become. Everyone seems to sense that and back away. But Tim is one person that steps towards you when you're in that position. And so, you love him for the commitment he has to his patients' recovery.

I still miss Pierce. I had a different kind of love for him – an affectionate kind, accompanied by jealousy over his ex-girlfriend. He talks about her often enough I know whatever feelings he has for her haven't been quashed. We had a good friendship – the healthiest I've found, in fact. But Tim saw something more toxic than we were able to. I knew Pierce had taken a startling plunge into depression recently. The time I saw him at the hospital, he looked like anxiety personified. He could barely talk to the staff without shaking all over – his arms, his legs, his voice. He barely looked me in the eye that day, and because we'd had some distance from each other – I could see it more noticeably. Why are we both falling apart when we're meant to be rebuilding ourselves? I guess with this illness, there are the weak and the strong, and we are just too weak to rise above it like Tim thinks we should be able to.

CHAPTER THIRTY-SEVEN

Pierce

I sat at my desk into the late hours, spilling my soul onto the page. I'd reached a level of honesty with myself that was too painful to face. I still had to keep writing it down – to write through it. It was the same as treatment – get through the bad to get to the good. I wrote page upon page and then I took a bottle of wine from the fridge. It had been a long time since I'd had a drink. You weren't meant to mix my drugs with alcohol, or so I'd been told. I'd had a bottle sitting there, unopened since Molly had lived with me. That was too many months ago to count. I'd done well to avoid doing what wasn't healthy for me, but today had tipped me over the edge. I needed numbness, and to find it quickly, so I took the quickest route there.

Next time I saw Tim, he looked blissfully happy. His face didn't really change, he didn't smile, his body language was the same. But his eyes looked more alive than usual. I wondered what had happened. I knew he wouldn't tell me, and that alone made me curious. How had he found the key to life – the one I reach for that always ends up being the wrong fit for the lock?

"Well, Pierce."

"Hi."

"Take a seat. Let's have a look at your work. You have done it, haven't you?"

"Yes."

"You're not very talkative today, Pierce."

"I don't feel good."

"Well, it's no reason to be uncooperative."

"Sorry."

"Let me see your notes. How many did you write?"

"Five."

"And did you gain any clarity from it?"

"I drank a bottle of wine."

"You're not supposed to be drinking, Pierce, not while you're in treatment."

"I know."

"You need to learn to react less to things. Someone prods you with their elbow and you're straight down their throat."

"I don't know what you mean."

"It's aggressive – and unsettling for everyone around you – your extreme behaviour."

It was hard to believe that I could be aggressive towards anyone. I'd always thought of myself as passive. But Tim knew what he was talking about. Maybe my illness had made me become a worse person – someone lacking tact.

The sun was strong that day and it came through the window like heat in a sauna. Tim didn't bother tilting the blinds. It mustn't have bothered him. I could feel myself getting clammy all over. I was wearing clothes that contained all the heat and I knew my face was red. I hoped Tim didn't put it down to embarrassment at being caught out. He was always right, and I was getting tired of it. But challenging him was out of the question. I needed him. I needed him like I needed my prescription filled.

The same lady I'd met last time came into the room.

"I was just bringing you a patient's file," she said. "You left it at the front desk."

"Thank you, Sara."

He took it from her hand and gave her what would have been a lecherous look from anyone else. She beamed back at him and I was convinced that something was going on between them. What if he talked candidly about me to her? What if she knew all my problems and told her friends? What if they passed around the town until everyone knew how bad I was?

She went out the door with her slinky walk. I didn't trust her. She looked too naïve to know better. Why did Tim have the same effect on everyone he took under his notice? I still wanted to please him, and I didn't know how to turn that off.

"Ok – first note," said Tim.

"It's not very good."

"This isn't a writing competition, Pierce – I'm just looking for honesty."

"Honesty about what?"

"I want access to your deepest thoughts – the kind that only come out on paper."

"Why?"

"How else can I help you?"

"I don't know."

Tim went quiet while he read the suicide note.

"This is better – but there is still something lacking."

"What?"

"Contrition – self-blame."

"Why do you want me to blame myself?"

"It's a normal component of a suicide note. You need to believe your value is lost, and that everything is your fault."

"How will that help me?"

"You'll see."

Tim picked up a pen and scribbled a line under my last one.

"What did you write?" I asked.

"This isn't anyone's fault but mine – I couldn't keep going any longer."

"What is that meant to convey?"

"We're role-playing, Pierce. I'm trying to make it sound convincing."

Tim held a valuable piece of paper in his hand. He went to get me an appointment card, and then came back, handing it to me, along with the letter.

"I want you to read over this tonight and let the words sink in – to show you how dangerously close you've come to suicide – to tackle the attitudes holding you back."

I put the paper in my pocket, and I didn't know what I'd do with it. I still failed to see the value in the exercise. I was witnessing first-hand the unconventionality of Tim's methods, and I still doubted how effective they were. But questioning him wasn't an option I could afford anymore.

CHAPTER THIRTY-EIGHT

Tim

I managed to ease my way into Sara's life, just like I knew I would. She didn't notice it happening because I came in under the guise of a caring boss. I wanted her to know everything about the office. I wanted to explain the context of everything – the types of patients we saw, her predecessor, how they didn't measure up to her at all. I could feel the energy radiating off her. It's a special kind of magic – watching someone's self-belief inflating because of you. Better still, knowing that you can take it away.

She was selling herself from the day she walked in; mini-skirts and tight shirts are asking for trouble. She should have known better, even if she was only twenty years old. The day I invited her out for coffee to discuss work was my opportunity to strike. I only had to get someone in a room once to persuade them of my goodness, of my value in their life. We sat down at the table, facing one another, like a business meeting. I had no intention of sharing my business with her. It was a chance to extract hers.

"So, how are you finding the job so far, Sara? You look well dressed for it."

She smiled, looking at herself proudly.

I didn't think she seemed like she had much going for her, other than her looks and her susceptibility to manipulation. You could tell she was one of those stupid girls – she mightn't have been blonde and big-chested, but she still had that daft doe-eyed look about her.

"It's great – the people are lovely. I felt at home right away."

I didn't know how anyone could feel at home in the workplace without any status – but that was her inadequacy, not mine. I thought of the lovely people to whom she was referring. Little did she know they were just as mindless as her – just not as good looking, or I would have tampered with their lives too. Every time I see something beautiful, I need to destroy it. Doing that allows me to absorb all its bright energy. Then I can let the person go and watch them walking away, just a small fraction of who they used to be.

"I'm glad you're settling in ok. Tell me about yourself – I'm intrigued."

"You are?"

"Of course, I'm always happy to learn about new colleagues. We spend more time together than we do with our friends."

"That's very true – I never thought of that before. You're a clever man."

I thought it was pathetic that something so simple could impress her, but I didn't let it show. I could see her lapping up my words, like each one I uttered was of more importance than anything she'd ever heard before.

"I just left college last year."

"What did you study?"

"Business studies."

"Was it a degree?"

"Not really."

"Did you not want to go into business?"

"I wanted to get some work experience first. This job came up and I thought it sounded good."

She was painfully dull. I knew it already, but she'd look good next to me. I looked at her legs. They were very tanned for that time of the year. I wondered if she was originally from elsewhere or if she just had good quality fake tan at home; it was responsible for most tans I saw in this country.

"Are you from near here?"

"I'm from near Ballynahinch."

"I thought I detected a bit of a rural accent."

She smiled.

"Yeah, I only moved to Belfast once I started my course."

"I'm sure if you'd been here before then, I would have seen you around."

"What do you mean?"

"Nothing, just that you're distinctive looking. Are your family from here?"

"My dad is, my mum is from Italy."

"I thought you looked a little bit exotic."

"Yeah, I guess I get a tan all year."

"Definitely."

I looked her over and I could tell she was half-enjoying the attention, half-embarrassed by it. I detected a whiff of low self-esteem. She might have been something special, physically at least, but I knew for sure at that moment that she had insecurities. Uncovering insecurities is like uncovering pearls in oysters to me. It doesn't take long to see them – you just have to watch the person more intensely than the average person has the patience to do.

"I know it's hard to learn the ropes at any new job – if you need any help, I'm happy to advise you."

"What about?"

"Anything – I know every role in that building inside out."

"I'm sure you do. I read about you before I started work there."

"You did?"

"Yeah, you were being recognised for your work in the Belfast Trust."

"Oh, I'm not sure when that was."

"I'm sure you have been too many times to remember."

I smiled. I was starting to like the girl's personality more than when we'd started talking. Somehow, the things she said were becoming more interesting to me.

She ordered a cup of black tea and no food. She must have been dieting.

"Don't you eat lunch?"

"I usually eat later in the day."

"You don't need to lose weight."

"I think I do."

"No, don't – you'll lose your best features."

She looked a little awkward.

"I'm anti-dieting – I've seen it affect too many of my patients. Eating disorders and mental illness often go hand in hand."

"Why do you think?"

"Distorted self-image, trying to control the uncontrollable."

She looked at me blankly, like she was wishing she had a dictionary handy, probably.

"You don't know what I'm talking about," I laughed, "Sorry."

"Yeah, you lost me. I'm just not as smart as you."

"You're smart enough."

She looked pleased by that, but it wasn't a compliment. It just meant that she was the perfect kind of project – of average intelligence, lumbered by emotions, insecure. I was getting excited just thinking about it - excited enough that for a minute, I almost forgot about Kate and Pierce.

CHAPTER THIRTY-NINE

Pierce

I finally got a draft I was satisfied with. It took hours to come up with it, but I knew it would get me Tim's approval. I'd got the right cocktail of regret, despondency and self-blame.

To whomever finds this,

After much consideration and trying to follow treatment for a year, I have decided it is time to give up. Tim has done everything in his power to help me, but I am not able to change. Even on medication and with weekly appointments, I still can't see a future for myself. This year has only highlighted my own uselessness. Tim has gone above the demands of his job to try to save me, and I'll forever be grateful to him for that. Some people just can't be spared, and they'll never be happy in this world.

Things have happened to lead up to my decision to end my life – my strained family relations, the effect I've had on Kate, the fact that I disappointed Molly – the person I loved the most. I've lost my job and my sense of self. I just spend my life attending mental health appointments and never developing a better attitude. Maybe I'm just lazy. Maybe I'm just never going to be good enough. I'm not waiting around any longer to find out.

Pierce Jones.

CHAPTER FORTY

Kate

I think I'm starting to see the truth. I don't want to admit it to anyone. I need to keep seeing Tim because I need to prove what he's doing. Even if I leave and he stops doing it to me, he will do it to someone else. I have to use my position as his patient to figure out what is going on. I've been involved with him long enough to know I'm not getting better. Surely by now things should be improving. Apologetic though his phone call was, if I'm honest with myself, I've felt afraid of him since the last day I went to his house. I don't feel safe going into his office. The thought of it makes me start trembling and sweating. I don't think you should feel that way about seeing someone who means you well, even if you think you love them. I know those feelings too well – and I've been reliving the scariest scenes of my childhood in every dream since. Maybe that's what Tim was trying to do – to bring every repressed memory to the surface so we could deal with them, but something tells me he gets some sort of sick enjoyment out of it too. I saw the look of triumph on his face – even when I was underwater, even when I was gasping water. Despite what was happening, water is still clear, and I could see straight into his eyes. They looked alive – more alive than they ever typically did.

When he let go, I was surprised. I'd believed he was going to kill me. He didn't look like he wanted to let go. I'd had similar situations my whole life, and if there's one thing I know to expect afterwards, it is the promise of change and touching apologies. My mum always came to me after she lost her temper with me, blaming me for causing her outburst, but promising not to overreact again, telling me how desperately sorry she was. When Tim phoned me to apologise for what he'd done, I believed his show of repentance. He sounded like he was on the verge of tears. It took me a while to process what had happened. It's like when you get hit by something and you're so stunned you can't see straight for a while.

I dream of getting out of this life now. Nearly as much as I did my parental home. I spent my childhood dreaming in my room, dreaming of being anywhere else. I created fantasy places that had nothing special about them – other than their calmness; that is special in itself. I've started to feel enslaved again, and like I need a fresh start. Will the fresh starts ever stop coming? I'd like a place to become dull and stale to me. Boredom would be a blessing – I've had enough activity for a lifetime.

I find it hard to trust my own beliefs. They seem to change as much as the tides. Tim told me it's a feature of my illness – I hold one belief one day, the opposing one the next day. I might think someone is a saint on Tuesday and the devil by Friday. They do one thing wrong and I devalue them, labelling them a bad person. I know this must be right. I read up on it during this period of distrusting him. It is listed as one of the main symptoms – all or nothing thinking. So, I guess Tim didn't make it up for his own agenda. If I could stop splitting everyone into all good or all bad, it would make it much easier to see people's intentions. I'm blinded to them because I think they're either all for me or out to get me. It's hard to tell which group Tim belongs to when he seems to oscillate between the two.

I know I need to talk to Pierce. He might have a clearer view of what's going on. But I feel like I can't take the risk that contacting him would involve. I feel like Tim knows when we are speaking – like he's watching and listening - how? I don't know. That could just be the paranoia creeping in. This is how I end up in the cycle of self-loathing – I think something's happening, then I'm sure of the opposite, I believe myself and then I don't trust myself with a single thing. As long as I can keep myself safe and start to get better, maybe the details don't matter.

CHAPTER FORTY-ONE

Pierce

I saw Tim today and he announced something new. He has done me the kindest of favours, he says. He has organised for a carer to come and stay with me. After reading my suicide letters, he has deemed me unsafe without supervision. I told him he got me to write them, but all he said was that I came up with the content alone. He'd needed to do the exercise to prove my instability.

"But you don't have the letters," I said.

It felt like the only bit of hope left.

"I have copies of them," he said.

"How?"

"I photocopied them before you left."

"I don't need a carer."

"Of course you do; you've been telling me for months that you can't manage alone, that you can barely get out of bed, wash or cook. You're isolated, you can't sustain friendships, no one in treatment can bear you, you are having dangerous thoughts. I've never had more conclusive evidence that someone needed a carer before, and I've had a lot of patients, Pierce."

It felt like he was enjoying what he was telling me, but that wouldn't make any sense. Maybe I was misreading his face, maybe he was just relieved to have released some of the responsibility for my wellbeing to someone else.

"Who is it?"

"A colleague of mine – Kevin."

"How much time would he have to spend with me? Is it just to come in and do chores and check I'm ok?"

"No, I want him there during your waking hours. He'll prepare your meals, structure your day and keep you company."

"I don't want to have a stranger in my house."

"He's not a stranger, Pierce – I know him well."

"I don't."

"I thought you were going to trust me this time, Pierce. If you don't have faith in me, how can I help you?"

"I don't know."

"You've been getting worse and worse lately – and that isn't for lack of treatment offered. We need to change tack."

"I can't cope with change anymore. I want to have my own home I can go to, to get away from everything."

"I can't trust you there after reading your notes. You couldn't be trusted with kitchen knives or managing medication properly, or anything. I never know what you're taking, or how much. You seem drugged a lot."

"It's my mind – it moves slowly on certain days."

"You hardly expect me to believe that's the natural state of things and not a drug-induced state, Pierce?"

"It is. I've never touched drugs."

"Now, we both know that's not true. You've begged me for them on countless occasions since you first started here. In fact, I have the times you have all logged."

"No, that's not why I asked for them. I just needed help."

"That's what all addicts say, Pierce. You're just going to argue with me at every turn, aren't you?"

"No," I said, looking away from him.

I couldn't help fighting for the truth, but sometimes survival is more important than getting to the bottom of things.

"What is he like?" I asked him.

"He's a pleasant guy – bland and inoffensive. You'll get on fine."

"Is he hard to talk to?"

"That's up to you. He isn't there to chat anyway."

"How many days a week will he come?"

"Five."

"So, he won't come at the weekend?"

"We'll reassess that when the time comes."

"I don't want a carer," I said.

"You don't want help, Pierce – that's your trouble. Just do what I tell you and everything will be ok."

CHAPTER FORTY-TWO

Tim

There's a guy that has been angling for my job for a while. He isn't highly qualified enough to take it over, but he has that level of determination to get him there. I didn't like him the instant I met him. He came to me under the pretence of wanting my knowledge and wisdom. But I know he isn't just asking out of interest. He's been on placement here for the last few months. He is studying at the moment and hopes to become a psychiatrist. He's been helping out with the menial things – signing patients in, organising files; but he wants to get above that. He wants to be me.

He was sent into my office on day one, and even then, I noticed something amiss. He had a cockiness to him I didn't like. How dare he behave like that in my building? How dare he try to step on my toes?

I don't think he's an intelligent type – there's nothing special about him. That doesn't threaten me in the least. It's that steely determination he has. That's the stuff that helps people go far in life. They'll walk on heads to elevate themselves. I know because that's the kind of determination I have.

So, when I saw the trouble that he was causing me, redirecting him felt like the best solution, and pushing him towards Pierce would solve several problems at once. I know they won't like each other. Pierce will be a source of irritation to him. Kevin likes quick fixes and Pierce likes to walk in circles until he's disorientated and dizzy. I need to present it in a way that isn't a choice to either of them. Once I have them in the same house, I can control the situation from the outside. I can make decisions on Kevin's behalf and stop Pierce being a nuisance to me.

So, I called Kevin into my office that day. He looked at me with too much confidence for an undergraduate. Only people who have the credentials to back it up have earned the right to that. I knew I had to take him down a peg or ten.

"I needed to talk to you about how your placement is going," I said.

I waved to the chair opposite for Kevin to sit down. He did. He sat with one foot on the other knee, a little too relaxed for my liking.

"Ok, what did you want to tell me?"

"Well, how do you think it's going?"

"Good, I'm learning quickly – I'll be your successor if I keep it up," he smiled.

I didn't like that. I felt the urge to bash his head against the wall, but sadly, I couldn't follow through on that.

"I don't share the same view, Kevin."

"Oh?"

"I think you've been a bit too much at home here. You haven't been respecting the boundaries of your role."

His eyes looked like mine probably do in a rage, but he didn't say anything. His face just seemed to swell, like he was holding back too many angry words. He tucked his hair behind his ear.

It annoyed me because he didn't have enough hair to justify doing that. He'd reached the point of no return – he'd become so irritating to me the only thing that would correct it was his eradication.

"Several members of staff have commented on it," I continued.

We hadn't discussed it, but how was he to know any different?

"Well, what is the problem?" he asked. "I don't see what I've done wrong."

"You're not respecting the hierarchy that exists in here. I've made the decision to move you to a different role for a while."

"What is it?"

"I need you to work as a carer for one of my patients."

"I don't want to do that. I'm not going to be a cleaner for someone crazy."

"We aren't meant to use that word in here," I said. "I could report you for that."

Taking the moral high ground – that was the way to win when someone had robbed you of your power. I was an ethical worker, as far as he knew, and no one could expose me as anything else.

CHAPTER FORTY-THREE

Pierce

I woke up in a hot sweat. I'd been having a dream that the windows of my house had bars on them. I was alone inside and trying to work out how to pry them off, but I didn't have a hope of doing it. I was panicking because time was running out. My carer had gone out to get bread and milk and would be back in ten minutes. I'd driven myself mad trying to think of another means of escape, but I couldn't. Finally, I heard him unlocking the door. I didn't have a key anymore. I wasn't allowed one. I jumped awake. Real life didn't feel so different. I was no less anxious when I remembered what was ahead of me that day.

We were having a hand-over meeting – Tim was handing over his care of me in the hours outside appointment times. Maybe that was his real motivation behind it – he wanted shot of me. The care he'd once offered me, he'd decided I wasn't worthy of. I was starting to feel unworthy of breathing, and all I could think of were things easier to do than living. I thought about phoning Molly. No matter how much time had passed, I still got the urge to reach out to her. I wanted to tell her what was happening, even if she'd never understand. I couldn't trust

Kate as much – I didn't know what she'd been thinking or saying about me.

The doorbell rang and I went to let my new companion in. I had a feeling without even meeting him that he'd systematically work against every natural way I chose to live. The wine would be thrown out of the fridge, my mealtimes would be at the same time every day, we'd sit side by side for hours in awkward silence. Thankfully, it was Tim who'd appeared first. Putting aside any questions I'd asked over Tim's treatment methods, I'd never had an awkward silence with him. I wondered if he had them with anyone – he seemed too self-assured for such silliness.

"Well, Pierce," he said, stepping inside.

He looked different than in his office. The natural light showed up a few more human flaws on his face. He didn't seem like someone who would ever have a blemish or forget to shave a patch on his chin, but no one is that perfect, and seeing him a little imperfect made me trust him more. I had to – he was the only person who was going to make this transition smooth. He was the connecting person – the one who could find the common ground between his friend and me.

"He isn't here yet," I said.

I walked into the living room. I didn't bother offering to make tea. I was shaking too much and too anxious for formalities. Tim sat down in the big armchair. I took the sofa bed. The armchair was usually my go-to seat in the house, but he didn't bother asking, and I didn't mind him sitting there. He was a greater man than me. I wished I could have an ounce of his strength. If I did, I'd tell them both to get out of my house and never come back. I'd be able to manage my life alone and not have to allow people to call the shots.

"You look nervous, Pierce," Tim smiled.

"I feel sick."

"Why?"

"I don't like change. This is the only place I have to escape people."

"That's part of what we need to address – your self-isolation. You need a bit of society."

I gave him a disbelieving look.

"Ok, I know I said he was dull, but any company is better than your own."

"I don't know if I'd agree with that."

"When you're left alone, you get dangerously depressed, Pierce. It's the only option."

"Will he get paid for this?"

"Of course – did you think he'd do it voluntarily?"

"I don't know."

"You need to apply for carer's allowance for him too."

"What do I have to do?"

"I don't know – you'll have to sort that out at the benefits office."

"Why should I do him any favours?"

"Are you going to start this again, Pierce?"

I shut up. I looked around the room, enjoying the last moments of having the place exactly how I liked it.

"What if I asked someone else to move in instead? They could keep an eye on me, but I could still live independently," I suggested.

Tim shook his head resolutely.

"Now that didn't work with Molly, did it? And what about your relationship with Kate? You can't seem to keep personal relationships appropriate."

"That was never romantic."

"That's not what I meant."

Pierce looked away from me impatiently, like he was tired of having to entertain me. He looked out the window at the view. It was just a row of houses opposite, but he looked strangely intrigued by them.

"Do you know your neighbours?"

"No, I don't."

"Why not?"

"I just prefer not to know anyone too close to home."

"Isn't it good to have them as a safety net?"

"If I'm having a breakdown, I'm not going to go to the lady at number fifty-seven and ask her for help."

"I don't think a lady lives there," smiled Tim.

"Why?"

"Oh, it doesn't matter."

"Do you know your neighbours?" I asked.

"I can't tell you about my personal life, Pierce – you know that."

The doorbell rang again.

"That will be Kevin," said Tim.

He didn't look in a hurry to talk to him and didn't get to his feet.

"Do you want me to let him in?" I asked.

"It's your house, Pierce."

I couldn't help feeling like it wasn't anymore, and that I needed permission to do everything.

I opened the door to a man whose face I didn't think I'd ever remember, no matter how many times I saw it. There were a thousand faces like his in Belfast.

"I know I'm a little late, but I'm here now," he said.

He was smiling like he expected everyone to be happy to see him. Maybe I should have been – he was giving up his day job to look after me. He walked through the hall without asking where to go. He seemed sure of himself – especially for his age. He couldn't have been much older than me, but he had that look about him, like someone starved of sunlight who spends too much time in front of a screen. He had a smell too. I know everyone has a different smell, but his seemed more pronounced. It smelled like staleness. He was sloppily dressed, in all grey. It didn't reassure me that he'd be fit for the role of looking after me.

"Sit down, Kevin," said Pierce, gesturing to the spot on the sofa bed beside me.

He gave it a disapproving look, like he imagined it could be full of fleas. It wasn't – the place was clean – sparsely decorated, better looked-after than they believed I was capable of.

"This is Pierce Jones. He has been a patient of mine for nearly a year now."

"Nice to meet you," I said.

Kevin nodded his head abruptly – maybe he just couldn't be bothered with etiquette, and that was refreshing. He took a seat beside me and the sofa creaked with the additional weight.

Tim explained all the rules and regulations. Then he handed me over to Kevin. Kevin and I had to sign a few forms.

"Well, that's all I need to do," said Tim, getting to his feet.

He looked happy – bright, hopeful, lighter. Maybe I had been like a dead weight around his neck.

"I'll leave you to get acquainted."

He let himself out and I sat in silence with Kevin.

"When do you have to start coming?" I asked.

"Now, but since it's a Friday, I'll be back again on Monday morning."

"So, you don't have to come at the weekends?"

"Not as yet – we'll see how you're getting on."

I decided to bury my pride and try to get along with him. After all, we'd be spending a lot of time in each other's company. Maybe he wouldn't be such a bad guy. He didn't really have any defining features that inspired me to like or dislike him.

"I appreciate you giving up your time," I said.

I thought about adding "to come here," but if I was honest with myself, I still wished he hadn't bothered.

"I'm not doing this out of the goodness of my heart," he said. "It's an assignment Tim gave me."

"Oh."

"Are you friends?"

"Colleagues… I suppose you could say we're friends, as long as there is a professional purpose to me doing this."

"Have you never worked as a carer before?"

"No, if I wanted to, I would have gone into that line of work. I'm not exactly the nurturing type – but I'll do anything to attain the same status as Tim."

I didn't imagine that Tim would like that, but maybe he was a more munificent boss that I realised. He must have been praised for his good works for a reason. People rarely bragged about someone who hadn't done anything for them.

"Well, what do you have to do while you're here?"

"I have to cook, clean, make sure you're alive, accompany you on outings so you can safely get there and back."

"I can do that."

"You're not allowed anymore – it's in the contract Tim drew up."

"But what if I want to clear my head, go for a walk or something?"

"You can't."

"Why?"

"You gave Tim drafts of your suicide note."

Either Kevin hadn't been told the details of my case, or Tim was a liar, but that couldn't have been the case.

CHAPTER FORTY-FOUR

Pierce

A week later, and I needed to escape. Kevin did things in his dull way at half the speed I would have. He always seemed lethargic, and he always had the TV playing. I couldn't picture him in a high-level job; he was too slow moving. Maybe that was why Tim had redirected his efforts. It was probably a fix-all for him – it got rid of me and it got rid of him in one stroke. I could imagine everything slowing up in the office if he'd been there.

He'd half-heartedly vacuumed the living room and then sat down for a break. He was watching breakfast TV. It wasn't something I ever thought to put on, and the voices from the speakers were grating. They were discussing feminist issues – something I wouldn't have thought would have interested him. He seemed like the type of guy to behave with superiority because of something as randomly allocated as sex.

"I'd love to go for a walk," I said, looking longingly out the window.

The air in the house was musty and I felt like I was going to perish there, right next to one of the last people I would have wanted to see me alive. A week's conversation hadn't allowed for any progression in our relationship. We didn't get each other, and we didn't want to. I couldn't help wondering if Kevin even believed in mental health problems. He said some dismissive things about them, making out that the mentally ill were just less intelligent. I hadn't met a patient yet who was less intelligent than him. People who act superior bother me, but when it's unfounded, it's even worse.

"Well, I could go with you," said Kevin. "But where were you thinking of going?"

"Just for a walk – I could walk for miles and miles."

"What's the point in walking if you aren't going anywhere?"

"I prefer it."

"That's why I'm going somewhere in my career and you aren't, Pierce."

I felt an increasing urge to get up and walk out, but would he let me back in again? It was starting to feel like it wasn't my house anymore. There wasn't much use in Kevin having his own house – he was like a lodger in mine. He'd started calling in at the weekend to check on me too and I wondered what he got out of it. He seemed to resent every minute spent with me as much as I did him.

"We can go for a walk around the block," said Kevin.

I nodded. It was better than nothing.

"You look anxious, Pierce," he said, as we walked along, side by side.

I was, but I wasn't going to give him the satisfaction of admitting to it. I didn't want him to think I was reliant on him. If I proved my independence, maybe he'd leave me alone sooner. I hadn't seen Tim since our transfer appointment, and he hadn't phoned me since. Any communication seemed to take place between himself and Kevin. When he phoned, Kevin always went into a different room and closed the door so I couldn't hear what they were saying.

We finished walking in five minutes and I'd never felt more trapped in my life. I just wanted to walk where I wanted, see who I wanted, be who I wanted. I regretted ever asking for help with my mental health. Had it ever done me any good? If I hadn't asked and I'd ended up dead, it would have been easier than all the complications that came from walking into the hospital.

We got back to the house and Kevin locked the door again. I wanted to do something, to make myself useful – but I wasn't allowed to anymore. Kevin told me I was over-exerting myself if I tried to wash a dish. He was like an overbearing flatmate – someone who was always hanging around when you wanted a bit of alone time to get your thoughts straight. I tried to imagine him having a social life outside of his work. I couldn't. I didn't know who he'd get along with. He was lacking too many key characteristics – and any characteristics I had detected were irritating ones. My first impression of him had been wrong – I was no longer neutral towards him.

We sat and watched show after show – all trashy TV I normally would have flicked past for a film or a documentary, or something I found worth watching. I looked at the clock – it was 4pm and we'd wasted the day. I was tired of time draining away, unused and unmemorable.

"Oh, I have something for you," said Kevin.

I straightened up – he didn't seem like a gift-giver.

"It's something Tim asked me to pass on to you."

"What is it?"

He handed me a plain lined notebook.

"What's it for?"

"Tim wants you to keep a diary – to log your feelings and

thoughts – to see if there is a pattern to them and help us gain more insight."

"I wouldn't know what to write."

"Just write about your day – it isn't anything complicated, Pierce. Anyway, I'm going to microwave your dinner and then I'll head on.

"You're leaving early today?"

"I have to go out tonight, and you seem ok. You'll be ok if I leave you alone, won't you?"

I nodded, eagerly.

He set a plate of plastic food in front of me before he started to pack up his bag.

"Those dinners are handy, aren't they?"

I didn't tell him the sight of them made me lose my appetite.

"Keep eating, Pierce – you're getting thin."

"I just don't have much of an appetite."

"That's psychological – it's because you're worrying about things. There's nothing to worry about. Let us do the worrying for you."

I hated worrying, a lot for a regular worrier – but I'd rather have ownership of my own worries than hand them over to someone else – especially Kevin. I didn't trust him – I just couldn't. There are some people who give you every reason to trust them, but you still can't shake the feeling of suspicion you have about them. I get that feeling more often than most; if I'm paranoid, I don't trust anyone – even the few people nearest to me that are still there.

"Well, see you on Monday, Pierce."

"Yeah, see you then."

"Just relax this weekend – don't try to go out – if anything happens to you, it'll be on my conscience."

"Ok."

As soon as he left, I planned to go for a long walk, to no destination, but on the way, I'd go whichever way I wanted. I thought about calling a locksmith once he walked out. I could have the locks changed and on Monday he wouldn't be able to get in. But something told me that a different lock wouldn't be enough to keep him away. If Tim instructed someone to do something, they'd better do it, or they'd lose their career.

I waited until I heard the front door slam shut and I watched out the window, waiting for Kevin to walk around the corner. I still didn't know where he lived – it could have been five minutes away, or fifty. He didn't have a car with him, but for all I knew, he could have parked it elsewhere. Maybe he didn't want me to know much about him – so I couldn't work out exactly who he was. If you were determined enough, you could find anyone's life story online nowadays.

It was dry outside with a slight breeze. It was getting dark, but there was no rain. I needed the wind to air out my thoughts. I passed a few people in the street. It was rush hour and most were busy blaring their horns and fighting their way home through the traffic. The shops around me were all open – probably selling drinks for everyone's Friday nights to be celebrated. I missed mine for a minute. I missed having a set schedule. Now 10 am was the same to me as 6pm. Monday was the same as Saturday. Breathing was the same as talking, and eating was the same as sleeping. My life was a block of samey, hopeless grey.

CHAPTER FORTY-FIVE

Tim

S ara is meeting me tonight. I wasn't going to risk taking her out in public outside work hours, so I invited her to my house for dinner. I'm calling it a "business meeting," but we have nothing business-related to discuss. Pretending that that's the case amuses me. Her role is so far beneath mine that the idea of that is preposterous. I told her my address. I'm not worried about her telling anyone I've invited her over – if she ever tells anyone, I will vehemently deny it. Why would anyone believe the new girl over the man who runs the whole office? She might have two shapely calves, but she hasn't got a leg to stand on.

She knocked the door. I had dinner underway and I was already dressed – I hadn't bothered wearing anything smarter than I usually did. I wanted to look casual – like I wasn't trying too hard to achieve anything. Tonight would be all about her choices, not mine. She was wearing a black short dress – the kind that is so short that bending over is the same thing as stripping off. Seeing her in it disgusted me – it made me respect her less than I already did. I can't respect anyone who tries too hard to impress me. I might use it as a tool – but

I'll never respect it. She had a bottle of wine in her hand and passed it to me. I noticed her hands were shaking.

"I don't drink, but thanks," I said.

"Oh, I'm sorry – I should have brought something else."

"More for you," I smiled.

She did too.

She was probably a closet alcoholic, who relied on drinking to get through any social interaction. How can anyone be so dependent on other factors to hold up their confidence? Her hair was scooped up into a loose bun. Some strands had come free and hung around her face. I realised that she had highlights. Maybe she didn't possess the natural beauty I'd thought she had. She was starting to slip from the top spot I'd put her on. Maybe that was for the best – that removed the temptation to make her into a conquest. I had a more important purpose for her.

"Let me get you some wine," I said.

I strolled into the kitchen to get a corkscrew and poured a generous glass for her. I needed her to lower her defences, so I was glad she'd thought to bring something alcoholic. When I drink, I get jealous and I lose my temper. That wasn't something I could afford to do tonight. Too much depended on that one night – she was going to be an important witness. You might wonder why I needed a witness, but that will all come clear soon. I want you to be as delighted as I am at the grand reveal. I kept the bottle of wine in a cooler next to her glass, topping her up every time she got low.

"Goodness, I don't know how I've drunk so much," she said.

Her words were slurred, and I could tell she didn't have a high tolerance for drink. What she'd thought we would share had become hers alone – wine, romance, trust. She played with her hair, pulling more and more strands from her bun. It irritated me and I felt like telling her to fix her hair, but I couldn't risk showing any sign of control that night. I knew she wasn't sharp enough to pick up on it, but I still couldn't take the risk. I turned on the electric fire and she gazed at the false flames.

"So, what did you want to discuss?" she asked, moving closer to me.

I stayed in my seat and didn't lean in. I wanted her to approach me, for her trust in me to grow of its own accord. I might be influencing that, but she would never know it.

"I mainly wanted to invite you here to let you know that I understand how hard it is to be the new person in a job. At one stage, I was the new person there."

"Really? And you've been promoted above everyone there."

"Well my qualifications helped with that."

Maybe that sounded too arrogant, so I added. "I needed them because I didn't have looks like you."

She blushed and hid her face in her wine glass. I hoped she wasn't a passive drunk – I was relying on her making the first move. I was delaying dinner and she didn't seem to notice. Or if she did, she was too polite to mention it. If I fed her, the food would absorb some of the alcohol, and that would work against what I was trying to do.

CHAPTER FORTY-SIX

Pierce

All I can hear is the voice. I can't hear the sounds of the house, I can't hear Kevin, I can't hear the drone of the TV. I almost wish I could hear it, even though the sound of it has been giving me a headache. The last few days, the voice has been growing in amplitude. I can't compartmentalise it – boxing it into a small corner of my brain like I usually try to do. It's taking over, and I don't know how much of me is left in my head. He's coming to life more than ever before, telling me what I need to do. I knew Kevin had spoken to me a few times that day; I could see his mouth moving but could hear none of the words coming from it. Eventually, I'd gone to my desk to work on filling out my journal. Maybe if I documented what was happening, someone sane could work out how to make it stop.

I'm scared. I wrote. *I'm scared of being alive. Every minute feels like days. I'm drowning in my own thoughts and no matter how many times I try to reach out, to cling to someone for reassurance, I can never reach them. It's like the world is contained in a place I can never travel to. Everyone is walking around, living their lives the way lives are meant to be lived. I still haven't figured out how to do that. I can just hear the chanting of the voice. He's becoming more unbearable each minute. I'd do anything to make it stop. At least if sound is so loud it hurts, you can remove yourself from external factors – you can walk away, you can use ear plugs, you can turn to louder distraction. But when the sound comes from within, there is no escape. He's been trying to take ownership of my mind. I know I've described him as determined before, but he has gone beyond that now. He is trying to drive me to death. Everything bad he ever thought about me has been multiplied by all the negative comments I've received of late. His voice is hollow sounding – like he has no feelings for me – other than an unexplained drive to end me.*

After a while, I couldn't write anymore. I didn't even know what I'd written – my pen had moved unconsciously across the page, writing without thought. Maybe Tim would be able to clear things up – to make sense of what I'd written for me.

"You're worthless – a failure at everything you've ever done. Look at you – look in the mirror. I know you can't stand to look at yourself. You're worse than what you were worried you'd amount to. Your looks were all you had left, and they're going now too. You're just like a sad old man, but without the experience or effort to look back on your time on Earth with pride. You're going to die alone, and when you do, no one will care. Your funeral will be empty. A few people might attend out of a sense of responsibility – but no one will because they want to. You've made too little impact in this world. You're a lazy waste of space. I knew you'd fail. I knew it from the first day I watched your life begin. I've always been here, over-shadowing everything you do, and no matter what you do, you'll never get away from me. I gave you the chance to get better – you've had the best doctor in the country and even he can't fix you. It's hopeless. Life isn't going to ever get better. You need to realise there is nothing worth holding on for. You'll continue to sit around, lifelessly watching all the others around you progressing in life, while you sit and decay in the same small room. You'll never be able to work again – you can't support yourself – you're not strong enough to. You should really be living at home with your parents. But you couldn't take that last shot to your pride. You aren't even humble enough to admit when you need help. You just try to keep going, but don't do anything to change yourself. There are so many things wrong with you that they could never be corrected. You're ugly, stupid, in bad shape, a failure in your career, a loner, an oddball. You'll never have a meaningful relationship – not with anyone other than me anyway. I'm the only person that can give you a consistent view of yourself. I see you for what you are because I see you from the inside. No one has ever known you as intimately as I do. I've been with you right from the beginning, hearing your every thought. I've tried to push you to better yourself, but you just don't want to. No one can force you to become a decent person. You need to find justification for the earthly space you occupy – but you can't even do that. What do you contribute to anyone's life? What do you contribute to the greater good? You've ruined everyone's lives around you, including your own. That's the true definition of destruction. You were given chances to form connections with people, but you broke them – Kate, Molly, Tim, your parents, your friends from university. They are all different people – you are the only connecting part. The fact you can't make it work with any of those people shows you couldn't make it work with anyone. You'll repeat the same pathetic pattern until you die. You're insignificant – less significant than the bugs that you consider pests. You've forced them out the window so many times – so why not yourself? Why don't you deserve to be thrown from the window? Maybe you think it isn't high enough, maybe you think you'll fail, maybe you just aren't brave enough. You like to talk about your mental health, but you never act on it. You just sit around, complaining and making the lives of those around you worse. You need to kill yourself - not just for you, but for everyone that has known you. They deserve to be unburdened of you forever. You are just a worry to people. No one loves you; no one even likes you but being near you makes them feel responsible for your survival. That isn't something anyone deserves to feel. Show the ones you claim to love that you're willing to rid them of yourself. You can't go on anymore – what are you going to do with the time you have left? You might only be a quarter of the way through your life, and you've already fucked it all up. Just make one plan and stick to it – pills, rope, jumping – whatever it is, follow it through, like you never have anything else in your pathetic existence."

"Shut up," I yelled, hitting my head against the desk in front of me.

Maybe if I hit it hard enough it would kill the voice and I'd never have to listen to him again. I thought about the doctors that had told me schizophrenics heard many voices – not just one. I couldn't imagine a chorus of voices being any less distressing than him. I thought about the people in life who had told me to just ignore it and keep going, and I wished they could tell me how the hell, under such conditions, that was possible.

CHAPTER FORTY-SEVEN

Kate

I walked into Tim's office. I had to convince him I was the same as usual. He was too good at reading cues when something was wrong. I was dreading seeing him. Usually when I saw him, I felt either excitement or relief, but that was gone. I knew things had irreparably changed, and all I could do was try my best to hide that.

"Kate," he said, getting up to close the door behind me.

Little gestures like that were what contributed to feeling special with him. He made you feel like he was cocooning you from the world, talking about your secrets in the most private way possible. But I didn't know if any of it was authentic anymore. Was he working alone, or did he have others overseeing his work? Were they recording the sessions? Were they gathering information to prove I was crazy and worthy of being locked up for life? So many questions were running through my head and I didn't know how to silence them.

"You look stressed, Kate," he said, staring at me with his unwavering gaze.

"I'm ok."

"You don't look it – did you look in the mirror before you went out today?"

"Why?"

"You look dishevelled – like you've been busy with something other than getting ready."

I shook my head. I didn't know what to say, so saying nothing felt like the safest bet.

"Do you want to tell me what's wrong?"

"No."

"Come on, Kate, I can't help you if you're clamming up from the minute you get here."

"I don't know who I can trust."

"Who you can't trust, you mean."

"Yeah."

"Well, who do you have in mind?"

I didn't answer and turned my head to the floor.

"Me."

"No."

"I know that's what you mean. What's making you question it? I already explained about the bath incident. You know what I was trying to achieve. I already apologised to you and *you* accepted my apology."

I'd never thought before that apologies meant unconditional forgiveness, for never giving the incident another thought so long as you lived.

"I've been sensing some resistance from you lately. Has Pierce put any ideas in your head?"

I shook my head violently.

"I never see Pierce now."

"Well, why the change of heart? When you walked in here, you were such an accommodating girl. You just did what you were told, and I saw you getting better even when you didn't."

"I don't know why it's different, but it is."

Tim moved towards me in a desperate manner. If he'd been in a silent movie, people would have supposed he was begging for my agreement to marry him.

"You know that I love you. I love all my patients – and all I want is their recovery. But I want yours most of all. You're special, Kate."

"Why?"

"I just have my favourites, and you've always been one of them."

He was laying the compliments on thick and I had to resist the urge to get up and run from the office. If I did that, I knew I'd never be allowed back, no matter the severity of my condition. I couldn't take that risk, so I did what I've always done – I suppressed my feelings.

I was trying to salvage my view of Tim so I could still look at him in awe and with respect. But it was gone. Sometimes you stamp on a flame, reactively, but it isn't enough to permanently put it out. It catches again, until you make a concerted effort to beat it out. This time, I knew I'd beaten it out – I couldn't see Tim in the same way anymore. That made me as sad as it did happy. That illusion I'd had to cling onto – the one for a better life without mental health issues – had died.

"So how are things?" he asked.

"Ok - nothing remarkable."

"Oh, come on, Kate – you've always been through something remarkable."

He smiled at me and I knew he was trying to suck me back in. He could probably tell I was aloof that day, and knew he needed to turn on the charm. But now that I saw the charm for what it was, it was impossible to be drawn in by it.

"What's wrong Kate? Did something happen?"

"No."

I knew I was being too short with him. If I didn't start talking, he'd figure out what I knew.

"No, I've had a quiet week – a bit lonely. Haven't really gone anywhere or seen anyone."

"That's maybe what you needed – some time away from everyone."

"Well, it's not like I see lots of people every week."

"I just mean – removing yourself from society. I know even doing a food shop can be too much for you."

It was true, but why was he reminding me of the fact? Everything he said now seemed like it was laced with agenda.

"I've thought about going to see Pierce."

"You know that's not an option, Kate."

"I don't know why I can't."

"I told you – he's a bad influence – he'll bring you down with him."

"Is he ok?"

"I can't disclose another patient's information."

It took everything in me not to roll my eyes.

I jumped to my feet and got close to his face. He backed away – it was the first time I'd ever seen him startled.

"I know who you are, and I know what you're doing. You can't fool me anymore. I'm going to expose you and all your patients will be transferred to someone that's actually trying to help them."

"You have no proof of any of this, Kate – you're being irrational

– and frankly, I'll be calling the office security if you don't back off."

I thought about launching myself at him. If I was already labelled crazy, I might as well live up to the title. But then I came back to the present moment and remembered why I couldn't.

Instead, in a level tone, I said, "I'm sorry."

"Do you trust me?"

"Yes," I said. It was like trying to swallow stones.

"Well, then trust my judgement – I know the people that are bad for you. I'm just keeping you safe."

"Why am I so special?"

"I told you Kate – you're my star patient."

I gave up. He wasn't going to admit to anything, and I was going to have to keep my opinions inside. If I wanted to reveal the truth about Tim, I'd have to gather as much evidence as I could. The only way to do that was to keep going to the appointments, to keep up the façade of closeness with him until I got what I needed about him.

CHAPTER FORTY-EIGHT

Pierce

I can't function. That's all I can think of – I can't, I can't, I can't. I can't sleep, I can't get out of bed, I can't eat, I can't talk. I'm just stuck, listening to whatever Kevin wants to talk about that day. He doesn't seem to notice I barely answer him anymore. Maybe that suits him fine. I don't remember how I was ever autonomous. He is the only thing keeping me alive. If he wasn't here, what would I do with my time? That's when you know you're done with life – when the thing you dreaded most becomes better than your own company. I've covered all the mirrors in my house. I can't bear to look at myself. The voice is unrelenting. I carry it with me back and forth between the same rooms, all day, every day.

"What's wrong with you today, Pierce?" Kevin said, impatiently.

He doesn't want to hear about it – he just wants me to be more vivacious. I don't matter to him. If I wasn't here, he'd probably be in a better paid position. I keep expecting him not to come back each day – and that's why I was so surprised about what he had to say that day.

"I have something to tell you about – not that you've been very communicative lately."

"Sorry."

"It's like sitting next to a mannequin. At least I don't have to force conversation," he laughed.

"Ok."

"Tim and I were talking and decided that it would be best if I moved in here. I'm going to keep my own house, obviously, but I'm going to stay here at the weekends too."

"Why?"

"You're getting worse, Pierce. Honestly, we don't think you have long left and we want to make your final days comfortable."

How did he know I was that despondent without asking me? It must have surrounded me like the smell of a storm coming. Quiet doesn't always mean you aren't a nuisance – that's what my parents used to say. You can be quiet and still affect everyone in the room. My mum used to call it brooding silence. I just thought I didn't have anything worth saying. Maybe they'd been right, and Kevin was picking up on the same.

"No," I said.

"No, what?"

"No, don't."

"I wasn't putting it to you as a question, Pierce – I was telling you that's what we're doing."

"No."

"You can say no as many times as you like – it's not going to change anything."

I couldn't even compose an argument, to try to resist. I didn't want to be left alone – when I was left alone, I didn't move around any more freely than when Kevin was there anyway. I didn't go out and mostly sat in silence, listening to the voice.

"Why?" I asked.

"I've told you why, Pierce. Anyway, it makes sense for me – I can come and go when I like but I'll be checking in on you often enough to ensure nothing happens."

I shook my head. I didn't know what I wanted anymore – I didn't want to be with Kevin, I didn't want to be alone, I didn't want to go out, I didn't want to stay in. I just wanted to be exorcised from my own body. It was like a cell that kept me continually trapped, gasping for contact, gasping for air. Something told me that I needed to see Kate, but I didn't see how that could even be possible. Tim and Kevin knew my every move. They'd never allow it. I just felt like she was the only way out – the key to what was happening and how to undo it all. After all, she'd been there herself, and seemingly, she'd survived. Maybe once Kevin moved in, he'd ease up on the amount of time he was spending with me. I could barely go to the bathroom without being questioned about it. The thought of leaving the house was terrifying, but if I could just get to Kate's door, maybe everything would be alright. If I figured out how to stop feeling like I was going crazy, maybe I had one last chance to recover my old life. It was the only thing I could look to as a template of what happiness must be – before I got ill, when I'd been with Molly, when I'd been a student, when I'd still had promise. Any clarity of thought I'd had, went away as soon as the voice got louder. The idea I'd just had was swept away, like pictures stolen from sand by an incoming tide.

"So, next week, I'll move the rest of my stuff in – everything I'll need while I'm here, anyway."

I nodded, staring at the screen. There were images moving on it and sounds coming from it, but I couldn't see or hear what they were. I was losing the last parts of myself. You can lose your looks as you age, you can lose your naivety, your strength, your health – but usually, you retain some sense of who you are, or of who you were. I was losing that. I was just moving around with no personality left inside me.

CHAPTER FORTY-NINE

Tim

Kevin is moving in with Pierce full-time. I wonder if it could end explosively, but that's what I need. I need to bring everything to a head to force Pierce over the edge. He kept coming so close, but since Kevin moved in and took over certain tasks, I think he's got complacent again. I need to apply enough pressure to break him. He's been a stubborn one, but I always win in the end. When I defeat a stubborn one it feels so much more satisfying. It's harder work, but that keeps me occupied so I don't have to think about getting bored. I just spend my free time plotting and planning. It's ironic that a lot of my clients believe people are plotting against them, when really, it's their doctor who is. That makes me laugh; it's the cleverest kind of irony.

Once I passed on my idea to Kevin, I left him to sort out the details. He's the kind of guy who'll enjoy making Pierce's house into his own little empire. There will probably be nothing left to identify it as Pierce's by the time he's finished with it. This will back up my suicide suggestion even more – I can say he'd worsened so badly he'd needed a carer to move in with him full time. It all ties in nicely together.

I discussed that with Kevin and urged him to be quick about it – time was precious when it came to Pierce's "recovery." It also kept Kevin too busy to have time to annoy me. He was still calling into the office, wanting to know what I could do to help build up his reputation there. I just told him to do as I said. That's my favourite phrase to use when I need someone to get off my back.

Then I could turn my attention to Sara. I sensed she was becoming more comfortable with me. She was using every opportunity to come into my office with absurd requests. You could tell she spent all morning at her desk, cooking up any excuse to talk to me. I was flattered by the attention, but I'd already decided she was beneath me. Her intelligence doesn't come close to equalling mine. Then again, whose does? But she was proving herself to be particularly pathetic. She couldn't see through my game at all. She was just like an eager child trying too hard to get an adult's attention. In some ways, I wish I'd found someone I didn't work with to use for the purpose for which I'd chosen her. At least then it would have been easier to keep them at arm's length. I was too accessible to her. But I couldn't complain. If I did, she might tell someone we'd been meeting outside work. No matter what she said, I'd deny it anyway, but I just don't need the bother. I can't be bothered constructing arguments to defend my corner.

That night was going to be the last one of prepping her. I couldn't bear to spend another unnecessary second with her. She was boring. Her attention was quickly turning stale to me. Usually it takes a few months for that effect to take place with my conquests – but she was just too simple to figure out. There was nothing challenging about it.

She walked into my house, without bothering to knock. I didn't want to answer the door, but I didn't like her audacity either. She was making herself a little too much at home. She was one of those types of women who manages to extract an engagement ring from lesser men than me without their explicit agreement. She just puts herself in your space, until she's taken it over, and it's so insidious most men don't notice it. She tried to do it with me tonight. She bought a bunch of flowers to "scent" my flat. She even helped herself to a receptacle she could use as a vase that she found in the back of a cupboard. I didn't even know that it was there, or what it was there for.

I don't like anyone changing my living space – even if it's with something that will wilt in a week. I don't want someone else's touches on my patch. I can be territorial like that – especially since my ex-wife and I divorced, and she got the house. That's why I live in this flat that is so far beneath me. But as soon as I get out of the debt that she put me in, I intend to live somewhere worthy of me. That fact just emphasises that women can't be trusted – they can't be allowed to unpack on your territory, or you might never get it back again. I'll never allow that to happen again. I don't know how my power game turned into her having the power over our assets. I guess we met when I was much younger – before I'd perfected my techniques – when I had stronger impulses than I had sense.

"Well, Sara," I said.

I always said hello like that. I wanted to convey from the first word to the listener that they would have to work for my approval. It was like I started on the assumption that they'd done something daft in our time apart, and they usually had, when they deviated from the advice that I'd given them.

Sara was leaning back against the kitchen counter. She was wearing a short black dress with a low neckline and a slit up the side. My mother had always said women should be dignified. There was the rule she told me that I use to judge a woman's worth. They can bare their legs, show a little of their décolletage – but never in tandem. If they do both at once, there isn't much else they won't do.

You might think I have old fashioned views about women.

I do, and I'm not ashamed of it. How often do you meet a woman that surpasses me in intelligence? Even if she does manage to hold a conversation, her emotions always let her down in the end. It's an impairment she can't move beyond. My dad taught me that at a young age – one of the only valuable lessons he ever taught me. Usually, he just thought the sun shone out of my rear and that I knew better than he did with half the life's experience. I didn't have a role model to respect. Is it any wonder I've ended up more predator than person? I'm not unhappy about that, in case you think I am. Being human is a weakness, and I can't respect anyone once they reveal to me that that's all they are.

I couldn't hear what Sara was saying – it didn't interest me, and I was too busy getting excited about the coming together of my grand plan. I'd master all of them, and I'd be the one that walked away with a smile on his face. I'd coordinated the whole thing perfectly. So, to reach that end, I put up with Sara's presence. She drank wine and talked about herself, her hopes and dreams, and I appeared to listen with interest.

CHAPTER FIFTY

Pierce

Kevin moved in with me this weekend. It's Sunday and I'm already sick of the sight of him. I didn't realise he was going to show up at the door with a removal van instead of an overnight bag. It feels like I'm slowly being effaced from this Earth. All day, I've watched him unpacking items, rearranging mine, "making room" for his own. I once had a bookcase filled with everything that I'd ever loved reading, or that I planned to read. I don't read anymore, but they were a reminder of an important part of me. Sometimes I glanced over the titles, imagining a time when I'll have read them all and been enriched by them. But now half of them are gone. Kevin packed them up into a few boxes and put them aside for charity. He needs to make room for his own literature too. He says I need to learn how to share again; I've grown too accustomed to living alone, to doing everything on my terms. I don't like anything he has introduced into our environment. Our tastes our like two angry animals at each other's throats. I just want to move away – to walk out unannounced one day. I didn't have to bring my possessions with me. Living like this is making me realise the only thing I value is my freedom – well - that and my sanity.

Kevin has taken the spare bedroom adjacent to mine. It is too close for comfort. I can hear every sound he makes as he moves around behind the plasterboard wall. I hope he never brings guests over – I don't need to hear their comings and goings and to know the parts of him I don't wish to uncover. He assured me that once he became a permanent housemate, I'd get some rest; I'd feel calmed, knowing that there was someone there to look after me. But the voice seems to be getting louder every day. I'm seeing things too. It's becoming hard to distinguish fact from fiction. Yesterday I saw one of the neighbour's houses burning on the other side of the street. I could smell the smoke like my own house was the one burning. It was that horrible charcoaled smell – of things burning that weren't made to burn. The flames were flashing up the exterior of the building, but there was no commotion. There were people walking past the building, without even giving it a second look.

"We need to call the fire brigade," I said. "Do you have your phone?"

"Why can't you ring them?" said Kevin.

"I don't know where my phone is – it got lost while you were unpacking."

"Are you accusing me of taking your phone, Pierce? Come on."

"I wasn't – it just got misplaced."

"Well, I don't have time to make personal calls for you, Pierce."

"That building," I shouted. "Look at it."

I pointed across the road, my hand shaking violently.

"What? I can't see anything," said Kevin.

He scanned the street and then sat down again.

"How can you miss it?" I pleaded. "Look again."

He came over to the window, lazily and peered out the glass.

"I don't see what you're talking about, Pierce."

"That building is on fire – look."

"No, it isn't."

"What?"

"You're imagining things, Pierce."

"No, I can see it, I can smell it."

"It's your imagination."

I was getting sicker than I'd ever been before. Why wasn't having a carer helping? Why did I feel like I was losing my mind more every minute? I knew I was losing the run of myself. I remembered seeing cases of mentally ill people long before I knew I was one. They had become so unwell, they had detached from reality, permanently. I didn't feel like that point was far away from where I was standing. All the words around me were coming together in the air, like they made up a swirl of sound that had no meaning. Sound was just loud, and images were all unnerving. Human behaviour was bizarre. I was overthinking everything – the shape of the walls, the fact that we were standing in a building built by people's hands. It had faults and could decide to flatten itself at any time, all because of one mistake someone made, and we'd be stuck in it forever. Every detail of life felt threatening, like everything had the potential to kill me. But maybe that would be easier than what I was currently facing. It would strip everything back to a simple skeleton - literally – no worries, no fears, no thoughts.

CHAPTER FIFTY-ONE

Kate

T oday I tried to see what I could find out about Tim. He invited me to his house again. I thought it was bold of him to suggest it after what had happened there the last time. Clearly, he had been less traumatised by the event than I had. Or maybe he just saw the opportunity for something else. Either way, I was afraid to go. But sometimes you have to stuff down your fear so you can confirm what you need to know. I got there after dark and let myself in. Tim didn't seem concerned that strangers could walk in unannounced, but maybe he knew his flat was too well concealed to risk that. It had a separate door to allow entry to the upstairs. From the outside, it just looked like one whole house. I felt like running away from the self-imposed responsibility of finding him out, but I proceeded up the stairs, pausing every few seconds to gather myself.

When I got to the top, I opened the second door and the smell of freshness hit me. It smelled the same as my house. It was eerie. How did Tim know what scents I liked without asking me? He must have known that the previous staleness of the house had triggered me, but was that piece of information in my notes?

"Hi," I said, walking towards him.

He was busy at his desk and he quickly gathered his notes and put them away in a drawer, locking it with a key.

"Why do you lock it?"

"I have sensitive information regarding patients here – if anyone was to break in and find them, my patients' safety would be compromised."

"Oh, are you allowed to bring them home?"

Tim shrugged me off like a sweet-seeking wasp making one approach too many.

"Would you lie down?" he asked, gesturing to the therapy couch.

I hadn't known they existed in real psychiatric offices – I'd thought that was a cliché that came from hospital scenarios in high-paced dramas. But my life was no less dramatic – just without the sharp lighting and costumes.

"Well, Kate."

The sound of the well-known phrase made me shudder.

"Are you cold?"

"A little."

"I just turned the heating on, so it should warm up soon. I just did it for you – usually I don't need it on. Women always seem to feel the cold more."

It was odd to me that he highlighted the fact I was a woman – I'd just thought I was a sexless creature to him – that everyone was. He seemed above noticing such trivialities. I wondered what he knew about women as a species. How many personal encounters had he had with them? When I first started seeing Tim, I'd noticed he was wearing a wedding ring. But I couldn't be sure if it was really a wedding band, or just a traditional-looking ring that happened to be on that finger. Anyway, it had disappeared shortly after that. I hadn't liked to ask – Tim had an air about him that told you if you asked the wrong question, you'd pay for it – certain topics were too private. But it was his business to know all of mine.

"I wanted to discuss something with you Kate."

"Oh?"

"It's about Pierce."

"What about him?"

"I think you need to make contact with him. He needs the extra support."

"But I thought you said he was a bad influence on me?"

"Well, sometimes friends need their friends, whether they are a bad influence or not."

"Ok."

His eyes didn't look the least bit shifty, but it wasn't in a way that inspired my trust. He just looked like he'd twisted things so many times it didn't even faze him anymore. Maybe it never had. Maybe he was just lacking a conscience since birth. I could suddenly see a lot of my mother in him, and I felt hatred rising to the surface. I'd never got to finally face her down before her death – she'd gone suddenly, with everyone feeling sorry for her. It felt like I was the last one Earth to know her true character, and to not go into denial over it. I knew who she'd been now, and I suffered for it. I knew manipulation intimately, like most people know what love feels like, and now that I could see through Tim's façade, I could see that's exactly what he was doing.

Still, I will play along with it, because I want to find out what his motivation is. Why did he drive Pierce and I together, to then forbid us to see one another? Why after repeating the importance of that distance had he suggested I move back towards Pierce? Why was I Pierce's saviour? Why not his girlfriend, his parents, or his psychiatrist?

"You're looking a bit brighter," he said, observing me.

His eyes moved in a circular motion, taking in every feature of my face. It made me a little embarrassed and I knew I was blushing, but he didn't look away and he didn't look self-conscious about it. Now that I could see through the superficial charm, I could see the depth of evil that existed behind the mask he wore.

"What's wrong, Kate?"

"Nothing, why?"

"You're looking at me strangely – don't you want to be told you're getting better?"

"Of course. I was just thinking about Pierce."

"I think for a time you were a bad influence on each other – but that time has passed. I think he needs someone he can trust to relay messages from me."

"So, you want to use me as a go-between?"

"Not a go-between - a friendly face."

Whatever I had to do, I was prepared to, to see Pierce again. I had no idea what form his life took now, but I just knew I missed him being in mine.

CHAPTER FIFTY-TWO

Pierce

There was a knock on the door. It was either Tim or the postman – Kevin was still in bed. I went to it and opened it gently. Maybe if I could get some conversation from the postman, it would remind me that there was a reality outside of my own. I didn't know anything anymore – what happened on the news, what happened locally, what I was missing out on. The only sign of life I'd seen in weeks, besides what I suppose you could call Kevin's company, were the pedestrians passing by when I looked out the window. Kevin didn't even like me doing that. He got up late in the mornings, so I made the effort to get up early, make myself a cup of tea and sit at the table next to the window. He said it was too risky letting me go where I wanted, to do what I pleased – heights, glass, knives, boiled water. All avenues of freedom had been closed off. If he knew I'd taken the liberty of making myself a hot drink and looking out the window, he'd be angry. But thankfully he was too lazy to get a chance to see it. I'd got used to his routines by then. That didn't make him any less irritating to me. He was one of those people that could wind me up by breathing. I knew I should respect him for the role he played in my life, but I couldn't. He was too detached from everything. He didn't let me run any aspect of my time. I was like a prisoner with constant supervision, and I didn't like that he had private conversations with Tim I couldn't hear.

I was shocked to see Kate. When the door was wide enough to see out, there she was, standing right in front of me. She looked otherworldly – serenely still. I hadn't seen her in a couple of months, but it felt like centuries, like we were being reunited in a different lifetime. Her face broke into a smile.

"Pierce, it's so good to see you."

She moved into me and clung to me for a prolonged hug.

"You too. What are you doing here?"

"Tim told me to come, to see if you were alright."

"Oh, I thought he didn't want us to see each other?"

"He didn't, but I guess he changed his mind."

"What about Kevin?"

"He has to do whatever Tim says. Can I come in?"

"Sorry, yes."

I stepped back to let her in. I hoped Kevin would somehow sleep through the whole meeting, so we'd get a proper chance to chat. But even if we did, how did I know for sure he wasn't pretending to be asleep and eavesdropping from the other room? Maybe the late sleeping was a pretence – a way of monitoring what I was doing without looking like he cared.

"Tea?" I asked.

"I'll make it," said Kate.

She seemed extra cheery and I wondered why.

"I don't mind making it."

"No, you look sick as hell. What happened to you?"

"I've just been – having a difficult time."

"Did you hear a door bang there?" she asked.

"Yeah that'll be my carer getting up."

"Why do you need a carer?"

"I don't know."

"But you can take care of everything yourself."

"I suppose, but that's not why I have one."

"Why do you?"

"Supervision – I'm on suicide watch."

"Do you still think about it?"

"All the time," I admitted.

It was a relief to be able to be candid with someone – it made me realise how rare it was that I got the chance to do that with anyone.

"Come and sit in here," said Kate. "We'll close the door."

She ushered me into the living room and shut the door behind us, peering across the hallway as she did.

There was banging around coming from Kevin's bedroom, but no sign of him yet. Maybe he was just reminding me of his presence – that I never had true privacy.

"I need to tell you something while we have a chance to talk," she said, in a rushed whisper.

"What is it?"

"Tim wants to use me to relay messages to you."

"Like what?"

"Like negative suggestions. He said today to tell you that I thought you'd got far worse."

"Why would he do that?"

"I think he's trying to beat you down."

"No, he wouldn't do that – it'd be unethical."

"He is."

"No, I know Tim and I haven't always got on well, but he's not evil. No one would abuse their job like that – not something as important as that."

"I think he is."

"I think you're being paranoid, Kate."

"I'm not – I know I'm not, because he has tried to wear me down too."

"Tim didn't think it was a good idea for us to see each other – was this his idea or yours?"

"He told me I had to see you."

"I don't know if I believe that."

"Well, he wants to meet with both of us in a few days."

"Here?"

"Yes."

"What for?"

"To talk about our options."

"Why would he talk to both of us together?"

"I don't know – I think he's trying to plant an idea in our heads."

"What kind of idea?"

"I don't know – I just know I feel uneasy about it."

"Look Kate, you have reason to be suspicious of people. It would be worrying after what you've been through if you didn't, but Tim has gone out of his way to help me now. He got me a carer - why else would he do that?"

"To drive you mad."

"Why would that drive me mad?"

"Well, doesn't it?"

Kevin walked into the room.

"Who's this?"

"This is my friend Kate - she attends the clinic too."

"What did we say about forming friendships with fellow sufferers, Pierce? It's not doing you any favours."

"Tim sent her here."

"I don't know why he'd do that – not without informing me first."

Kevin looked like someone had just bumped into the best car he'd ever bought and torn off down the road.

"Maybe he wanted it to be private between us – to give us a chance to talk first."

"Tim doesn't do anything regarding you without running it by me first."

He looked wounded and I knew for sure that there was no sinister plan of Tim's. If there was, Kevin already would have known about it.

CHAPTER FIFTY-THREE

Tim

Today was my final meeting with Kevin, Pierce and Kate. It seemed easier to allow them all to converge – to deal with them all at once. They're all in a weakened mental state now, so I knew they'd really listen to what I had to say. When I walked into the house, I noticed the change right away. Pierce's personal effects were hard to spot. They'd been pushed out by Kevin's. It's funny how little direction he has needed to do what I wanted him to do. The fact he's so ambitious works in my favour. He'll do whatever is required of him to get the praise he needs. So, he'd taken care of the house move and I could see that Pierce was vanishing into a corner, like he was getting smaller and smaller, until he was nothing. Kevin seemed a little bit off with me when I walked in. But you can't worry about pleasing people. Manipulation isn't for the purpose of pleasing anyone but me. As long as I don't push them too far away and annoy them enough that they won't do my bidding for me – that's all that matters. Anyway, it's easy for me to correct the dynamic. I knew what had bothered Kevin – he'd wanted to be informed of Kate and Pierce's reunion before it occurred.

"Kevin," I said, fixing my eyes on his. "I'm sorry you weren't kept abreast of this – I had a reason why I held off telling you."

"Oh?"

"I wanted to discuss it with you in person when I got here, to see how you think the friendship is affecting Pierce, objectively."

Kevin nodded at me, like he was beginning to understand where I was coming from. He'd never know where I was truly coming from. Every time he thought I was coming from China - I'd be coming towards him from Italy. Keeping them confused – that's the key to success.

Kevin brightened up a bit and he looked at me with renewed respect.

"Oh, I understand what you were doing now."

"Ok, if you need to discuss it further…."

"Not necessary. One psychiatrist understands another."

That comment was like a sting from an angry hornet. He wasn't on my level, nor would he ever be. He wasn't intelligent enough, but even if he had been, I would never have allowed it to happen. I don't need rivals in my work – I need subordinates.

"So, Pierce – how are you finding the friendship after months apart?"

"I think it's healthier – I can see more. I can question Kate's opinions on things without blindly going along with them."

"That's good – just don't be swayed by love."

"I won't," said Pierce.

He didn't look embarrassed, so I could see that he still didn't love her. He might have liked her a lot – he might have seen shades of himself in her, but he wasn't in love with her. I'd pinned my hopes on that happening because it would make them cling more to each other. It would make them sacrifice more for the other person. I knew Kate had a certain type of love for him – but romantic? I couldn't be sure.

"What's your impression of Pierce after some time apart?" I asked Kate.

She answered slowly, like she was trying to be overly careful with her words.

"He looks exhausted."

"That's probably from our treatment regime."

"Why?"

"It causes great changes in you, but it takes a lot out of you too."

"Undoubtedly," she said.

It had a bitter undertone to it, but I let it go. She was always a stubborn one, but I needed her on-side, so I'd bypass a few things I usually would have stopped to point out. I didn't understand why Kate looked energised that day. Her hair was in good condition, she'd put on her makeup and she looked like she was coping. I hoped that wouldn't interfere with the plan. The plan had been to separate the two of them and allow them to deteriorate alone until they were reunited. Then they'd be primed for what I needed them to do.

"I can see that treatment must be working," said Kate.

Her whole demeanour changed. She gave me a friendly look again.

CHAPTER FIFTY-FOUR

Kate

I was told to be at Pierce's house around eleven this morning, but I decided to go a bit earlier. I wanted a chance to talk to him alone first. I knew Tim was holding a meeting to try to impose his ideas on us as one. That's all we were to him – one; not even one person – one assemblage of objects that served a use. I had to warn Pierce about what I suspected was happening. But I knew he had a live-in carer now. How easy would it be to talk to him in private? I didn't know whether he was allowed to move freely around his house, or if he was followed in every bit of his routine. I had to try anyway – to warn him of the danger he was in.

I got to the door and it was strange being back there. It had only been a couple of months since I last was, but it felt like years. The look of the place had changed even from the outside. Hadn't the door been yellow? It had always cheered me up seeing it. Now it was white PVC and it looked like every other house in the neighbourhood. I knocked and waited for an answer. I was pleasantly surprised when Pierce was the one to come to the door.

We exchanged hellos and he looked afraid to see me. He kept looking back over his shoulder and spoke at a low volume. I wanted to meet his carer. I was curious to see who he was – what kind of person Tim could have recruited to live full time with Pierce. I knew that was part of a greater plan. Nothing Tim did was ever random. He was too smart to do anything at random.

Pierce took me into the living room, and we sat down. There was no sign of his carer – maybe he hadn't woken up yet. It seemed unlikely considering the meeting was taking place. Wouldn't he be waiting on tenterhooks for that? I didn't know how much time we had, so I got to the point quickly.

"Tim is getting me to relay messages to you."

"What kind?"

Pierce looked like he didn't believe me. Maybe my disappearance had caused him to mistrust me. Who knew what Tim had been saying about me in my absence? But perhaps Tim was too clever for clear-cut complaining – he worked in a way that was more insidious than that. He made us doubt each other, so he gained no enemies and pitched us against each other instead. The more I thought about it, the more I saw my own mother's behaviour. I saw the scenarios she set up amidst siblings, and it was the same kind of behaviour. Pierce looked at me with a growing expression of doubt on his face.

I didn't know what he'd gone through with Tim since I'd last seen him. From the outside, it was apparent he'd been isolated, likely, with no one else to turn to for help. Why wouldn't he defend him? I felt embarrassed for showing up and being honest. I knew he thought I was just paranoid, or manipulating him, or both. I wished we had more time, so I could get into the private details of what had happened to me. But I got the feeling he wouldn't believe what I said, no matter how much supporting evidence I had for my story. I made a few quick attempts to convince him, and then we were interrupted.

Kevin came into the room. He wasn't what I'd imagined at all. He looked less in control than I'd thought he would. I'd pictured a lesser version of Tim, but he didn't have any prowess. He looked like he paid little attention to his appearance and like he was too lethargic to do more than the basics. He was pasty and ill-looking himself. Maybe that was part of the plan. If Pierce was being looked after by someone sickly, it would make him sicklier just by association. Maybe I was reading into everything too much. I had to stop myself slipping back into self-doubt. Self-doubt was what allowed Tim to operate as he did; it was what allowed him to persuade me of anything and to continue along his destructive path.

I knew the facts – I knew what he'd done to me in his flat, and I couldn't allow that to fade from my memory, even if I wanted it to. Kevin was surprised to see me. The fact I wasn't a professional and I was female probably raised alarm bells for him. He treated me like an intruder, but I got the feeling he did the same to Pierce. Being in that guy's company for too long would drive anyone crazy, diagnosed or not. He was offended when I told him Tim had arranged my visit – he looked like a prideful person – like someone who'd want to be included in every part of the process. I wondered where Tim had found him and how he'd convinced him to take on the role of carer.

Tim arrived last. He had a way of walking in late to things that didn't make you question his tardiness. No would have dared ask him what he'd been doing; you just got the feeling it was something especially important. He looked like he'd put a lot of time into getting ready that morning. He smelled fresh, particularly in contrast to the stale air in the house. I wondered when Pierce had last ventured outside. Was he even allowed to leave his own home now? Tim sat down in the main seat – we were all still standing, trying to make sense of the situation. He put himself right at the centre of it, which felt right, considering he was the one connector between us all. He took out his notes and his powerful pen, writing uninterrupted, like we supplied him with a stream of comments to make just by us existing.

He asked us how we were finding the resumed friendship. He seemed to know I'd been there for a while before he'd arrived. I wondered what he thought we'd been discussing. Did he trust me alone with Pierce? Did he know I knew what he was? Even if he did, he didn't look perturbed by that. Maybe he was used to people mouthing things to each other behind his back; he remained above all that, looking down on us. I could see for the first time that he did. He didn't want to be there, but he needed whatever it was we were able to give him: reverence, respect, worship?

We spoke about Pierce in general terms – so general they could have applied to anyone in the population. I didn't want to get into specifics with him. If I revealed I knew anything about Pierce, it was only supplying Tim with the information he needed to exploit him. Last time I'd been in Tim's office, I'd taken the time to look around. He kept a collection of newspaper cuttings on the wall, marking every mention of him in local papers. Some were positive reviews, but I'd been surprised to see negative ones included too. Why was he trying to present himself in a balanced way when he was all about power imbalance with his patients? Did it make him seem more trustworthy, the fact that he acknowledged his failures? Or was there another reason I didn't know about that made him hoard bad reviews?

At the end of the meeting, Tim had to run. He said he was late for an important seminar he was hosting. I wondered where it was, and who would be unquestioningly taking in his advice. It was worrying to think he held that much power over people. I hadn't even questioned it myself until I was already embroiled. I hoped I'd realised what was happening soon enough to undo the negative effects of it. Maybe my parents weren't the only ones to blame for my aged skin and dark circles under my eyes. I'd been living the same patterns, with different people, in a different country. Once something is engrained in you, it's hard to break away from it, even when you start over with something you think is new.

Tim was looking at me intensely. Maybe I'd gone too quiet for too long. I noticed he didn't like when people were too quiet – maybe he worried what they were thinking about him or if they had figured out what he was doing. If you were quiet because you were listening to him, that was something else entirely. But quiet by choice wasn't acceptable to him. Before Tim left, he gave me a book. I couldn't tell what it was about from the title or cover. It was one of those types of books that tries to hook you with its mysterious title more than its known content. I flipped it over to look at the blurb, but Tim blocked it with his hand.

"Read it later when you're at home – it might help you on the way to self-discovery."

"Thanks."

I hadn't decided whether reading it was a good idea, but I knew curiosity would make me do it. I needed to get as close as I could to Tim's truth, even if it burned me when I finally reached it.

"I hope you'll continue meeting up and support Pierce in everything," said Tim.

He walked out the door, making his apologies to Kevin. He hadn't involved him in anything – maybe he was realising he'd better acknowledge him. Kevin blushed as soon as Tim's hand touched his to shake goodbye. How did he have that effect on everyone? It was like a special kind of magnetism – if you got too close you were immediately under his spell.

After Tim left, the three of us sat in awkward silence until I realised Kevin wanted me to leave. It was like a silent protest to get me out of the room. I wished I could have stayed as a fly on the wall, watching his private interactions with Pierce.

CHAPTER FIFTY-FIVE

Pierce

After the meeting today, I felt hopeful. I'm allowed to have a friend again, and I hoped that would progress to being allowed out on solo outings. Maybe I was proving my improvement to Tim. I couldn't get any information from Kevin. It bothers me that I know he has phone conversations with Tim, but he won't tell me what any of them are about; I know they are all about me. I know I'll not be able to talk honestly with Kate. If Kevin is always there, he's always listening – whether he's in the same room or in the farthest corner he could get from me. When I remember that, it makes me despondent again. How will I ever tell Kate how much I've deteriorated? How will I ask her advice? How will I find out her side of the story of our separation? Had she chosen to stay away from me or had Tim enforced it? I had so much about my life I wanted to know but wasn't allowed to know. That's one human right I'd never imagined losing. It was like living in a supervised setting with every decision made for you, and I'd come to crave the life I'd feared before living like this. I had chosen to avoid going out unless I had to, but at least then, I'd had a choice in the matter.

I could tell by looking at Kevin that he didn't like Kate being there. From the first moment they met, he was unfriendly towards her. He didn't even offer to shake her hand. Maybe he'd come to view me as a possession, and he didn't like anyone else getting access to me. Maybe he viewed me as a friend, and he didn't want any other influences to distract me from his. I could only speculate because he never told me anything. The only things Kevin told me were inconsequential – the weather forecast, that day's news, dinner options for that night. It was like knowing someone for years without ever progressing beyond the stage of small talk.

I desperately wanted to have a chance to look at the book that Tim had given Kate. Why had he presented her with one, but not me? I couldn't tell by glancing at it what it might be about, but I wanted to read it. That was the only thing that had come from my confinement – I wanted to read stories that allowed me to experience other lifestyles. I hoped that Kevin would leave us alone soon so I could get a chance to look at it. Surely, he'd have to use the bathroom sooner or later? Or he'd have a phone call to make or somewhere to go? But no, he stayed squashed up beside us on the sofa, invading our space. Kate looked uncomfortable; so much so that she eventually made up an excuse and left.

CHAPTER FIFTY-SIX

Tim

Today, I gave Kate an important book. It's one that is deeply important to me. The characters represented in it are mentally ill. They closely resemble Kate and Pierce, actually. Maybe that influenced me choosing them as my project. I could cast them in roles easily – I'd already seen how it could all work out on paper. The novel shows how two people can influence each other through their flawed thinking patterns. If you're surrounded by depression, the only thing you can become is depressed too. The story begins with a young man who shows great promise in his career and love life. He sharply declines when his mental health deteriorates. The descriptions of the hallucinations he has always struck me as made up, but I see a lot of that in my profession: attention seekers that make no better use of their time. He develops a friendship that borders on romance with a young woman with similar struggles. They get treatment but work against the doctor at every turn. At the end of the book, their doctor announces that they are both untreatable. The only way out of their predicament is suicide. He doesn't have anything else to offer them. He doesn't suggest it, of course – that would be cruel. But they have the general understanding that it's the only solution to their troubles. They agree to a suicide pact. It prevents either of them pulling out at the last minute – strength in numbers and all that. I thought the ending of it was pretty powerful. You see the contrast between the turmoil they cause and the peace that reigns after they pass. It helped the seedlings of ideas to flower in my mind. I wanted to make a real life film adaptation of the book.

I'd introduce the concept to Kate through passing on the book. I wouldn't lend it to both of them – that would be too obvious a suggestion. Kate's tougher than Pierce, so she was the one I wanted to pass it on to. She has more influence over his decisions than he does over hers. Using the book would save me a lot of work – it was all written down for me – but it was coming at them indirectly, of course. Anything more than that would cost me more than just my job, and even though I know I have the right to do what I do, others aren't as open-minded. They're living in a less advanced world, and they don't have the brain capacity to understand my sound techniques.

I have Sara lined up. I know she has her hand wrapped around her phone, day and night, waiting for me to call. I brought it all to a crescendo and then backed away from her. Not fully – I couldn't risk turning her against me. I just had to look busy for a while, to guarantee that the night I wanted to see her, she'd be free. In fact, I know that no matter what else she has on, she'll cancel it to run to my flat, thinking we're finally going to become something special.

You can make your moral judgements of me. They don't apply to me. I'm just made differently to you. I'm not encumbered by guilt, and I know that deep down, you're jealous of that. How many times has your guilt hampered you when you've been close to doing something immoral you desperately wanted to do? That crappy conscience was the only thing that stopped you, and I know you still think about the things you could have done, if only you'd had the bravery to do them. Maybe by living vicariously through me, you'll get a glimpse of what it is to lead an exciting life.

CHAPTER FIFTY-SEVEN

Kate

T he book that Tim gave me is a bit close to home. I know there is a reason behind him giving it to me. Tim doesn't do anything without hidden meaning behind it. He's just that kind of twisted guy – the same breed as my parents. I should have known him a hundred miles away, but those types of people are just so knowledgeable, so charismatic, so plausible. I'm not lacking in intelligence – but I'm lacking in confidence – and that's where I fall down in front of people like Tim.

I wonder how many of his ideas are authentically his. How many has he adopted from films and books? Maybe he isn't as smart as he appears to be – maybe he's just like a parrot collecting sayings and passing them off as his own. The content of the book worries me with each fresh page I turn. It's all so familiar and I can't help seeing myself in the female protagonist. I'm convinced the male character is supposed to be like Pierce, and that it's to put ideas in our head that we haven't yet come up with on our own.

I can't figure out why he gave it to me and not Pierce, but

there must be a reason. Maybe he knows Pierce puts things off – he likely wouldn't read it for months, and Tim must have a tight timeframe to what he's doing in "treatment." He knows I'll read it right away – I'm too curious not to. He also thinks I'll do anything he asks me, on command. That mightn't have changed – but it's no longer for the reason he thinks.

I sit in my house in the strange silence and I'm ok with it for once. It feels safer than where I've been spending my time escaping it. I would have done anything, for years, to avoid my own company, replacing it with God knows whom. But it's hard to trust people. All the people I've trusted have been silent predators. I need to etch out a new kind of life for myself, and I can only do that by starting from scratch. As soon as I prove what Tim is doing, I'm going to start a new life. I can't take Pierce into it, but I hope before that time comes, I'll have managed to get him out of this hole too. As soon as I figure out what Tim is trying to tell me in the book, I'll pass it on to Pierce.

I spent all day in bed, glued to the book. I had to finish it today, to get to the bottom of it all. Maybe all the questions I had about Tim were hidden in the pages. If I just concentrated hard enough, I'd finally understand everything that was happening. As much as I had an emotional need to find out what was going on, I have a need to understand the ins and outs of everything. That is what keeps me stuck in a situation, long after I emotionally break away from it. If you can understand why something happens, you can close the file and return it to your mind's shelving system, never having to read it again – in theory, at least.

I think that is why it is so hard to cut negative influences from my life – I've spent so long trying to make sense of the nonsensical, that until I do, I can't let go. Tim seemed too pragmatic to cause such confusion, unless it was intentional of course. I wanted to study him, like a subject I was dying to know about. What made him do what he did? How did he switch between being so charismatic and so cruel? Why did I still like him when he turned up his good qualities? My mum always said, "even Hitler had friends." That was one truth she'd taught me. She could be charming when she wanted to be too.

As I progress by page number, I can feel things becoming more sinister. What starts off as mutual understanding becomes a toxic connection. The characters are going to bring about each other's downfall – it's inevitable. I feel the urge to climb into the story and shake them for refusing to see what can save them, but then I remember they aren't real. The characters aren't real, but they are to me. They too closely resemble Pierce and me to be able to remain fictional.

The only difference I can see between them and us is the minor role of their ineffectual doctor. He barely makes an appearance for chapters at a time. Why doesn't he do more to help them? I start to think about Tim and remember that if nothing else, he is present for us. He devotes all his time to treating us. But then I start to feel sick about that, as I remember recent events and realise how subtle and gradual his control is. It's hard to get rid of every trace of influence he has pumped into my brain, but I know I have to break away from him for good. But not without Pierce; I won't leave without helping him leave too.

CHAPTER FIFTY-EIGHT

Tim

I just have to bide my time now. I know that Kate will devour the book I gave her. She told me once that she was a voracious reader, but I know that she is also curious to know everything. She would love if I sat down and told her my life story. Unluckily for her, I know better than to do that. I'll never tell anyone the things they are dying to know about me. That would break the spell and would diffuse the mystery. Every time I think about certain scenes from the book, I feel the same kind of childish excitement most people get over new ventures or their infant's first moments. Most people get a kick out of things coming to life – I get a kick out of taking the life out of them.

I wanted to check in on Kate, to see how she was progressing with the book. But I know she'll come to me in her own time, and she'll be much more receptive when she does. I sometimes still think about the depth of her eyes – you can tell by them how smart she once was, but smart doesn't always mean sensible. Sometimes I worry she'll expose me, if she gets to the bottom of everything. But I think her self-doubt is too strong to allow that to happen.

I hope she is spending adequate time with Pierce. I know she will be – she feels such a sense of responsibility to other people. She also can't face being alone. Anything that presents itself as an alternative to that will immediately be snapped up by her. I find it funny how little she thinks she is capable of now – she thinks she can't have a relationship, that she can't function normally in society and that she can't support herself. I don't know how true any of that is – I only said those things to feed into her self-doubt.

I'm hoping the book will complete the rest for me – that Kate will finish it soon and act on it. How often have people changed their lives because of books? How often do they make snap decisions after reading the conclusion? The only worry I have, is that she will see through the transparency of what the book is meant to achieve. I'd hoped she would unconsciously draw parallels between herself and the protagonist, and between Pierce and the male character. But do the mentally ill have the self-awareness to do that? If not, the plot might influence their actions on its own. Maybe neither of them had the bravery to end their lives up until this point, but the idea of a pact will change that. Facing anything is less scary with someone you know next to you – if they're going through the same suffering you are, it's bound to reduce the fear you feel. At least, that's what I imagine ordinary civilians do. I'm not sure what fear is like – I've never felt the sensation of it. I suppose the closest thing I could compare to it is the worry that my reputation will be destroyed – that someone will see through the glossy veneer and that they'll expose it to everyone; that a person of importance will believe someone else's story over mine.

I feel like everything is on hold until the book is read. I wish there was a way I could control my patients' reading speed, on top of everything else, but I've done all I can. I can't phone Sara to invite her over until I know it has all been set in motion.

In the meantime, what keeps me going is submerging myself

in my fantasies and patting myself on the back for a job well done. Before it even happens, I know it simply cannot fail.

CHAPTER FIFTY-NINE

Pierce

Today Kate showed up unannounced at my door. She looked like she was desperate to talk to me. Unfortunately, that wouldn't be possible for her. Kevin was there and he was hanging around me like a fly on food. I thought about suggesting we go for a coffee to talk, but then I remembered I wouldn't be allowed to go out unsupervised. Kate stood in the doorway for long enough it was obvious she didn't want Kevin to be there. He didn't move from his position behind me, waiting for what she had to say.

"Can I talk to Pierce in private for a minute, Kevin?"

"No."

"No?"

"That would be negligent of me. I need to make sure Pierce is safe at all times."

"Didn't Tim suggest we see each other again?"

"He didn't say without my supervision."

"Ok."

They stood in a standoff, like they were both expecting the other to back down first.

"I think it would be best if you went home – unless you want to come in for a cup of tea while I'm here," he said.

"I'm ok, thanks – I just have something to give Pierce."

"What is it?"

"Oh, just the book that Tim gave me. I found it immensely helpful for my condition – I think he might too."

"What is the book about?"

"Doesn't the fact that Tim chose it tell you all you need to know?"

Kevin nodded deferentially. It seemed that Tim was one person he respected. At least we knew if we brought up his name often enough, Kevin would back off. I knew he was there for my benefit, but he was becoming increasingly irritating. I didn't think he was anything more than a pest, and he was a determined one at that.

"Thanks," I said, taking the book.

I didn't know how I'd ever have the concentration to read it. That wasn't something I managed to do anymore. I couldn't remember reading a book cover to cover since before I'd entered mental health services. What was the point in wasting my mind on activities that I'd never need to use again? My education was long gone – wasted like everything else.

The book didn't look like a self-help book. It had a dark cover with trees overhanging water on the front cover. It didn't look uplifting, but maybe that was the point. Maybe it wasn't meant to serve us up niceties; maybe it was to make something inside our minds click, like a necessary lesson. I'd give it a chance – at least it would give me something to do to fill all my empty time.

I started on the first chapter that night. It was interesting, but the storyline was upsetting. It was like I was reading thoughts I'd had, all assembled on a page – ones I didn't want to have to confront again. I hoped it would end with the solution to our troubles. Maybe that was the point of it – Tim knew Kate and I would identify with the characters and then he'd show us through it how to get better. Even though the book interested me, I still couldn't read it. I kept reading the first few pages over and over, but by the time I got to the end of the chapter, I couldn't remember the start. What was wrong with me? It was like there was a mental block stopping me reading. I couldn't even ask Kate to help. If I wanted to be alone with her, I'd have to sneak out of the house while Kevin was sleeping. That was my only chance of talking to her in private. But I didn't have a key anymore. What if he woke up and shut the door? I'd be locked out. He'd never forgive me for putting his job at risk, for breaking the rules, for daring to do the opposite to what Tim had advised.

I had to read it, or I'd never know the important thing Kate had been trying to tell me. Even if it took months to do so, I had to try to see out of the mental fog and finish this one thing. So, I waited until Kevin was asleep, and then I sat up, reading. I knew the sleep deprivation would do me no favours, but things couldn't get much grimmer than they already were. I was already seeing frightening figures around me, hearing that voice, failing at everything I wanted to do. I'd gone from leaving work to leaving society. This would be my life until the end – living in this small house with the man whose company I enjoyed the least, monitoring my every move. People say reading is escapism – sometimes reading is the only exit from a world where you don't want to be. I made it through the first chapter that night. I had to read and reread. My concentration was terrible. How had I ever had the brain power to get a degree, to work a job, to think for myself? I felt as dependent on Kevin as the elderly probably feel on their carers. Independence was a concept so distant I couldn't imagine it. It was something that belonged to other people – not to me. The voice started getting so loud I couldn't hear my own voice reading the story in my head. "You're worthless – you're a failure – you can't even read a book anymore – how are you going to amount to anything in life? Your days have passed. You should just put yourself and everyone else out of their misery."

I was getting beyond despair. I hoped there was something in the book that would fix that. Otherwise, everything was hopeless. As I read, at least I felt less alone, watching the main character and his behaviours. I understood his thinking process; his behaviour didn't seem irrational to me. Irrational actions are only irrational to people with a different thinking process. If you're acting in response to a thought, isn't that always perfectly reasonable? I was starting to think the only rational action I could take was exiting the world. If I couldn't live freely, what was the point in living at all? At least in death, that was what you got – freedom, not just from your body, but from your circumstances, and from other people.

Johnny, the male character, wasn't a likeable guy. I wished he was, because if he wasn't, that reflected badly on me. It was clear that Tim linked him to me. We were the same types of people, and he wanted to direct me away from the same kinds of mistakes. Johnny had a close friend called Beatrice. When I read the descriptions of her, I mentally pictured Kate. She had the same kind of look, and same kind of character. Johnny was dependent on her – he couldn't allow a day to pass without seeing her. She was constantly on the end of the phone when he needed support. She was his Kate. Maybe that's what Tim was trying to tell me – we were essential for the other's survival. I'd always thought he warned against co-dependency – but maybe he was realising it was necessary for some people to function. We weren't made to be solitary beings, and maybe I was too hard on myself about that.

I missed Kate as I read it. I remembered the times we'd spent together, and my aloneness stood out. I knew Kevin was asleep next door, but it wasn't the same thing as companionship. Maybe that had been Tim's intention, but it wasn't working. I wondered if he knew it wasn't, or if admitting that would be the same thing as admitting defeat in his profession.

"Let's go to the riverbank," said Beatrice.

"What for?"

"I walk there sometimes – it always clears my head."

"Oh."

"You should try it – it might be the one thing that helps."

Johnny was growing less sociable and it didn't sound like a bad idea.

Why did rivers keep coming into play? It felt like they had an expanding significance in my life. I'd never taken them much under my notice, but lately they were like a recurrent theme in a book. I felt drawn to them more and more. I thought about the spot where I'd been with Tim. I wanted to go there then, but I couldn't. I felt suffocated. Nature could save me from my imprisonment, if only I could get there. There was something about the steady flow of the river that comforted me. I thought about the grave marker. I wished I knew more about the guy who rested there. I'd never thought to bring Kate there, but maybe if I got the chance to, she could tell me why something pulled me towards it. Maybe the guy that had died there had answers we needed, but I didn't know how I'd ever reach anyone who knew him. Tim wouldn't tell me any specifics about him. He wanted me to know that I was following in his footsteps, but not anything more personal than that – for reasons of confidentiality, probably. But since being there, he had haunted me, like he and I were one and the same. Was that what the book was meant to teach me too? Was it a final attempt at shaking me out of my failure? I was too immersed in my own problems to look out and see the world in a broader sense. The more I read of the male character, the more I cringed. He was weak – pathetically so. He was like someone whose growth had been stunted, and he'd never reach adulthood, because he was too feeble to do it. At least the female character had some strength to her – she came up with ideas and she tried. Johnny didn't try. He stayed in his house like something less functional than the furniture that filled it.

As I read it, I was falling in love with Beatrice. Her character was too charming not to notice, and she was like an angel to Johnny. I thought about Kate for the longest I had before. I'd never considered her to have romantic potential, but maybe I had underestimated her. Maybe I needed to be more welcoming to the people who wanted to be in my life, and to pine less after those that didn't. Molly wasn't someone I could imagine myself with anymore. She was too much of a success to consider someone like me. I needed to spend time around people who accepted me in my current state – not people who wanted better for me. Pierce, Kate, Kevin – they were the only people who fitted that description. I closed the book for the night – whatever there was to learn from it wasn't going to happen in one night, or so I thought.

CHAPTER SIXTY

Pierce

I've tried to come up with excuses to see Kate, but Kevin won't agree to it. I tried to bypass him and go straight to Tim, but he caught me out. He was angry when he found out I'd tried to use his phone. He'd left it unattended on the coffee table while he went to the bathroom, and it was a temptation too great to resist.

I'd picked up the phone and searched for Tim's number. I couldn't find it, so I scrolled through the phonebook, until I found it labelled "Mr Hanlon." Why had he given him such an official form of address in his phone book? It was like they didn't know each other, like they didn't talk as often as Kevin led me to believe. Just as I hit the button to dial Tim's number, Kevin burst out of the bathroom. I turned the phone over and set it quickly back in its original position – but I hadn't exited the phone book. I didn't have time. When Kevin saw it, he was angry.

"You *do not* go through my phone – I could report you for this," he said.

"Sorry."

"What were you trying to find?"

"Tim – I need to talk to him."

"No, you don't. Any talking you do with Tim goes through me – you know that."

"But I need to ask him something in private."

"There is no private anymore, Pierce – not here anyway."

"I need to spend some time with Kate."

"What for?"

"Just for some advice."

Kevin shook his head.

"I'm never going to agree to that – so you might as well give up on it."

"If Tim finds out, he'll not be happy."

"Well, he can bring her to the next appointment."

Kevin shifted around uncomfortably, like he sensed that everyone was tripping on his toes. Why were there so many politics involved in getting treatment? I remembered my old expectations – I'd walk in, be assigned a worker, they'd know what they were doing, put me on appropriate medication, and help me to rebuild my life. But here I was, lying in the rubble that had been there when I'd first come in. Why was I un-help-able? Was my life running in parallel to those in the novel?

The scene with the doctor's appointment stood out most to me.

"What do you think about treatment?" the doctor asked. He looked like he was ready to hide behind his desk, should he come under siege.

"It's not working for me," said Johnny.

"Maybe treatment isn't the problem – maybe it's something else."

"What like?"

"Something that only applies to you and Beatrice."

Beatrice sat, holding my hand to help me through the appointment.

She had a worried look on her face, like she knew more than I did, and it was nothing good.

"You're untreatable," the doctor said, simply.

"What?"

"You're resistant to treatment – it happens sometimes."

"It does?"

"Yes, you both are."

"How can you be sure?"

"You're getting worse as treatment goes on. On a subconscious level, maybe you don't want to get better."

"I do, I promise," pleaded Johnny.

"No, I'm discharging you," said the doctor.

"Well, what other options do we have left?" Johnny asked. His voice sounded sad and hollow. He looked at Beatrice, but she just looked at the floor.

"It's ok," she whispered, "I have a solution."

Johnny squeezed her hand – he trusted her with his life, never mind with anything simpler than that.

She got to her feet. "Thanks for your time anyway, Dr Graham."

"That's ok – I did all I could," he said. It was like he was assuring himself of that, as much as he was them.

The door closed behind them, and Beatrice immediately started sharing her plan. She didn't call it suicide – that was the thing that made it feel like a healthy answer. But in short, that's what it was.

The story was progressing, and I was making my way steadily through it. I was jealous of Kate for having finished it. She was a fast reader and absorbed everything quickly, even with her mental disorder. I wanted to know what the main point was that she wanted to share with me. Did she see us in the characters too? They were written as if someone had based them on us. I looked at the author's name: "Rich Clarke." I'd never heard of him before. How could he write about something so personal to me without ever having met me? I did a search of his name. My internet access had been restricted. I was allowed to use it for a few minutes in the morning and a few in the evening. I had to remember to clear my history, as Kevin would be checking it. You got smart about keeping your privacy when it was invaded in every possible way. I couldn't find much about him. It appeared that he only had one book.

"Rich Clarke is a writer of fiction. He uses a pseudonym and his real name is not known. He has chosen to remain anonymous, but he is rumoured to have worked in psychotherapy."

So, there was a reason for the book's knowledgeability of mental health issues. He had worked with them first-hand. I wanted to know what his real name was. It said that he was a local writer but didn't state anything by which I could identify him. It was strange how the story almost mimicked my own, but it was fictional, and I had no way of finding out who had written it.

Maybe that wasn't the important part – the writer was irrelevant – it was the content that mattered. I wished I could ask Tim what the main message was that he was trying to convey, but I knew he would have condemned my laziness – expecting me to do some of the work for myself. He couldn't place the answers in my hands and then expand on them for me – that was my job.

The more I read, the more hopeless I became. The two characters were in love with each other. I didn't feel like I was in love with Kate, but maybe I was without realising it. How could I betray Molly like that? What if I was doomed to follow the same path as Johnny? He was going to a darker place every day. I knew I was too. I could barely hear my own voice anymore. Maybe people aren't aware of their own voice when they're thinking – most of the time, but when you have another voice taking over, you suddenly realise your thoughts have an identity, just like you do. My thoughts no longer had the one I identified with. I don't think there is anything more frightening than being trapped inside your own mind for your whole life with someone that isn't you. There is no exit door; none other than death. Death – that was developing into a word of comfort for me. I equated it to peace, rest, silence. How much longer could I escape it? The book was pressing me towards it. The more I saw Johnny learn, the more that was what I deduced from it. We were untreatable and death was the only way out.

CHAPTER SIXTY-ONE

Kate

I have to see Tim today and I don't know how I'm going to uphold the pretence. I know he's driving Pierce and me to end our lives, and I can't let him win. But every time I'm in contact with him, it feels like he's embedding himself more deeply in my head. I just need to find something condemnatory in his office. I'll wait for him to use the photocopier, get my proof and get out. I don't think I'm smarter than any other patient he has had. It isn't arrogance that makes me think I can catch him out – it's determination. He's tampering with lives and it's more dangerous than any of his patients or colleagues realise. He's getting more confident with it the more he goes on.

I've been reading about one of his former patients this week. He was called Paul and he ended his life in the river. I saw stories about Tim, looking sombre around that date, but never grief-stricken, and certainly never guilty. The photos said it all. He was playing along with what everyone expected of him during such a sad time, but you could tell he didn't have a hint of empathy for his patient. I need to do something before he does the same to Pierce. I'm not in danger now I see what he is doing, but I don't think Pierce does, and he's so isolated I can't warn him.

It's bad enough playing with the lives of other people but playing with the lives of people already contemplating the fact life isn't worth living is indefensible. Now I've realised what he's doing, his shiny look has turned to matte. I see through him, and I wish I could tell him that.

"Well, Kate," he said, in his sluggish way.

"Hi."

"How are things?"

"Ok."

"Ok?" he smirked at me. "Something's not adding up."

"I'm ok – I'm managing."

"Are you hiding something important from me?"

"No."

I panicked – obviously I wasn't doing a good job of hiding my shift in attitude. I had to pretend to be in awe of him, to ask his advice for everything I did – to act like the people pleaser I'd always been.

"I finished the book you gave me."

"You did?"

"Yeah."

"What'd you think?"

"It was revelatory."

"How so?"

"The untreatable patients."

"It's a real problem."

"Why didn't you tell me you thought that?"

"How do you tell someone that to their face?"

"Could you do me a favour?"

Tim looked at me, affronted.

"That's all I do for you, Kate."

"Could you photocopy my treatment plan for me?"

"What for?"

"I just wanted to look over it – to see that I'm doing all I can do."

"Well, if that's the case, I'll copy it for you. I'll be right back."

As soon as Tim left the room, I rifled through his drawer. I didn't even know what I was looking for. Did I think I would find evidence sitting waiting there when I slid it open? I was surprised it wasn't locked. There mustn't have been anything important in it. As I went to close it, I saw a corner of a page sticking out. Had I done that? Had it already looked like that? I didn't want Tim to suspect I'd seen anything, and he noticed everything. I pulled it out to look at it. It was a copy of a letter with Pierce's signature. It was handwritten but had been photocopied. Where was the original? I didn't have time to look. I folded it up and put it in my bag, shutting the drawer. I hoped Tim hadn't seen me. I was frightened about what would happen if he did. He was an imposing person – you didn't want to get on the wrong side of him, even if you hated him. And that's what I did now – I hated him. Any admiration I'd had for him was dead. His spell on me was broken, but there were others still hypnotised by him. I was doing this for them.

CHAPTER SIXTY-TWO

Tim

Kevin phoned me today. I'd told him to update me on Pierce's behaviour. He told me he'd become even more withdrawn. He was hiding in his room reading the book – the one that Molly had given him. I told him if anyone asks, Molly was the one who recommended the book to him. I knew she would give it to him – that's why I'd encouraged them to get back in touch. But officially, I had never allowed her to pass it on to Pierce – it hadn't come from me. I wasn't sure I had Kevin's full loyalty yet, but I knew if I promised him something big, he couldn't turn me down.

"I've spoken to a friend of mine in a different surgery. She is going to line up a placement for you soon. That's the place you want to work in – you can only advance so far in our office."

His face changed when I said that. He even seemed warm for a minute. I'd given him access to what he wanted, and he was going to protect my name in exchange. I didn't have to worry too much about him saying the wrong thing to the police anyway – the police all know me on a first name basis – no one would listen to him. I just like to cover all bases, just in case.

That day, I was confident Pierce was going to commit suicide. Don't ask me how I knew – I can just sense things about my patients the way others can about their soulmate. I got a strong feeling the day that Paul died. It's hard to explain, but it's unmistakeable. I contacted Pierce just to be certain. There was no point in wasting a day on an alibi I didn't need.

I asked Kevin if he would let me to speak to Pierce, and he willingly did. After the post I'd offered him, he'd probably have offered me the keys to his car and the contents of his wallet if I'd asked him.

When I talked to Pierce, I could sense the change.

"I'm untreatable."

"It's ok, Pierce."

"No, I'm untreatable, and it's dangerous for me to be around Kate. I can't go on."

I hung up, pretending the line had gone dead. I didn't want to say anything that proved I was trying to push him over the edge, but I didn't want to change his mind either. When I phoned back, I apologised to Kevin for getting cut off, asking him to let Pierce know I had a meeting and couldn't talk. Then I went away to arrange my final date with Sara.

"Hi Sara," I said.

She'd picked up on the first ring, and that filled me with confidence. I knew I'd barely have to ask her the question and she'd meet me.

"I'm sorry I've been so busy in work the last few weeks. I was wondering if I could take you for dinner tonight?"

"Is it ok for us to go on a date in public?"

"Who's to say colleagues can't be friends?" I said.

I was smiling as I said it, and I hoped the flirtatious undertone came through on the phone.

I knew it was safer to stay in, but it was worth the risk of going out, to ensure that plenty of witnesses had seen me around town on the night of Pierce's death.

"I'll meet you at Rosa's at seven," I said. It was a busy Italian restaurant in town. I'd book a table to make sure we got in. I'd probably bump into twenty faces I knew in there – it was all well-thought-out.

When I got there that evening, Sara had made an extra amount of effort. She was wearing a sequined gown. It was a bright emerald colour, and even though I disliked it, I was glad she wore something that would draw further attention to us that night. I would act like the perfect gentleman – I'd treat her so well she couldn't complain, and then I'd pull the "inundated at the office" excuse as soon as she went home, and hopefully never meet up with her again.

We were seated at the centre of the restaurant. It was perfect – Sara would feel like the most treasured person in the world that night, and all our witnesses would have the best view. I ordered some wine and encouraged Sara to order anything she wanted on the menu. We were going to have a fine meal, but more importantly, I was going to have a fine alibi.

CHAPTER SIXTY-THREE

Pierce

During the evening, I finished the book. The first piece of literature I've finished in years. I wished the message had been something more uplifting, but at least it confirmed what I'd already known. Maybe it was what finally gave me the courage to do what needed to be done. I got the note that I'd composed with Tim's help and put it in my jeans pocket, inside my wallet. That night, I was going for a walk. I wanted to see Tim, but I knew I couldn't. Looking at him would be like looking at the truth of my collapse in the face. He was made for better things and I was getting off his books. I started walking. It was raining heavily, and I wasn't wearing a raincoat, but that didn't matter. Chills and colds only matter when tomorrow is a concern. It was freeing knowing that only this minute mattered – that I could just enjoy the rainwater saturating my clothes. A car pulled up beside me. I could feel it hovering behind me like a less-than-subtle stalker. I turned around to face the driver. He wound down the window. I'd never seen him before.

"Do you need a lift?" he asked.

A final act of kindness – maybe it was meant to tell me something, but I was too far gone to ever come back from that ledge.

"No thanks, I like the rain," I said.

He looked confused and looked at me sadly, with my wet hair in my eyes. It might have looked like I was uncontrollably crying, but the rainwater was just streaming down my face.

"Are you sure?"

I nodded. "Thanks."

"No problem, take care of yourself, man."

The car drove away, and I didn't even wish for a chance to redo it. I had nowhere worth going to and no reason to change my mind. I walked and walked until my legs ached. The river was my destination and I had nothing else to think about. If my legs hurt, it didn't matter. It gave me a last reminder of life's discomfort.

I got to the river and I walked along the tow path. I was going to go back to Paul's plaque. It was dark from all the early rain, but I knew where I was going. I got to the spot and brushed the weeds aside to see the plaque. I used my phone screen as a torch. I'd got it back, but by the time I did, there was no one I felt like calling. I examined Paul's face. Maybe everyone had forgotten about him by now, but I hadn't. He was significant to me even if we had never met. He was like a younger version of myself. I tore away some of the weeds, hoping it would stop his spirit getting lost. But maybe people don't care about those things. Maybe once you commit suicide, you're not worth remembering anymore. I thought about my own parents. They hadn't spoken to me since my dad's birthday party. That had been months earlier. I wondered if they ever thought of me, and I knew if they did, it would only be with disappointment. That thought just drove me forwards. I walked towards the river, further along than where Paul was. I didn't want to step on his toes. Death is where I think people deserve the most respect – more than they were ever awarded in a lifetime. It shows that they have reached the end, under whatever circumstances they needed to and that they've made it out. That has always been my aim – not to achieve anything in particular – just to make it out. I try to remember feeling differently than that, and I can't. It must have been the way I'd always thought. When you're depressed, no earlier thoughts exist – you are, have always and will always be depressed. I felt sick to my stomach – not with nerves - just with emotional discomfort.

I took my wallet out of my pocket and placed it on the ground next to my feet. I set a rock on top of it, just to hold it in place. The river was rushing along, the rain making taps like an impatient pencil on the sheet of water.

"Hurry up, Pierce – this is the moment everyone has been waiting for", said the voice. "You've waited too long for this – so long it's possible that no one will notice now. Don't forget the ending of the book – the characters both commit suicide. You have to, to save Kate. If you stay here, the same will happen to both of you. You can't allow that. She deserves a life, even if you don't."

My hands were shaking now, and they slipped off the wet railing when I tried to grip it. I kept trying anyway. I couldn't stop – nothing could deter me from what I had to do. The rain pounded down so hard it hurt when it hit my skin. I pulled myself upwards and stood on the railing, looking down on the water. From that angle, it looked more peaceful. It had a mysterious depth to it, and I knew I wanted to find out how it felt to plunge myself into it. I took a moment to regret everything I'd ever done wrong, and then I jumped.

CHAPTER SIXTY-FOUR

Kate

I didn't make it in time. I should have tried harder. Timing becomes dangerously important when death is involved. I got a phone call from Tim today. I hadn't planned on answering, but for some reason, I picked up.

"Kate?"

"Yeah?"

"You're ok?"

"Yeah, why?"

"I didn't think you would be."

"Why?"

"Pierce is dead."

"What?"

I went quiet for what felt like hours.

"Kate?"

"Yeah?"

"How could you allow this to happen?"

"What do you mean?"

"He wasn't meant to be on his own."

"What did he do?"

"He jumped into the river. His body was found this morning."

"What?"

"He committed suicide."

I couldn't speak, I couldn't try to say a sentence – I was just lost in a crowd of words.

"I'd encouraged you to repair your friendship – didn't he say anything to you about it?"

"No, Kevin doesn't let me talk to him."

"Well, maybe you should have tried harder."

"I did, I gave him the book."

"What?"

"The book you gave me."

"That book wasn't for Pierce – it was for you. He was never meant to read it."

"So, you gave it to me to put ideas in my head?"

"No, you know I'd never do that. Kate – you're paranoid."

I wanted to scream that I wasn't, to tell him that I had the note I'd found in his drawer, that I knew he was trying to drive Pierce towards suicide, and that he'd succeeded. But no, I'd save that for the police.

Tim didn't sound the least bit shaken – he was jovial, considering the circumstances. Maybe he had wanted it to happen so he could get rid of the workload. Maybe Pierce and I had been too much trouble. But he hadn't allowed for the fact that I would see through his ruse. I just wished Pierce had too.

"What else do you know about Pierce?" I asked.

"Nothing – he left a note, but I haven't heard what it said yet."

"When is the funeral?"

"It's to be arranged."

"Are you going?"

"Yes, but if you do, I think it would be best if we avoided each other there, Kate."

"Why?"

"It just doesn't look professional if we're seen there together."

"But I'm your patient."

"Exactly – I'm not meant to socialise with you outside appointments."

"Ok."

"I have to get back to work, but I thought you'd want to know."

Tim hung up and I didn't bother to say bye. Pierce was dead. That was all I heard in my world. I thought about him, wishing I could have been there. Was it because of the book? Was it because of Kevin? Was it because I had let him down? It was ironic that he'd chosen the river as his place to end his life. Why had Tim's patients gravitated towards the same suicide site? It couldn't be coincidental. How had Pierce even known about it? Did Tim tell him? There were so many suspicions running through my mind, but I didn't have the evidence to back them up.

I was scared to go to the police – afraid that they would dismiss the "ravings" of someone as mentally ill as me. If it was my word against Tim's, I knew whose would win. He had influence and there was no topping that. I still had the suicide note. Maybe it was time to step forward with what I knew. But I was afraid of no one believing me.

I found out about the funeral through Tim. How did he always have all the insider information? I supposed he was trusted with such things since everyone still believed he'd been taking care of Pierce. I wished he could be exposed for what he was at the funeral, but I knew that wouldn't give Pierce the goodbye he deserved. Part of me hoped he wouldn't show up. I wanted to say my goodbyes to Pierce without him watching over us. Now I knew his true character, he was a dark and foreboding presence. There could be no room big enough to create a large enough distance between us.

The morning of the funeral, I put effort into getting myself ready. I pulled a black dress from the back of my wardrobe. I hadn't worn it since I used to work years earlier. I hoped it would still fit. When I put it on, I realised I'd got skinnier since then – stress I suppose. I still looked the best I had in a long time. I almost would have passed for someone without anxiety or depression. But appearances are nothing. You can't read anything about the state of anyone's soul from their appearance. I had no one to go to the funeral with, so I set off later. I didn't want to awkwardly wait about for someone to talk to me. When I got to the crematorium, I was surprised to see barely anyone there. Pierce was right – he didn't have any friends. An older couple were there, who I assumed were his parents, but they didn't look like him at all. They had a proud and stuffy look about them, and I didn't like to approach them. If they didn't know of my existence, I didn't feel like explaining it to them then. There was a girl standing next to them, welcoming everyone in. When I got closer, I could see that she had Pierce's smile – it must have been his sister. She was dressed sharply – in heels, a pencil skirt, what looked like an expensive jacket. She must have been a lawyer or someone of importance. The parents looked proud of her, and I wondered if they'd ever looked at Pierce like that. I hadn't heard much about them, and from what I gathered, their relationship with him had been an unhappy one.

"Hello," said the tall girl, shaking my hand.

It was like looking Pierce in the eyes, only without the depth.

She didn't look like she'd think herself into a bad spot the way he did. Some people just find it harder to navigate life than others, even if they're closely related. I offered my apologies and was then ushered into the room. It was a secular venue. Pierce wouldn't have wanted any religious undertones. I was filed into a row of seats and waited for the service to start. There was dreary organ music playing in the background, and it made being there all the more depressing. I looked around at the dark wood, the dim lights and the cheap furniture – it all made the room a scene you wanted to flee from as soon as it was over.

"This is a service of thanksgiving for the life of Pierce Jones," the director began.

There was silence in the room apart from a few coughs and sniffs and whispered conversation.

I listened to the eulogy, but it didn't resemble Pierce at all. I could have walked into the funeral of anyone I had yet to meet and it would have felt just as impersonal. Did anyone really know Pierce? His parents certainly didn't seem to. His sister looked like someone who would have thrived as an only child. The parents looked snobbish and I thought about their reputations. I imagined they'd want to shrug off the association of suicide and their son. It would be a shameful truth to accept if you were used to living so perfectly.

I sat towards the middle of the room. It was too empty to sit near the back, and it felt like it would have been audacious to take a seat near the front. None of Pierce's family knew me, but I didn't know them either – neither did Pierce, it seemed. Funerals can be like that – the hierarchy is all muddled up – the ones with the blood links take centre stage while the dead's dearest are kept furthest away.

The room remained empty. There were no latecomers, no one last to find out. I sat, feeling as alone as I imagined Pierce had done in his final days. Kevin wasn't there, and that didn't surprise me. I'd sensed that deep down, he hated Pierce. He might have posed as someone who wanted to help him, but really, he just wanted control over someone's movements. It could have been Pierce, it could have been me, it could have been anyone – it all satisfied the same need.

As I listened to the description of Pierce, I couldn't believe how edited it was. There was no mention of his depression, no mention of his treatment – just an illusion presented of who he had been. The suicide had been a "shock" to the family. They were still insisting it could have been an accident. There were no definitive answers – apart from the ones given in the suicide note. The parents sat silently at the front, listening but not participating. They kept their heads to the floor, but they didn't look like they were crying or moved by it at all.

I stopped listening to the lies they were telling about him. They could say whatever socially acceptable things they wanted, but I knew who Pierce really was. And in that moment, I realised I would never see him again, that his house was now vacant, that it would be sold to a stranger – and that made me indescribably sad. Life is always changing, but not necessarily for the better. Sometimes new changes replace old things you needed.

I regretted not trying harder to see Pierce in the last months. I was angry – angry at Tim for keeping us separate, for creating the divide between us. I could see what he'd been trying to do now, clear as crystal in daylight. He'd been isolating us, so we couldn't question anything he was saying. He was targeting us individually, because it was easier than doing it together. Then he created our reunion, to make it look like it was his idea and like he supported our friendship, but all he wanted to do was to bring us back together, broken, so we'd decide to leave the world together. I thought about that book and how it would haunt me. It was probably hidden by now. Kevin would have got hold of it once Pierce left. Tim would have instructed him to do so.

But why had Tim got Pierce to draft a suicide note, and why not me? Was it just to put the notion of it in his head? Maybe if he got caught with more than one it would look suspicious. I wondered if he would lie when he was confronted about it. Would he admit to forcing Pierce to write it, or just say that Pierce gave it to him, scared he'd reached such depths of despair? There were so many stories Tim could make up to cover himself and I didn't feel smart enough to challenge them. He was a master story weaver, and I'd only found one small piece of it. Who was I to try to get him arrested? But every time I thought about giving up, something inside told me I had to stop him before he did it to someone else, and he would – he had before us.

I wondered how long it was until Tim planned out his next design. How long had it taken him to orchestrate this? Had he planned it from when we first met or was it just a way to dispose of difficult patients? He was sitting feet away from me, but I couldn't ask him. I wished if I made him trust me the way I'd trusted him that he would reveal it all to me, but I knew he never would. Tim had probably never trusted anyone with anything in his life. People like him didn't; killers. Could he be classed a killer? I remembered watching a documentary once about the Manson Family and Charles Manson had convinced his followers to kill for him, but he had never lifted the knife. He'd been convicted of murder, so it must have been possible without physical involvement. Tim's influence was something so gradual you didn't see it happening until it was too late. I wondered if Pierce saw it in his final moments, or if he left this world naively thinking he was helping him. It made me saddest to think he might never know the truth.

I've spent my life seeking truth from the mouths of liars. I can feel a lesson coming together now, like fragmented pieces of a picture finally being assembled. Tim reminded me of my mum, and that was what made me feel safe with him. Ironically, that was the thing that made me least safe. You can't repair a broken relationship with someone you loved using a substitute who is exactly the same as they were. It just multiplies the brokenness until you break yourself too. I know removing myself from the situation is the only thing that will start to make it better. But not until the time is right. In the meantime, I'm detaching slowly from Tim. I can see his false smiles, his looks I used to think were caring but that were just invasive. Once you've seen evil, it's hard to find any of the good again.

The funeral rounded up. I'd missed most of it, but it didn't feel authentic anyway. I knew that Pierce would have hated every minute of it. It was probably good that so few people had seen it play out. I wished Pierce could be better represented. He shouldn't just become another number on Tim's "down by the river" list. Who remembered his quick wit, his empathy, his kindness? His parents sat side by side, their lips pursed like the mouths of two cold-blooded creatures. They seemed to have enough friends around them to make it look like they were decent. Now I was seeing through one thing, I was seeing through many. I guess that's what happens with the truth – you can't face a fraction of it – you have to face the whole thing.

• •

I noticed a girl sitting on the other side of the aisle. She was hard to stop looking at once you'd seen her. You felt compelled to look at her twice and three times. She had a Scandinavian look about her, and I instantly knew who she was. It was Molly. She had an effortlessly glamorous look and I was drawn to her. But I envied her too – she'd experienced a level of closeness with Pierce that I hadn't. I crossed the aisle to talk to her.

"Excuse me," I said.

She turned her head slowly and met me with her ice blue eyes.

They were like the clearest pools of water.

"Are you Molly?" I asked.

"Yes," she said.

"I'm Kate – I was friends with Pierce."

"Oh, nice to meet you."

She got to her feet.

"He talked about you sometimes. I don't think he ever really got over you."

"Thanks," she said, pressing her eyes together, like she was trying to hold back tears. "I didn't know if he still thought about me. I'm still in shock."

"Me too," I said.

I offered my arms to her and she accepted the hug. She looked very alone sitting there – even more than I did. Had no one thought it important to accompany her to the funeral of her ex-boyfriend? Maybe she didn't have anyone she could tell. There were so many people in life keeping the dark parts of themselves a secret.

"I knew this would happen," she said. A few tears dripped down her face and somehow her makeup didn't run in the process.

"You did?"

"Yeah, unless he got away from his doctor. I knew Tim was bad news from the start. Pierce got worse while he was with him."

"I know," I said. "Have you met him?"

"No, but I just knew that something was off. I could see Pierce getting worse. He was worse in treatment than without it. Did you meet his doctor?"

"Yeah, he was my doctor too."

"He was?"

Her face opened up.

"Was he the same with you?"

"Yes." I lowered my voice. "He's here."

"Which one is he?" asked Molly, scanning the room. She looked a mixture of fearful and fascinated.

"Oh, wait, I know," she said. "Is it the bald guy sitting near the front?"

"Yeah, how did you know?"

"He looks like the type."

"I wish I'd seen that as quickly."

"It's hard to when you're immersed in it."

She picked at what was remaining of her nail polish.

I looked down at her hands. She had hands that even formed bad habits beautifully. You couldn't help but follow them wherever they went.

"Nervous habit," she explained. "Pierce used to tell me off for it."

"It's hard to remember the mundane moments once someone is dead," I said, sadly.

I tried to recall minor events between us, but my mind was blank – taken over by the fact of death. I couldn't think of anything else. Pierce was already almost becoming like a mythical creature.

"I loved him – even when we didn't get along," she said, with hollow sadness.

"I know, I'm so sorry for your loss."

I hated clichés, but it felt like there was nothing better to say at that moment. I realised then that clichés must have been invented for whenever you're at a loss for words.

"Do you want to help me with something?" I asked.

"What is it?"

"It's to do with Pierce."

"Yes," she said, eagerly. "What can I do?"

"I need to meet you in private to discuss it. There are too many listening ears here," I said.

When you looked around the room, it was hard to tell who was on Pierce's side, and who wasn't. It was a strange mix of people – it felt like the people who wished him well were outnumbered by those relieved by what had happened. And Tim still sat there, staunchly. He didn't look a bit ashamed to be there. How did he have such constant confidence, even in the face of events that proved his guilt? I felt like crossing the room, not to talk to him – but to grab him and shake him, to beg him for answers, to hear the motivation for what he'd done. I knew if I did that, he'd turn the situation around to make me the guilty party – I'd be removed from the room, he'd accuse me of harming him, he'd blame me for Pierce's death. Confronting him was pointless. Anything less than arresting him was pointless.

CHAPTER SIXTY-FIVE

Molly

I met up with Kate today. I can't tell whether the story she tells me about how she featured in Pierce's life is true. Did he have a romantic interest in her? Was it purely platonic? Those were questions I'd never know the answers to for sure, but it didn't matter anymore. We were on the same team – any competition that might have existed between us had been annihilated by Pierce's death. It was nice to have someone who understood the pain I was going through, to remember his good qualities with. She'd known him at the end, so I could ask things I otherwise would never have known the answer to.

We sat side by side in the library. I'd decided against going to Kate's house. I didn't trust Tim – he could be watching us, particularly with one of his patients off his hands now. He had more time to put into illegal pursuits. I was terrified of him finding out our meetings were based on anything other than pure friendship. I never would have exchanged more than two sentences with Kate in any other setting in life. It's funny how shared trauma can rid you of any social awkwardness. I just wanted to sit and speculate about Pierce's last thoughts – about what could have been if he'd just stepped in the other direction, but Kate had something important to discuss with me.

She had proof that Tim planned Pierce's death. I knew he hadn't killed Pierce, but I also knew that he was the driving force behind his suicide. Was that just as bad in the eyes of the law? I waited, quietly, hoping that whatever Kate had to show me was enough to have him convicted. There's nothing more galling than seeing someone you know is guilty walking free.

Kate pulled out a piece of paper. She tried not to touch it too much – it looked like a letter. She read it aloud to me. My stomach churned as she read it. Had Pierce been planning his suicide? How did Tim know about it beforehand and do nothing to stop it? How had the person I loved been so hopeless and I hadn't even sensed it? I stared at the letter, lingering on every one of Pierce's familiar letters. There was no chance that it had been written by anyone else. I knew his writing too well. He used to leave me notes around the house all the time before treatment. He'd been thoughtful like that. I wished the words weren't his. If they had been Tim's, we could have proven his involvement – but he was too smart to get caught over something like that. Still, everyone leaves a weak spot somewhere – something they haven't thought to cover up. We just had to keep looking for that.

"What can we use this for?" I asked. "Doesn't it prove that Pierce was suicidal?"

"I found it in Tim's drawer in his office."

"How did you do that?"

"I waited until he left the room and looked through it for evidence."

"That was brave of you – I'd be too afraid he'd walk in."

"What have I got to lose? I've already lost my life to this man."

"You haven't," I said. "You won't."

CHAPTER SIXTY-SIX

Tim

"Well, Kate."

I was annoyed with Kate. I hadn't seen much of her lately. She'd cancelled our last two appointments. How dare she have the cheek to waste my time and still expect me to be sitting waiting when she decided to come back? My plan hadn't panned out as promised. She was meant to be off my books by now. I'd thought she was smart enough to be trusted with my book. I didn't tell her I'd written it, but she should have taken from the story that the suicide pact was the safest way out for them. They could leave together – she could support Pierce and influence his decision – and none of it would be linked to me. I pictured them jumping in tandem, holding hands. That was a better way to go than how Pierce had departed in his own lonely way. And she didn't even appear guilty for leaving him to do it alone. She was a less kindly person than I'd thought her to be. I'd thought self-sacrifice was her life's purpose, I'd thought she'd loved him more than herself.

Now I can see that she is a selfish woman. She doesn't display any emotion now. When I phoned her to confront her about her missed appointments, she didn't even apologise. I don't know how I could have been so wrong about her. But I remain confident that I will win in the end. I have a back-up plan, and it will punish her even more. I'm just glad I had the foresight to think of it.

She looked at me, brazenly, like when you stare at a criminal waiting for them to own up. I hadn't done anything criminal – purging the world of its badness is a favour to all humanity, and I won't apologise for it. I didn't lift a finger in the process, so no one can hold me responsible for anything.

"I saw you talking to Pierce's girlfriend at the funeral," I said.

"You did?"

"You forget I miss little, Kate."

"Well, she seems like a good person."

"Do you know what makes one?"

"What do you mean?"

"Do you know about goodness?"

"I don't know what you mean."

"I'd advise you strongly against meeting up with her."

"I haven't."

"Don't lie to me, Kate."

"I haven't. Why would I meet up with her?"

"Because you want to form a pressure group."

"Of two people?"

I didn't like the tone she was using with me. She was too sure of herself. Something was going on – I just didn't know what – and I wouldn't own up to knowing anything if that was the case. I must retain the image of intelligence at all costs.

"If you get involved with Molly, I will report you."

"What for?"

"For inappropriate patient relations."

Kate shook her head but looked a little worn down. I was winning again. I had to make sure they didn't see each other – doing so would be dangerous for me. I've become too lax about things since Pierce died, but I'm going to address that now. I won't let Kate out of my sight. I won't let her poison Molly's thoughts about me either. She is a single woman now. I can be the person to help her get over Pierce. I'll give her personal insights into the workings of his mind. I'll tell her he never loved her, that he was just using her, that he was much more callous than she'd ever believed him to be. And then she'd look at me with that beautiful awe on her face – the hero worship I crave so much. I'll win – not just at beating Pierce down, but at taking what should have been mine in the first place: Molly. Some people don't deserve the goodness that comes to them, but I've worked hard for it, and I'll deserve every bit of mine.

CHAPTER SIXTY-SEVEN

Kate

"We have to go to the police now," I said.

I was feeling nervy as hell. I could feel Tim with me even when he wasn't there. Was that just my own paranoia? Whatever it was, it felt as real as today is Thursday. What if he was watching everything we were doing? What if he knew I met in secret with Kate? What if he'd pre-empted what we were going to do, and had spoken to the police before we got to them?

"Yeah, we need to hurry up, before something gets in the way," said Molly.

"Like what?"

"I don't even want to think about that," she shuddered.

I hadn't seen anyone visibly shudder unless they were thinking of Tim in a long time. It was the material of nightmares. I oscillated back and forth between having conviction in what we were doing and doubting myself. What if I'd imagined it all? What if the police didn't believe me and had me locked up instead? They could probably put me into a mental institution, and no one would raise an eyebrow.

"It'll be ok," said Molly. She placed her hand on my arm and I could feel the warmth of it through my sleeve. "They can't turn us away when we come to them with the evidence in hand."

"Ok," I breathed. "Let's go now."

I checked, double and triple checked that I had the letter. I hoped I hadn't wiped off anything that could have been important in an investigation, like fingerprints. I hadn't thought far enough ahead to erase my emotions. I'd read over the letter many times, memorising it. They were the last words of Pierce's I'd ever see, and I wanted insight into his mental state. Did he write the note inspired by Tim, or did Tim make him write it under duress? I wished I could have walked into his office at that moment and put an end to the questions that tore me up internally, haunting me with Pierce each time I went to bed and each time I woke up.

We walked to the police station. I wore a heavy coat with a hood pulled up. Thankfully, it was dark and raining. The weather conditions were on our side, at least. We moved quickly. It was a time at which Tim should have been in his office, but you never knew when he might be mulling around. He never seemed to miss so much as a photo moment. He had eyes and ears that reached every hidden corner.

We got to the police station. It was intimidating walking inside – even the barbed wire that formed a skirt around the buildings made it feel like something terrible was about to happen, like their defences were up against us. We had to go through a security system and the guy manning it was someone to be feared. He was well-built – not just vertically or horizontally – both. He had a set jaw and dirty fingernails. He looked like a caveman, but with brains – the most dangerous combination. He took our bags and coats and put them through a scanner, and then, with a sharp nod of the head, he let us past. Why did I feel like the criminal walking into those buildings? Why did I feel so unsure that I would make it out again? I hadn't done anything – but by association, it felt like I had. What would Tim say about me when he was accused? He would weave the most convoluted story – one so detailed and with so many diversions that no one would doubt its truthfulness. I couldn't think about that – thinking about that would stop me trying. Once I stopped trying, there was no point left in existing. I could hear Pierce's voice – not like he was giving demands – more like a quiet prod at the back of my mind. I had to catch him – not just for Pierce – for everyone who might come under his care.

We walked inside the station and waited at the desk for someone to greet us. A female police officer appeared.

"How can I help you?"

"We have something we need to show to the police."

"What is it?"

"A letter that incriminates someone in the death of a friend."

"Ok, I'll get one of the officers to speak to you now."

"Thanks."

"Take a seat," she said, waving to the plastic chairs.

They had a curve in them that hurt your spine while you sat. They weren't built for anyone sitting there for any length of time. I didn't know how long we'd be there, but I felt the overwhelming urge to run back outside, race down the street and get as far from Belfast as I could. It had become as insufferable to me as England had once been. I looked at Molly. She looked less nervous than I felt. She seemed to have greater conviction that we were in the right, and that the police would know it But I'd been in state systems too long to trust them. I knew how much illegal activity went on. And it wasn't just condoned – it was praised.

We waited for a few minutes and a policeman came out to talk to us. He was in full uniform and looked ready for the worst, but the station was strangely empty and peaceful. It was so quiet you could hear keys tapping at computers and drawers clicking closed.

"Come with me," he said, walking ahead of us.

We went into an office and he shut the door. There was nothing official about the place – it was like a film set with the props yet to arrive. It was plasterboard walls, brown carpet, cheap furniture.

"Take a seat," he said, pointing to two chairs, side by side.

I sat down. My anxiety was taking hold. I was shaking so hard you could have seen it from the other side of the city.

"What can I do for you, ladies?"

"I have a letter I think might be important."

"Ok, let me see."

"Don't you want to hear the background first?"

"I want to see the letter first."

He read it several times.

"This is the guy who committed suicide last week?"

"Yes."

"How did you come to have this letter?"

"I found it in the office of someone I think killed him."

"He committed suicide."

"I think he was driven to it."

"What makes you think that?"

"I found this letter in his doctor's office."

"Maybe he gave it to him."

"I think he encouraged him to write it."

"What makes you think he would try to do anything other than help his patients?"

"Because I was his patient too."

"Can I ask the doctor's name?"

"Tim Hanlon."

The policeman went quiet and looked severely at me for a few minutes.

"I know who you mean."

"You do," I said. "Thank God."

I stopped shaking and gripped Molly's hand. He believed me. He knew who he was dealing with. He remained silent for a long time, like he was realising the full weight of what I'd just told him.

"Tim Hanlon," he said. "Is a man known to the police."

"He is?"

"Well, yes, he's known to everyone in the country."

"Yes, he's made quite a name for himself."

"He's the most revered psychiatrist in the country."

"I know."

"He has an enormous amount of influence."

"That's why I think he's managed to get away with this. He coerced Pierce to kill himself – he'd done it before with another patient."

"Well, mentally ill patients kill themselves. That's nothing surprising. I'm sorry – what's your name?"

"Kate Thompson."

"Miss Thompson, you have no idea what you're doing – you can't try to get this guy arrested – for something he didn't do. If you have a personal problem with Mr Hanlon, you need to go to him yourself. This is beyond anything I've dealt with before."

"I know – that's why we came to you."

"Well, you shouldn't have."

"What do you mean?"

"You're playing with fire – not even just fire – the bluest part of the flame."

"I don't care – I have to do this for my friend, for all of his patients. I know the damage this man is doing – I suffered from it myself."

"Who is going to believe that?" asked the policeman.

I still didn't know his name, but it didn't feel like that mattered anymore, they were all one and the same – all part of Tim's security team.

"I have this letter," I said. "It was in his office – he gave me a book."

"If you're talking about the book that was found in Pierce's house, there was a note from you found inside it."

"I passed it on to him after I'd read it."

"You gave it to Mr Jones as a gift."

"No, I didn't. Tim gave it to me."

"You expect me to believe that a psychiatrist gave you a novel to read? That wouldn't fit with his profile of professionalism."

Molly jumped in. "That's all the more worrying, don't you think?" she said. "He was personally involving himself with his patients. He knew them too well – inappropriately so."

"What is your connection to all of this.. Miss …?"

"Aagard. I was Pierce's girlfriend, a few months before he died."

"So, you have a personal interest in this – you want someone else to blame for your boyfriend's death."

"He wasn't my boyfriend – anymore."

"Miss Aagard – is that how you pronounce it? The only person to blame for your boyfriend's death is Pierce Jones. He was the one who did it. Now, I advise you to go home, if you don't want to create more trouble for yourselves."

"Why?"

"If you don't leave now, you'll be sorry you stayed."

"I have to stay," I said.

I felt sure of that now. Now that I'd made it into the station, that I'd got the listening ear of a police officer, that I'd had the bravery to confront it, there was no turning back.

"Miss Thompson, how did you come to be in possession of this note?"

"I told you – I found it in Tim's office."

"But why were you looking for it?"

"I was trying to find evidence because I knew he killed Pierce."

"Do you know it's a crime to search someone's private property without a search warrant?"

"I didn't," I said.

I looked away from him – his eyes seemed to be boring through me – right to the root of all my insecurities. He thought I was mad – he didn't believe the testimony of someone diagnosed with a mental illness. We were the lowest of the low. Complaining wasn't allowed, neither was reporting anything. You had to keep your nose in your own problems and let everyone else attend to theirs – or there would be punishment for it. The punishment was coming to me – I could feel it like I could feel one of my mum's rages coming on.

"What you have done today puts you in a difficult position," said the policeman.

"Why?" asked Molly. "She's just telling you the truth."

"She's telling me her story – the story that protects her from being suspected of anything."

"No, I was there," said Molly. She was getting tearful now. I hoped she could gather herself, so her story had more reliability to it.

"I was with Pierce for years before he met Tim Hanlon. I saw the decline in him once he became involved in treatment with him."

"Surely Pierce must have had significant problems to involve himself in services in the first place?"

"Yes – but not to that degree."

"Well, why not deal with it himself, if it wasn't that difficult?"

"He needed help – but not that kind of help. Just because he asked for help doesn't permit his doctor to do anything he wants to his life. He kept him in servitude – he wasn't allowed to make any decisions for himself – he controlled who he spent time with, where he went – he even got a carer for him at the end to control his freedom."

"Maybe Mr Jones needed a carer."

"That wasn't what he got."

"If you're talking about Kevin Connolly, he was selected by Mr Hanlon because of his specific skills."

"He selected him because he saw him as a threat to his job," I said. I was getting hysterical now – but there was no holding back.

The policeman shook his head.

"Did you know he was training to be a psychiatrist? He was on placement in Tim's office before he ended up caring for Pierce?"

"Well, maybe he decided to change career path, or to gain expertise."

"No, he was an ambitious guy – you could tell he liked having authority over Pierce."

"Well, maybe it satisfied something in him."

I waited for a minute, thinking of what to say. I was losing a war and anything I fired out would only result in worse coming my direction.

"Miss Thompson, I'd advise you to go home and just forget about all this."

"I can't do that – he was my best friend."

"There's nothing you can do for him now and trying to label someone guilty for his death isn't a tribute to him. He made the choice – allow him that."

"But I don't think he did."

I started crying. "I'm not moving until you do something about this."

Molly looked like she was weakening, but she still gave me a glance that was like a nudge of encouragement. Her ice blue eyes were filling up with water and it was like watching the sadness of the ice caps melting, all alone - all while knowing there was nothing you could do to stop the devastation.

"Miss Thompson, since you've brought it to my attention, you've done me a favour."

"What?"

"The letter you brought – I have to ask, how did you come upon it? You say you found it in Tim's office, which is bad enough on its own, but how do I know you're telling the truth?"

"Because I was his patient – I found it in his drawer."

"Did anyone else see it there?"

I shook my head.

"So, there are no witnesses – all we have is your word for it. You say you were a patient of Mr Hanlon?"

"Yes."

"Well, that proves that you must have a mental health condition if he was treating you. How do we know you're a reliable source of information?"

I looked down at my feet. I knew I must have looked abashed and that that wouldn't strengthen my story, but all the things I'd feared were coming to the surface. I was mentally ill, undependable, delusional, dishonest. Why was I always crippled by this illness – not just in my own life, but by the attitudes of others, and how they viewed me because of it?

"I suppose you believe me, or you don't. Molly can back up what I'm saying – she saw what happened to Pierce once he got involved with Tim."

"Pierce got so much worse after meeting Tim," said Molly. She looked like she was losing faith in what we were doing.

"I find it extremely disrespectful that you address Dr Hanlon by his first name. Who gave you permission to do that?"

"Tim did."

"He did? Well, doesn't that show what a good guy he is? I don't know many psychiatrists that would stoop to your level, never mind willingly."

"I don't know – that's just what he called himself. Maybe he wanted us to see him like a friend."

"Maybe he was a friend."

"Why are you defending him?"

"I just think – someone with his reputation would never abuse his role. I don't even know who you are, what your history is, who you associate with."

"I just live quietly – I've no reason to cause any trouble."

"Unless he said something that you didn't like, and you're the vindictive type."

I looked at Molly and she had the same hopeless look in her eyes I imagined I had. Was it time to leave? Maybe we wouldn't get anywhere, but at least we'd cause no trouble for ourselves.

I sat, thinking, watching the unmoving face of the policeman.

"What's your name, if you don't mind me asking?"

"It's Hanlon – Detective Hanlon."

"Hanlon?"

"Yes."

"Are you a relation of Tim's?"

"No – it's a common name."

"I'd never heard it before."

"It's just a coincidence – like everything else you're here about."

I lowered my head. Who was he? How was this happening? It was like a film where all the doors you think are escape routes are actually entrances back into the same place. I couldn't bring myself to look him in the face. I knew if I did, I'd see that same look on his face – that look of triumph that Tim had when he said something sadistic.

"Maybe we should just go," I said to Molly.

"No," she said. Her face was set like concrete and I knew something had shifted inside her in that moment.

"You can't get away with this," she said. Her voice was getting louder and Hanlon shushed her.

"No, I won't be quiet – you're related to this criminal – and you're protecting him. This is illegal."

"I think I'm the one who knows the ins and outs of legality."

"I'm not backing down," I said. I felt spurred on by Molly's burst of bravery.

"You will."

"I won't."

"Trust me – you will."

"Why?"

"You aren't leaving here today."

"What?"

"I'm keeping you in. We have evidence that you were involved in Pierce Jones' death."

"What?"

It felt like my voice was getting so distant from my body it belonged to someone else.

"You have a copy of his suicide letter – if that doesn't incriminate you, I don't know what does."

"I told you where I got that."

"That's what you say, but that doesn't mean it's true. You don't know about the other information we've come up with in the meantime, obviously."

"What information?"

"You gave a book to Pierce before his death."

"Yes, one that Tim gave me."

"You expect me to believe that Dr Hanlon gave you that?"

"Yes, he did. Kevin can tell you that."

"Kevin says you gave it to Pierce – that you dropped it to the house a couple of days before he died."

"What? I did give it to him, but it was after Tim had given it to me."

He shook his head, looking at me like I'd made up a story that was too flawed to pass as believable.

"You can't keep her in," said Molly.

"I can, and if you don't back down, I'll keep you in too."

"Just go home, Molly, you can do more there than in here," I said.

She gave me a hug and I could smell a scent that reminded me of Pierce. There must have been a little of her lingering in his house when I'd been there. It felt like she was my last friend on Earth, and I dreaded to think what was up ahead of me, without her.

CHAPTER SIXTY-EIGHT

Molly

I went into the police station today, prepared to come out empty handed, but not alone. I'd thought that letter would be enough to convict Tim, but I guess I don't know the system well enough. It hadn't occurred to me that they could ever pin it on Kate. She's such a kind soul – just a misunderstood one. You can tell she's one of those people who never properly developed because she didn't get the treatment she deserved. I always had a deep-seated belief that things have to work out in the end, and I'm not ready to let go of that belief yet. Maybe that's what keeps you living more than good outcomes – the hope of good outcomes. I don't know how I keep going, in spite of losing the love of my life, but what choice do I have? I can't succumb to the same fate as him. I don't have it in me anyway – I'm more of a person who plods along with their discontentment than someone with the courage to check out early.

I stand in front of my mirror, looking myself in the eyes. It makes me uncomfortable, because I've never really done it before. I prefer to go about my life in a methodical way. I get up, work, and don't overthink anything. It has worked for me so far – I have never fallen into depression, dejection, or despondency. I still have my job and I have to keep going in. I'm scared to face my deepest feelings in case they consume me. Sometimes it's easier to tuck things away than to allow them to hang out, spoiling you, preventing you living your life. So, I break the gaze with myself and go about putting my makeup on. I look tired. My skin looks a sicker pale than usual. It's normal – it's all part of the grieving process.

I hate feeling powerless – like there's nothing I can do to help the people I care about. I hadn't planned to ever like her, but somehow, I've come to care about Kate. She's my one ally now. Everyone else I know has turned away from Pierce. That's what happens with suicide – I guess it makes people uncomfortable, so they prefer to skim over it, acting like it was decades ago when it was only last week. I'm still staying with my parents. I feel no urgency about moving out now. I hadn't wanted to find a place of my own, in case Pierce and I got back together. Now I know that won't happen, but I don't want to venture out on my own yet. Even if my parents don't understand, it helps, hearing the sounds of life around me – the sounds that remind me that life goes on for other people. I haven't told anyone about Kate yet. I know they'd disapprove of me associating with her. They'd think she had an agenda, or that she was mentally unstable and that was why she'd targeted me. I know she had an unhealthy attachment to Pierce. But I had an attachment I couldn't cut off either, so I'm not the right person to condemn her for that.

When I think about Kate, I imagine her sitting in a cell. I've never seen one in real life, but I imagine it to be a room filled with nothing – nothing to watch, nothing to listen to – just your own memories and thoughts to mull over. I can't think of anything more maddening. What would I do if I couldn't bury myself in work to avoid my problems? Kate might not know it, but she's resilient. Strength is more to do with what you've been through and survived than your ability to avoid upsetting situations. I know that now. I wish I'd spent more time with Pierce, trying to get through to him, but it's too late. He was strong, but some circumstances become too much for anyone. Everyone has a point at which they crack.

It's terrible, not knowing what's happening to Kate and not being allowed to visit her. She's in a holding cell while they examine the evidence. They wouldn't trust me alone with her – they think I'm somehow complicit in all of this. I know she didn't influence Pierce, and it doesn't matter what comes of this – I'll always believe her, because I knew Pierce and I saw what Tim did to him in a matter of days. In months I can only imagine the destruction he could have caused. She's lucky to have made it out alive.

CHAPTER SIXTY-NINE

Tim

The end is near. Any questions raised over Pierce's suicide are about to be forgotten forever. I tried to call Kate, but her phone was switched off – confiscated I suppose. That was what the intention was. Did she really think I'd be stupid enough to leave Pierce's letter sitting in an unlocked drawer for her to get her hands on? I knew she had changed towards me that night that she was at my house. I'd expected her to get her revenge somehow. I'd known for a while she was starting to resent the wedge that I drove between her and Pierce. She can be vindictive – nice as anything until you cross her, and it isn't hard to do. She interprets everything as an attack – like the night when I tried to wake her up in the bathroom. I wanted her to realise that I was in charge, and that if she disobeyed me, I was capable of dark things. It didn't cause her to develop more respect for me like she should have. She has a vengeful side to her that doesn't let things go. Maybe I reminded her of her mother – that was the point – to remind her of how much control I have over her life. She needed to listen to me if she wanted to have a good life. I knew when to let her close to people and when to keep her away. I was skilled at monitoring her mental health condition – I knew when she was amiable and when she would drive everyone away. I know how to balance it out for her – she just does everything with her foot to the floor – there is no natural development in her relationships – it is all horribly intense.

For a short time, I'd wanted to use her as a tool to pull Pierce in. He seemed like he had too much of a mind of his own, and I thought she'd become institutionalised under my care. She knew the rules, she knew what was up to me to decide – and she could sell it to Pierce. For a while, I thought she was my strongest supporter. She lapped up everything I said, like every word I spoke was given immense thought. Sometimes it is – sometimes she just sees meaning that isn't there. You can toy with someone so much when they think that way. You just have to say a sentence and they'll find fifty layers of meaning to it without you having to do any of the work. I'd wanted to finish them off together, but once I noticed her demeanour change towards me, I knew that wouldn't be possible. So, I gave her the book. I told her to read it by herself – knowing she would give it to Pierce – she'd have to share the suicide pact theory, to warn him. In the meantime, he'd read the book, just seeing too much of himself in the main character and being driven to the edge that divided life and death. I'd been doing so much work along the way – in the slightest of ways. I hinted, I shared memories with him, taking him to the site of Paul's death. That place is spooky itself. It always had a bad feel to it, even before that happened. That was what had made me suggest it to Paul. I'd spent a lot of time there as a kid, killing mice and things. I'd been a bit of a loner. As influential as I was, I think people must have envied me, because I found it hard to make friends. Maybe it was because I liked to pitch people against each other. I spent long days there alone, and when you get bored, what else are you going to do? Throw stones in the river? Walk in circles? Draw in the ground with a stick? It doesn't satisfy as much as stealing the air out of something's lungs. I was just playing at it in those days, testing the boundaries and learning about what it felt like to snuff something out. Maybe I still had some goodness left in my heart then, but it was already being taken over by the badness. I love to find someone who thinks I had a tough childhood. I tell them my stories of being alone to pluck at their heart strings. They think of me as a poor, neglected thing, but they don't see that my aim has always been to destroy others. I'd never admit that of course. I know that I have badness running through me, but it doesn't bother me. I don't have a conscience so why would I feel bad about it? It's just a special skill to me – something that enables me to do what I'm programmed to do. If you were a hunter it wouldn't do you any favours being plagued by guilt after each animal's execution, would it? It's the same for me.

There are ways I can be sensitive. I can understand other people's feelings, without feeling them. People often mistake my deep understanding for empathy. Empathy is a concept I recognise as weakness, but that I've never experienced. What is it to feel sorry for someone? Feeling sad because they're pathetic? Is that something desirable? Thankfully, I'm not slowed down by emotions like that. I'm like a cheetah – quick, sharp, to the point. I see prey and I strike – nothing emotional holds me back.

The day after Pierce's death, I went to visit the river, once I knew the crime scene had been cleared. I knew people would congregate there – friends and family, people with their curious questions. Why are they so interested in the lives of people they never knew? That always perplexes me, when you see someone crying about the fate of a stranger; how can you care when you never knew them? I don't care even when I did. I just go to catch the last whiff of death hanging in the air. It's like someone polishing their trophies. I get to look at the cordoned off scene, and the chaos, and feel proud that I created that. All these people in turmoil, asking questions about why it happened – I have the answers, but I'll never tell. That's what makes me so good at what I do – I'll never tell the wrong information to the right person.

CHAPTER SEVENTY

Molly

It has been weeks, and I thought I'd have seen Kate by now. The case goes to trial tomorrow. I think they believe she's guilty – that she actually killed Pierce. I've gone down to the police station a few times, begging someone to listen to my side of the story. But no one believes me. They keep escorting me from the building. They think that Kate paid me – to help her maintain her appearance of innocence. I know her diagnosis holds her back – I just hope it doesn't cement her fate. I want to go to court with her – to hold her hand on the defence, but I know it's out of the question. I just wish in the meantime that I could move on with my life. It's hard to; it confronts me everywhere I go. On every news channel, the story runs constantly, on every page of every paper, every snippet of conversation I hear when I go out. It's the talk of the town. I guess not much happens in this small place – nothing too shocking anyway. And if it does, the details of it are rarely revealed. Most murders that occur are in a bad area, in a back street, forgotten as quickly as they went to press. In this land of one million people, everyone clutches to whatever scraps of scandal they can get, and it doesn't have to be homicide to get full coverage. This is the most unimaginable story; it's pure plot: a mentally ill girl murders a fellow patient, after posing as his friend, and makes it look like a suicide. She even tries to frame their doctor. That's how it's being presented when I read it. I know that Kate hasn't given up fighting, especially now she's inside and has nothing to lose. She will have told anyone who'll listen that Tim is guilty. But with no hard evidence, who is going to believe a girl with a mental illness? She has years of documentation showing she has one. I watch the news and every time I see a photo of her, my heart seems to contract, and I think it might just stop one of those times. There is nothing I hate more in life than seeing injustice prevail, and that's what it feels is happening. I just keep hoping that it will turn around. Some piece of evidence has to come to light; someone has to have witnessed what was happening. Tim hasn't been working in isolation – he shares a building with fifty other health service employees. Someone must have noticed his bullying tendencies. Or are they afraid of him too? He has too many high-powered politicians backing him. Maybe that is what makes him untouchable.

All I can do is keep praying that he will be revealed for the monster he is. I don't have much faith in prayer, or faith, full stop, but who else can you turn to when the justice system isn't working? I'm so tired of this place and I know I need to get away - even for a holiday. Just looking at different scenery that I don't associate with the nightmare would bring me some respite. But I can't – I can't allow myself to flee, or to unwind until this is all over and the right verdict comes out.

No one seems to know who Kate is. Thankfully no one knows I was associated with her. I don't think I could cope with the onslaught of questions on top of everything else. If I was her friend *and* I'd known Pierce, people would have too many prodding questions. Nosiness is something you can't escape in Belfast; not unless you cross a sea to get away from it. I know I have family elsewhere. I've never lived in Norway, and it would be a chance for a fresh start. I have family who would take me in. But I can't leave Kate alone to deal with this. In doing that, I'd be betraying Pierce too. But I've also developed a union with her too. The worst thing that has ever happened to me has equally shaken her. That's what makes me even angrier at Tim. He's still more of a symbol of evil to me than he is a real person. I've never exchanged a sentence with him, but I know what he's capable of. I've seen him on the news a couple of times, stating and restating his case. He isn't suspected of anything – just seen as a poor, helpless victim of Kate's wickedness. His reputation has come out unscathed – if anything, his persona has just been publicised by it all. He gets regular interviews where he gets the opportunity to publicly dissect Pierce's mental state before his death, and Kate's mental state before she killed him. It all points towards suicide. That's one thing I have to give him credit for – he can outsmart the entire country. If I hadn't known Pierce, I would have believed him too.

I seem to spend most of life now how Pierce spent his days: lying in bed, straining to get to sleep. No matter how long I lie there, I never fall asleep, and I never get any rest. The only thing worse than being arrested for a crime you didn't commit, is knowing the true story and being unable to do anything about it from the outside. I'm silenced – sitting in my room, plagued by memories and a feeling of fragmentation. My soul was shattered into pieces with Pierce's death, and with Kate's arraignment, I feel like all our souls will shatter together on the ground, like three mirrors, forever broken, the pieces mixed up, one no longer distinguishable from the others.

CHAPTER SEVENTY-ONE

Kate

I've made my peace with the fact that I might end up stuck in here for life. Tim has outsmarted me. I know I can't conquer him. Looking back on it, I was silly to ever think I could get him arrested. Bad circumstances make you try things that were doomed to fail before they began. Deep down, I'd known no one would view me as a reliable source. I'd just hoped the system was fairer than it is. I haven't seen anyone since I got in here – not socially at least. I keep getting visits from the first policeman I saw, under the pretence of checking on me. I think he enjoys the fact I'm here, in a sick way. I still wonder how he is related to Tim, but I'll probably never know. Tim is one of those men with so many fine layers to him that you'll never get to his core. I half-expected him to visit me, purely for the satisfaction of seeing me there, but he has stayed away. I don't know whether he put me here on purpose or if it was just an unlucky outcome of my trying to get him caught.

I wonder how many patients' deaths he has been involved with. He has picked the right industry anyway. Death is overlooked amidst mental patients – it's just part of the routine.

Why would anyone question him? They'd pity him instead, knowing he is working in a profession that offers little reward or recompense. When I try to sleep at night, I can't. I'm haunted by night visions of Tim. His polished bald head, his wide smile, his studious eyes. If only being locked up meant I was finally free of him. Sometimes I wish I'd taken the opportunity he'd offered me – taken up his idea of the suicide pact. At least I would have died on my own terms. Now I was stuck. I'd been told I'd only been there for a matter of weeks, but to me, it feels like much longer. Time comes to a standstill when you're staring at a blank wall. I've requested some books to keep me occupied, but nothing has arrived yet. Maybe they don't think I deserve them. They seem like guards who only grant kindnesses to people who've earned them through asskissing. I'll never do that. I don't have any interest in making friends with the people who have unlawfully locked me up.

I wish the trial would arrive. Waiting is the worst part. Even if I'm found guilty, at least I'd have the certainty of knowing that I was here to stay. I don't mind fighting for a good cause, but when the pay-off is imprisonment, it's hard to feel like it was for a reason. I imagine Tim sitting, happily working away in his office, unhindered. He can still do what he wants in his little kingdom, and that terrifies me. I feel powerless, but at least I know there's nothing more I can do. I know that Molly is still out there. I wonder if she has given up yet. Maybe Pierce has become a closed off memory to her – something she only allows herself to access when a fond memory of him springs up.

My room is better than any I've stayed in in a mental hospital. It's relatively peaceful in comparison. In mental wards, there is never any rest. You have to listen to the unhappy voices of the mentally disturbed. At least here, the dull silence belongs to me. It's only interrupted by the jingle of keys when someone comes to feed me or check I'm doing what I'm told. I perch on the edge of the bed I'm sleeping in. It's the most uncomfortable thing I've ever sat on – sometimes I prefer the floor. It's so thin it feels like something that should be a coverlet rather than a seat or a bed, but I can't be picky anymore. I'm just glad I have somewhere to lie at night and that they can't take my thoughts away from me. They are the one thing I always wanted to lose. I was exhausted from thinking so many thoughts, bad memories, going through mental strife, but now that is the only thing that belongs to me. They can control everything I don't do, but they can't control what I think about. In my mind I can visit the best places I've ever been, like they're happening now. I can pretend to myself that life is still worth surviving. If I were to walk out, would I even know what to do with myself? I feel like I was pre-conditioned for imprisonment. I lived my own form of it through Tim, through my mother. The only difference is the person guarding me now. I keep hoping a note will arrive from Molly, letting me know she's ok, telling me whatever she knows, but even if she tried to send one, it would probably be intercepted. I know they're nearly as suspicious of her as they are of me. I keep hoping she won't end up here too. Hopefully she will have the good sense not to challenge them anymore. Keeping quiet keeps you safer, except in cases like Pierce's, of course.

I'm developing patience here – patience I never had before. That's one positive thing I can think of. I don't have the option to let someone else fill the void. I can't reach out to anyone; I have no means of doing it. Maybe if I end up being transferred to prison, I will have company, but for now, I'm forced to sit still with myself. And that is the one thing I have always avoided doing, and that I've needed to do the most.

CHAPTER SEVENTY-TWO

Molly

I t's the day before Kate's trial. I didn't bother going near the building. I knew they wouldn't let me inside anyway, and if I stood outside, I was worried someone would spot me and it wouldn't help her case. They still think I was somehow involved; that I was at least trying to support her lies. No. I will lay low, watching everything unfold on TV, like every other stranger to whom the whole thing is impersonal. But it will never become that way to me. If I allowed it to, I'd never bring about any change, and I'm determined to do that. I'm just waiting for the right time. You might wonder when I consider that to be – Kate's court case is upon us and I haven't made a move yet. But I know in that respect, I'm helpless. I want to rush to her aid, to knock my way to the front of the courtroom, yelling with all the power in my lungs that I know the truth, but I can't. It would only hurt her, and I can't cause Kate any more hurt than she has already had. Instead, I will work in my quiet, practical way, and no one will even connect me to her – to see that I'm standing up for the same cause.

The hopeful part of me keeps telling me that maybe Tim will still get caught. Surely, he has made enough enemies in this small place that someone will have evidence of wrong-doing? You can't be that accessible to the public and avoid ever slipping up. That's how I view it, at least. There is always a weakness in every chain, even if it is made of something robust – some single scenario will be enough to break it. I decided to go into his office today. Risky though it was, I felt compelled to talk to him face to face. Part of me regrets not doing it at the funeral, but I didn't understand the full picture at that point. I didn't know what I wanted to say; I just knew I needed to say something.

I know where his office is, so I got up early and walked there. I hope he'll be in work today; I know he is vain enough to want to watch something on TV where there might be mention of his name. He will probably be praised on the back of it all – for his efforts to save Pierce, and the thought of that sickens me.

As I walk into the clinic, it feels like I've been there before. It's like I can sense Pierce in the air, and I hope that means I have his support, wherever he is now. I go to the front desk. I know I'm going to have to look confident if I want a chance to talk to Tim. They won't just let anyone in, especially with everything that is happening at the moment. But at the same time, I know he'll want to talk to me. I remember him from earlier days than he realises. I remember that he was watching us in the park that day, long before Pierce knew who he was. It took me a while to connect the dots – I just remembered he had that bald head, those piercing eyes, that heartless stare. I'd seen it before. At first, I'd thought it was when I'd been with Pierce. I'd recognised him right away at the funeral. But then I remembered, Pierce never introduced me to Tim. In fact, I wasn't allowed to attend any appointments with him. So, I must have known him from somewhere else. I thought long and hard, and it took a lot of memory-digging to retrace it, but I finally got there. It's hard to place people when you see them out of context, in a place you've never met them. Then, I remembered a neighbour of ours. He lived in one of the houses across the road. I couldn't be sure which one, but I'd definitely seen him going inside before. He often paced up and down the street, like he was inspecting the neighbourhood. He was like a one-man team of neighbourhood watch, without the good intentions. Had he been watching us exclusively, or did he just watch everyone? That wasn't the only time I had seen him. I knew the details of his face better than that. From that distance, you couldn't have made out any of his defining features. He had been watching me before –closely, intensely – disturbingly so. Then, I vaguely remembered sitting in the park one day with Pierce. It had been the tail end of summer and he'd seemed happy for the last time I'd remembered. We had been enjoying each other's company that day, before he ceased to notice me. Everything about the day was blissful, until it was marred by the stare of someone strange: Tim. I remembered the gleam of his bald head – he must have shaved it religiously. It was like a work of art. But even more than that, I remembered those eyes. The sharp eyes that picked things up at the speed of an eagle, that dissected things with equal indifference. He had been looking back and forth between Pierce and me. He looked at Pierce enviously, and at me with lust. It had made me uncomfortable, I remembered, but I hadn't made anything of it. Those situations present themselves; everyone encounters someone whose gaze makes them uncomfortable. It hadn't been something worth cataloguing in my memory bank. But now I needed to work out what the connection was, I was able to bring it to the surface again. Usually memories that cause you discomfort, no matter how trivial, are still there waiting for you when you need to access them again.

I waited for what felt like an age until I was called in. I expected to be turned away up until the last minute. But maybe Tim wanted to see me. Maybe he wanted to quiz me on Pierce or move onto manipulating me now that Pierce was out of the picture. I could still remember those lustful eyes – the thought of them still frightened me. How could someone capable of desire also be capable of killing? How had the humanity in him been erased?

Finally, Tim came to the door and opened it.

"You wanted to see me?" he asked.

I know he knew who I was. If he lived on your street, he'd know your comings and goings more intimately than you did. I wondered if it would stop him letting me in. I was sure he reserved the right to refuse to speak to anyone he didn't want to. But he didn't.

"Come in," he said, "I had a cancellation anyway."

"That was lucky."

"Yes, that's the thing with this job – you never know who's going to show up and who's not."

"I guess it depends on how patients are feeling on the day."

"You used to be Pierce Jones' girlfriend."

"How do you know that?"

"He talked a lot about you – I saw a photo of you on his phone screen once."

I didn't say any more until we were sitting down behind the closed door.

"I'm assuming you want more information about Pierce – his mental state before his death – some sort of explanation. I'm not allowed to give that kind of information out, I'm afraid."

"Actually, that's not why I'm here."

"Oh?"

He shifted towards me until I felt like he was invading my personal space.

"Well, what are you here for?" he asked. He said it in a way that I supposed could have been seductive if you didn't know who he really was.

"I'm here to talk about Pierce – and your involvement in his death."

"What involvement is that?"

"You drove him to kill himself."

Tim laughed. "That is completely preposterous."

I thought about the fact that I hadn't heard that word used since my childhood – probably in some quaint children's fiction set during the war. His unnatural use of it just highlighted his dishonesty to me.

"It isn't. I just wanted you to know I'm fully aware of what you did. I know you're the reason he's dead."

"You don't know what you're talking about. I was his doctor – I was devoted to his care."

"We both know that isn't true – you were devoted to destroying him."

"You aren't making any sense, Molly."

"How do you know my name?"

"I told you – Pierce told me it. I rarely forget things as important as names."

"Or weak points."

"There's no need to get snide with me, Molly. I'm on your side."

"My side of what?"

"I wanted what was best for Pierce too."

"And that was ending his life?"

"I didn't end his life – Pierce chose to end his own life. I can't be held accountable for that. That's part of my job description – I have to treat the patients that won't get better, just as much as I have to treat the ones that will."

His mouth became set with every sentence he finished, and it irritated me. He didn't look like he had the least hesitancy about anything he was saying. How could someone tell such outright lies to your face and not even flinch? I could see just how dangerous he was and imagined how much that danger would increase if I had been having delusions too.

"I was living with Pierce when you started treating him," I said. "I saw him get much worse in a short space of time. You can't deny that – I was there."

"All patients get worse before they get better."

"Pierce only got worse before he got worse."

"Some patients are weak, Molly, and there's nothing to be done about it."

I got up from my seat. I was getting so angry I didn't know if I could physically contain it for much longer. It was time to leave. But I didn't want him to be sitting over me when I left, like he was placing his power over me too.

"I just came here to tell you that even if you get away with this, even if you're not convicted, even if you frame Kate, I will always know it was you and I'll know the truth."

Tim shrugged. "Who are you going to tell?"

"That part doesn't matter – what matters is that I know, and as long as I know, it exists as truth."

I turned and walked away. I knew Tim had got to his feet to walk me out, but I didn't bother turning to look at him as I left or to acknowledge him. He didn't deserve it.

CHAPTER SEVENTY-THREE

Tim

T oday, Pierce's ex-girlfriend had the audacity to come to my place of work and confront me. I don't know how she could have come to hold me responsible for Pierce's death. What was it that had allowed her to piece everything together? I would be worried about how much she knows if I thought she would pursue it. But she knows that would be pointless – I know too many people in high-powered roles. I could destroy her in minutes – more than I already have. Kate is already lined up, ready to take the blame for all of it. The police would never backtrack, jeopardising their reputation just to catch the right guy. It wouldn't look good arresting a highly regarded psychiatrist. It looks better arresting a mentally deranged patient who poses a threat to society. It won't just be the family of the victim that will be thankful for this – the benefits will reach across the entire community. People will rest better at night, knowing that a murderous mental patient is behind bars.

I didn't want Kate to be put into a mental hospital. That would be letting her off too lightly. So, I made sure to put in her notes that she was coherent and that she rarely showed signs of delusional thinking. I might have started by writing the opposite, but I had to tamper with them once I knew I was going to try to get her arrested. I need them to know that she is responsible for her own actions – not her illness. I think I've got enough proof to back that theory up. I released my notes on her to the police last week, and they are using them as evidence against her. I made sure to make mention of the friend of hers who reported her for stalking. If you've been a stalker, the chances are, you have the potential to do worse. Maybe Pierce didn't know how to escape her influence, maybe he couldn't see another way to disengage from her – she was just so evil.

Of course, I know that isn't true – Kate has problems, but she'd never harm a soul – not even the ones that deserve it. I knew the distance I created between her and Pierce would cause her enormous heartache, but it was necessary to the story. Did the police realise that prior to Pierce's death, he and the defendant had had an extended falling out? They hadn't been speaking - then she had been reintroduced into his life, and suddenly, he was dead. It didn't sound good, did it?

Pierce's family have already shown me their support. They want the murder case to hold up, because it emancipates their son. If he was murdered, he was a victim – if he committed suicide, it brought them disgrace in their constrictive world. They wanted to look clean again. It was hard to look clean and pure when your son had done something so dreadful. It naturally followed that people asked them question upon question, verbally or through judgemental looks. Why hadn't they been there for him? Hadn't they intervened before it reached that point? Why hadn't they been seeing their son in the months leading up to it happening? If it was murder, those questions turned into "How are you coping? What can I do for you? Isn't his murderer monstrous?" That was the kind of image they were aiming for, so I had their support, whether they knew it or not.

Pierce's family sounded like a superficial lot, but that worked in my favour. If all they cared about was maintaining the appearance of the family, they'd do anything to avoid looking bad. I understand that – I'm the same way. I'd thought about trying to recruit them for the witness stand, but that would have been pushing things a bit too far. I don't want them to think that I have a personal interest in it. I think I've done enough preparation work that I should be able to sit back and watch it unfold without interference. At least, that was what I thought until I got a phone call today, requesting my presence in court, and I was happy to go – I didn't want to miss anything good.

CHAPTER SEVENTY-FOUR

Molly

I'm sitting, glued to the TV, waiting for the outcome of the trial, and there's nothing I can do about it. It's like being part of the audience for a horror screening in the cinema. You can gasp, and scream and cheer the right person on, but it makes no difference. The story evolves how it is going to, with or without your help. I've been in a state of inertia today. I feel like I'm almost experiencing what Pierce used to describe to me. I'd always wondered how he sat for such long periods of time, apparently doing nothing. I'm always on the go, always achieving something, no matter how small. But since all of this has happened, I've realised sitting still isn't something you have to try to do when you're paralysed by anxiety. It just happens. You sit there, at the mercy of things beyond your control. I guess that's how Pierce felt about living. I wish I could return to that period in time, when he'd tried to express himself, and I'd failed to understand. Maybe now I could better relate to it. I'd gone through mental agony of my own – not chemical, but painful all the same. I thought about Pierce even more than usual that day, and I felt sad for him. Today should have been like a day of victory for him. From the outside, it appeared to everyone that justice was being served – the person who'd caused his death was finally being punished for their crime. But it just felt like the unfairness of the case was quadrupling before me. I wanted to rush in, yelling about injustice to the whole courtroom. But no one would listen. I'd be labelled unstable too, and sent to a mental hospital, or worse. We were stuck, unable to change our fates. In some ways, I envied Kate a little. At least if she ended up in prison, she'd be paying a fine that lessened the hurt of losing Pierce. I wondered if she resented him at all for what was happening to her. If he hadn't died, she wouldn't be up for murder. For the thousandth time since his passing, I wished that Pierce could come back, not just for me, but for Kate's sake. She didn't deserve, after the life she'd led, to have this as the last episode of it. How long did people get for murder? I didn't even know. Life, probably. I should have researched it more. I wished I could go there, to hold her hand and support her through it, but at the same time, staying away was best for me. I'd get so infected by the negativity surrounding the case that it would be like losing Pierce all over again. I had no choice but to wait for the verdict, and then carry on with life. Whether Kate went free or not, I knew that I would likely never see her again. She'd become like a poster girl for my boyfriend's death, and I didn't know how to separate the two.

I had to go to work, but I couldn't that day. The place would have to keep going without me. I'd begun to see managers in a different light anyway. Were they necessary or were they just an excuse to exercise power in little ways? I'd thought about going into a different line of work. It's hard to keep going in the same vein when the world has become so changed to you. I waited for news. I couldn't move from the one spot. I'd never been so bound by something before, or by someone – someone like Tim. Even from afar, he was running the show, and I hated that he'd succeeded.

CHAPTER SEVENTY-FIVE

Kate

W hen I walked into court, everything was what I'd imagined it to be, but bigger. The room stretched from the entrance of my small stature right up to the judge. I wished I had a chance to talk to her personally, instead of sitting behind all the evidence she had available. Maybe I had more to give, but she wouldn't want to hear it. I wondered how she was connected to Tim. Everyone was, in one way or another. I scanned the room, looking at everyone in their smart clothes, feeling even more worthless and disposable. They were likely going to dispose of my future, and there was nothing to be done. Then I saw a familiar face. I walked towards the front, my feet moving but the rest of me paralysed. It was Tim. What was he doing there? And on the opposite side of the room? I'd half-expected him to show up, to make it look like he was there for my benefit, but secretly gloating as he watched everything evolve. But no, he was on the other side of the room. Was he a witness?

I sat down, looking at him. He looked at me too and our eye contact was unbroken but lacked intimacy. Just because he was looking into my eyes didn't mean I'd let him into my soul again. Whatever he had to say, I wouldn't give him the satisfaction of seeing it bother me. I broke eye contact with him, turning to face my lawyer. I'd been appointed one I didn't know. I didn't know if she was brilliant or bad. She got to her feet and put across my defence. There was little to support it, but it sounded good. The professionalism of it made me hope I still might have a chance. But if I did get out, then what? I'd already grown accustomed to my contained little life. I didn't know what I wanted to do or who I wanted to be, and this way of life spared me that worry. Maybe that was the only way left to win: to decide that this was the life I wanted. Maybe it was preferable to wandering around on the outside, lost and looking for someone to help me that never would. As I thought about that, all the words being said melted away; they didn't have importance anymore. Not until Tim emerged, of course. When he took to the witness stand, I had to hear what he said against me. He swore on the book and took a seat.

"Please state your name and why you're here."

Even as an interviewee, he took charge of the conversation. Tim didn't look pleased about having to introduce himself – I wondered if he'd ever had to do it before, or if people always already knew who he was.

"I'm Tim Hanlon – Pierce Jones and Kate Thompson's psychiatrist – I treated both of them. I was invited here today because I have extensive evidence on Kate. I've been treating her for the past eighteen months and I know her better than anyone. I have notes on her that no one else would have ever had access too. And they'd have remained confidential if they hadn't been needed under such serious circumstances. You won't get information as in-depth as mine anywhere else."

"Ok Dr Hanlon, please proceed."

"Well, I treated Kate in good faith – I thought she was just a patient needing help, but she used that as a tool to gain control."

"How so?"

"She used me to get access to Pierce, knowing that she would ultimately cause him to end his life. Ms Thompson has a long history of abuse. Her parents were abusive, and she has spent her entire adult life trying to wrest that kind of control from them – she has been looking for a new target."

"What makes you think she had bad motives?"

"I have notes here that show that Ms Thompson is consistently inappropriate where boundaries are concerned. I have proof that she forced her way into my home before, demanding treatment. How she found out the address, I'll never know."

I knew my mouth was open, but I couldn't close it. It felt as lifeless as my soul. How could he tell such horrendous lies? But I didn't even know where to start with defending myself. I'd sit and take it and then I'd be left alone in my new cell. At least once I was convicted, I'd have no reason to see Tim ever again. On the outside, he might be harder to escape. Maybe in a way, imprisonment was the freedom I'd been looking for.

"Ms Thompson selected Pierce as her victim. She met him at a walking group held by the mental health team. It was meant to be a social outing for people with mental health conditions, but she used it to ensnare Pierce. I've spoken to several other patients, and they don't even know who she was. She didn't talk to anyone there, apart from him. After that, she systematically drove his girlfriend away, I suppose with her stalkerish tendencies. If Kate wants something to happen, she'll make sure she gets it. She's ruthless in that way."

During his monologue, Tim never looked me in the eye, but he didn't look ashamed either. He looked confident in his story, like the fact that he'd created it automatically made it credible.

"Did you ever witness any other behaviour that made you concerned about Ms Thompson's intentions?"

"Yes, I have records here of a case where the police were involved because she was harassing a female friend. She had tried to coerce her into being in a romantic relationship with her, and when the lady refused, she kept turning up at her house. Ms Thompson has had problems respecting boundaries long before now, and she has shown signs of pursuing her victims to a dangerous degree."

"Why didn't you report her before?"

"I did report her for repeatedly turning up at my house, but I decided not to pursue it. I was trying to help her."

"And what do you know about Kate's relationship with Pierce?"

"It was intense – so much so that they had to stop seeing each other for a considerable amount of time."

I was in shock, but I kept looking at the judge's face instead of Tim's. I didn't want him to know what he was saying was bothering me. I knew that would give him the enjoyment that ignoring him would deprive him of.

"They finally got back in touch, and Kate gave Pierce a book."

"What book was it?"

"A book about a suicide pact. She was trying to plant the idea in his head – that he needed her and that they'd kill themselves together, to urge him to kill himself. But she never had any intention of doing it herself."

"Do you know who wrote the book?"

"No, I tried to research the author, but I couldn't find anything. They seem to have chosen to remain anonymous – maybe it was a message they didn't want to be associated with."

"And do you think this book influenced Pierce's decision to kill himself?"

"Absolutely – before he did, he had drafted several suicide letters, one of which Ms Thompson came to have in her possession. He also kept a journal (which is now with the police) that documents his dangerous state of mind."

"And where were you on the night of Pierce Jones' death?"

"I have someone who can vouch for where I was," he said, smugly.

He waved over a young girl in a tight skirt, and I knew I recognised her from somewhere. Then I remembered – she was one of the front desk workers in the clinic – the one I'd suspected Tim had a romantic interest in. Obviously that romantic interest went further than I'd realised.

"What is your name please?"

"Sara Lin."

"Where were you on the night of Pierce Jones death?"

"I was at *Rosa* – a restaurant in town with Mr Hanlon. He's a colleague of mine."

"I oversee her work," chimed in Tim.

"And during which hours was he there with you?"

"He stayed all evening. We met at seven and he didn't leave me home until one. He'd had a drink after dinner, so I let him sleep in my flat."

"Were you romantically involved with Mr Hanlon?"

"No," said Sara. "It was purely professional." She answered without deliberation.

"Ok, do we have anything else to add?"

The novel was held up in a plastic bag, like something anyone decent would be ashamed to touch.

"I've been told that several more drafts of the suicide note were found in Kate Thompson's home."

"Yes, a search was performed recently, and they were."

"What?" I asked, but my voice came out so small even I

couldn't hear it.

How had the letters ended up in my house? Had Tim put them there? How had he got inside? I was in such disbelief over it all that I almost had to give him the praise he was due. He was the best of the best – a master of manipulation.

CHAPTER SEVENTY-SIX

Molly

Kate got life imprisonment for murder. I'm still in shock that something so unjust could happen. I thought the system had to save her in the end, but as with everything else in life, Tim has won again. Innocence doesn't prevail over persuasiveness, I suppose. I feel like the world has been irreparably altered today, and it's somewhere I can't stand to be – not in its current state. When I saw Kate on the news and she was being escorted from the courtroom, she almost looked serene. I wondered if she had already made peace with what had happened. She looked too calm to have been in inner turmoil. I also noticed Tim in the background. I didn't know in what capacity he had shown up, but I could be sure that it had only hurt her case. He looked proud and stood tall – taller than I've ever seen him look. His head shone in the sunlight, like the crown of a dictator. That's what he was – someone who'd exercised the utmost control a person could, but who did it in such a masterful way it felt like something that could only be created by the supreme. Watching him on TV made it feel like he'd almost become a figure of legend; he was no longer part of ordinary life. Neither was Kate – she had become an icon of self-sacrifice, to me at least. You could tell she'd battled no one over the verdict; she just accepted it graciously. Someone had to be punished for Pierce's death, and if it couldn't be Pierce, she was content for it to be her. Sometimes injustice is served to find a sentence for something more unjust. As she walked away from the camera, I admired her bravery more than anyone else would ever admire Tim. Once this was over and the scandal of it had settled down, he'd be forgotten about. People would remember Kate more than they remembered him, and that was what he deserved. That's the only way to punish someone like Tim: to take the attention away from him.

Now that it's over, I had to sit down with my own circumstances and examine them. I didn't want to live the life I did before. I had to do something that felt more significant, and that worked against people like Tim. But I won't seek revenge – it is pointless to do that with a person like him. That would only delight him: the fact that I'd sacrificed my own life to make sure he paid for the actions in his. Instead, I need to do something useful, something that prevents him striking again.

So, I put in my notice at work, and I became a mental health advocate. I stand up for anyone vulnerable I can. I don't want to see the report of another Pierce, or another Kate. Their unfortunate fates have to be for something good. Otherwise, what's the point in any of it? I think that evil is always conquered in the end, maybe just not in the way you would have thought, and I'm ok with that now. Sometimes doing the right thing isn't about making a grand gesture or doing something news-worthy. It's about quietly working away in the background, preventing the things that would make someone want to send a news crew to the scene in the first place.

This week, two years after the worst period of my life, things look neither bright nor bleak. I am walking into a courtroom, standing beside another mental health patient. She claims her doctor was tampering with her medication - purposely making her unwell, wearing her down until she was committed, or ended her own life. Whether it is true or not, I don't know. I just need to stand at her side and give her the support she doesn't feel she gets from elsewhere. Whether it is the truth of what's happening or a delusion of hers doesn't matter; the fight to survive continues either way. Tim walks freely, but he isn't important anymore. He's just a symbol for the continual crusade of the mentally ill – against their doctors, against their illness, against themselves.

Printed in Poland
by Amazon Fulfillment
Poland Sp. z o.o., Wrocław

49182857R00195